T0048998

Why Earls Fall in Love

"With its shades of *I Know What You Did Last Summer* and strong gothic overtones, Collins's latest is a chill seeker's delight. Along with the surprising climax, readers will thoroughly enjoy the well-crafted characters, the charming setting, and the romance that adds spice to the drama."

—*RT Book Reviews*

"Sparkling romance amid mystery."

—*Publishers Weekly*

"Combining love, wit, warmth, suspense, intrigue, emotion, sensuality, interesting characters, romance, and plenty of danger, Ms. Collins's has created another enthralling story."

—*Romance Junkies*

"Award-winning author Manda Collins brings sensual historical romance to a new level with wit, heat, and beautifully written detail, finely drawn characters, and a flair for fun."   —Examiner.com

Why Dukes Say I Do

"Witty and smart, Collins's prose flows smoothly as she merges a charming, compassionate love story with gothic suspense . . . Add strong pacing and depth of emotion, and there's no doubt this is a winner."
—*RT Book Reviews* (Top Pick, 4½ stars)

"Collins has a deft touch with characterization, and she expertly weaves a thrilling thread of danger throughout the story. *Why Dukes Say I Do* is highly recommended for readers who enjoy their historical romances with a generous soupçon of suspense." —*Reader to Reader Reviews*

"Manda Collins pens a charming, romantic tale with *Why Dukes Say I Do.*" —*Single Titles*

"Totally engrossing, witty, and suspenseful."
—*Tulsa Book Review*

Also by Manda Collins

Good Earl Gone Bad

Manda Collins

St. Martin's Paperbacks

This is a work of fiction. All of the characters, organizations, and events portrayed in this novel are either products of the author's imagination or are used fictitiously.

GOOD EARL GONE BAD

Copyright © 2015 by Manda Collins.

All rights reserved.

For information address St. Martin's Press, 175 Fifth Avenue, New York, NY 10010.

ISBN 978-1-250-24983-8

St. Martin's Paperbacks edition / October 2015

St. Martin's Paperbacks are published by St. Martin's Press, 175 Fifth Avenue, New York, NY 10010.

P1

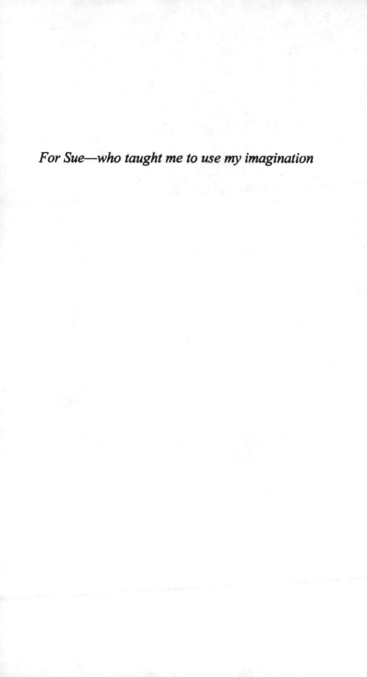

For Sue—who taught me to use my imagination

Acknowledgments

So many people are there for me along the road from idea to finished book. Thanks first and foremost to my lovely and wonderful editor Holly Ingraham, who went above and beyond the call of duty for this one. Congratulations, lady! To Lizzie Poteet, Amy Goppert, and all the team at St. Martin's Press who work tirelessly behind the scenes. To my awesome-sauce agent Holly Root for always knowing just the right thing to say. To my friends and family—especially my sister Jessie—without whom I would not be able to do this job I love so much. And to Stephen, Tiny, Toast and Charlie, for keeping me company during the long hours at the computer and for not getting too annoyed when I push them off the keyboard.

Prologue

"For a club called the Lords of Anarchy," said Miss Ophelia Dauntry wryly as she scanned the Paynes' crowded ballroom, "they seem remarkably well behaved."

As the current president of the once notorious driving club, Lord Payne had done much to repair the club's image in the eyes of the *haute ton*. And part of that campaign had been the invitation the club had extended to Lady Hermione Upperton, whose new membership was the reason for tonight's celebration. They had even gone so far as to fête her induction with a rout instead of what they might otherwise have done—taken the excuse to drink to excess in their favorite tavern on the Brighton Road.

"I think we all know why they are behaving so prettily," Lady Hermione said with a speaking look. She was under no illusions about the reasons for her warm welcome into the brotherhood. But as a driving enthusiast with a desire to take her place among the sporting elite, she was happy to seize whatever chance she could get.

Especially since her father had done his level best to keep her from fulfilling her dream by threatening every other club with a lawsuit if they allowed his daughter to become a member. Only the Lords of Anarchy had ignored the Earl of Upperton's threats and extended the invitation.

"I believe you should be chatting with your new compatriots," said Mrs. Frederick Lisle—more commonly known as the celebrated poet Leonora Craven. "Especially since you are looking so lovely."

Hermione smiled at her friend's compliment. It was true that she felt far more fashionable than usual in her deep blue silk gown. The color contrasted with her creamy complexion as well as bringing out the blue in her eyes. And she'd chosen to have her maid dress her dark hair in a newer, softer style which was more becoming than her everyday utilitarian chignon. Though she was now a member of a club that was known for its masculine pursuits, she didn't wish them to forget that she was a lady. And as such she hoped to bring a more equitable sensibility to the membership.

"Thank you, Leonora," she said, suppressing the urge to twirl. "I was sure Ophelia would faint dead away on seeing me rigged out in such finery."

"I always knew you had it in you," Ophelia said primly. Then in a lower voice said, "I'm just happy you chose to put away your dowdy gowns on an evening when there are so many handsome, eligible gentlemen around."

"Are we interrupting?"

Ophelia colored as she realized Leonora's husband, Freddy, was behind her.

"Of course not, darling," said Leonora with a twinkle in her eye as she made room in their little circle for both Freddy and the two men flanking him: the Earl of Mainwaring and the Duke of Trent. Friends from school, the three had once been four—

with Leonora's late brother Jonathan having rounded out the group before his death.

"I am surprised to see you here, Mainwaring," Hermione said with a raised brow. "I thought you were firmly against the notion of ladies participating in such rough pursuits."

As if he knew how much it would irritate her, Mainwaring raised his quizzing glass and surveyed her with it.

"I do not believe you are showing any signs of masculinity, Lady Hermione," he drawled. "So I suppose I must withdraw my objections."

That he was as handsome as he was provoking vexed Hermione even more than his grudging approval. With dark unruly curls that cried out to be tousled and the fine-boned features of a Renaissance angel, he would have been called pretty if he were a woman. But he was most certainly a man —as his wide shoulders and trim waist attested. Yet, Hermione could focus only on his maddening personality.

"You are the most infuriating man," she said with a scowl. "Do you really have to enjoy setting my back up so much? It's most unbecoming."

Mainwaring gave a shrug. "Perhaps not, but it's far too amusing for me to give up."

She wondered if it would spoil the party in her honor if she were to start a brawl. Likely not, but knowing that the Lords of Anarchy wanted to rejuvenate their image, she could jeopardize her membership. And though it would feel wonderful to snatch away Mainwaring's quizzing glass and smash it into tiny pieces, she would not risk her new place, even for the satisfaction of erasing Mainwaring's smug grin.

"There is more to life than amusement," Hermione retorted. "In fact, I would find it most amusing to—"

"Children," interrupted the Duke of Trent. "I believe our host is approaching his guest of honor."

Hermione, without the height of the duke to let her see above the crush, stared in the direction Trent had indicated, and soon saw that he was correct. Lord Payne, accompanied by his lady wife, was headed their way.

"My dear Lady Hermione," said the viscount, "I hope you are enjoying yourself."

He smiled politely at the circle around her, but without warmth. He and Freddy had crossed paths during the tenure of the previous club president, who was also Freddy's cousin. And it was obvious there was no love lost between the men.

"I am pleased to see so many of the membership come out to support you, Lady Hermione," said Lady Payne, her hand possessively on her husband's arm. Hermione wondered if her hostess was warning the club's sole female member away from her husband. It could not have been easy for her to stand by his side through the wilder exploits of the club. "I do wish you will consider me a friend during your membership. As the only lady, I know it will be difficult for you to find your footing."

She need not worry though Hermione could hardly say so aloud. She had no designs on any man, much less the boorish Lord Payne.

Aloud, she said, "Thank you, Lady Payne. It is most kind of you to think of me."

"Nonsense," her host contradicted his wife. "I foresee no issues for Lady Hermione with the other chaps. We are not the first driving club to admit ladies, after all. So long as she knows her way around a coaching pair, she'll be fine."

Lady Payne flushed in embarrassment at his contradition. Hermione exchanged a speaking glance with Leonora—not a happy match, that.

Before Hermione could break the awkward silence, Payne gave a brisk nod. "We'll leave you to it, then. I shall see you later this week at the first club muster of the season in Hyde Park. We meet by the Queen's Gate."

And just as quickly as the couple had appeared, they disappeared back into the crush of guests.

"Well, that was awkward," Mainwaring said once their hosts were out of earshot. "I wonder if he is that charming with all ladies or reserves such bombast for his wife."

For once, Hermione couldn't argue with him. But if she were going to succeed in the club, she'd need to accept the bad with the good. Even if it meant suppressing her dislike for the way the club's president treated his wife.

"Once a bully, always a bully," said Freddy grimly. "I had hoped he'd become a bit less difficult with my cousin Gerard gone, but it would seem that the leopard does not change his spots."

"Don't let's spoil Hermione's night with all this dark talk," Leonora said, linking her arm through Hermione's. "I see champagne over there. Why don't you gentlemen go fetch some for us?"

"Ahh, I see how it is," Freddy said with a much-put-upon sigh. "Now that we're wed, you think you can just order me about."

"Trent and I aren't wed to her, but she's ordering us about as well," Mainwaring pointed out with a shrug. "I think she just wants us gone so that they can talk about lady things."

And since none of the three ladies denied the accusation, the three men soon took themselves off to find the champagne tray.

"Are you sure you wish to be part of this club, dearest?" Leonora asked Hermione once the men had gone. "I know you are desperate for some place to show your skill with the reins. And I do most certainly think that you are any of these men's equal, if not superior. But I cannot like it that you will be associating with Lord Payne. He was not blameless in all that went on with the club when Jonathan was murdered. Though it's true he was not responsible for the worst of it."

But Hermione had already made up her mind. And though she, too, found Lord Payne troublesome, she had decided that until she saw evidence that the club was sliding back into its former bad habits, she would give them the benefit of the doubt.

"I know it's difficult for you to understand," she said aloud. "But I am doing this with my eyes open. At the first sign of trouble, I will sever my ties, I promise. But until then, I would like the chance to determine whether a club like the Lords of Anarchy can give me what it is I'm looking for."

"But what is it that you're looking for?" Ophelia, who had remained silent until now, asked. "What do you want from them?"

"What every woman wants." Hermione smiled sweetly. "To win."

One

"Damn me, Mainwaring," an aggrieved Mr. Percy Edgerton groused, throwing his cards to the table. "I should have known better than to bring my winning streak to any table that included you as a player."

But Jasper Fawley, the Earl of Mainwaring, had heard it all before. With a shrug, he scooped up his winnings and began methodically counting them into his purse. "You cannot say you weren't warned, Edgerton," he said when he was finished. "By me and others. And it's not as if you cannot afford to lose it."

Percy, the wealthy heir of Viscount Edgerton, persisted in the delusion that he was something of a virtuoso at the tables. From what Jasper could tell, he wasn't all that bad when his opponents were on his level. Hence the earlier winning streak. But the Earl of Mainwaring was accounted to be the most skilled player in the *ton* and as such had proceeded to annihilate Percy trick by trick until the other man was left with only a few coins on his side of the table.

"Come now, Percy," said the blowsy widow at the young man's shoulder, her rouged lips close to his ear. "I'll have my cook prepare you a nice supper to make up for it."

Despite his winnings, Jasper felt an unaccountable stab of envy. A warm woman and a nice supper sounded damned inviting.

What did he care that a scapegrace like Percy Edgerton was destined for a more comfortable night than his own? Clearly he'd had too much brandy.

It wasn't as if he couldn't find a willing woman if he wanted one. His dark hair and handsome face had served him well with the ladies since he was a halfling. He wasn't a vain man, but he knew that regular bouts at Jackson's and fencing at Angelo's had honed his lean frame into something more than one woman had found pleasing to the eye—and the touch.

But he'd begun to feel bored of late when it came to the practiced wiles of that kind of woman. Perhaps he'd been on the town for too long. Been the recipient of too many come-hither looks and calculated smiles. Or it could very well be that seeing his friend Freddy—Lord Frederick Lisle—settled down with a woman who had more to recommend her than bedroom skills and a fine bosom had given him an itch for something more permanent than the sort of relationships to which he'd become accustomed.

Whatever the reason, he was happy enough to go home alone if it meant avoiding the sort of liaison that would leave him temporarily sated but ultimately empty.

Before he could bid farewell to the unhappy gamester and his mistress, however, the Duke of Trent stepped up beside him.

"I think there's something you should see in the back room," Trent said, his naturally saturnine face even darker than usual.

Why had Trent even come to Mrs. Wallingford's hell tonight? Jasper wondered as he followed the other man through the throng toward the rooms reserved for high-stakes games. Trent never seemed to enjoy himself when he played, and he lost more often than he won.

Even so, years of long friendship had led Mainwaring to accept the other man's presence on such occasions without question. At the very least they could both avoid matchmaking mamas in such establishments, which was a high recommendation in and of itself. And when necessary, the duke did what he could to extricate especially reckless young pups from the clutches of sharps.

"It's not young Lord Dalrymple again, is it?" Jasper asked in a low voice as they wended their way through the crowded card room. "I vow I've stopped his skiff from going over the falls so many times I'm beginning to think he should give his bloody family estate to me."

But Trent shook his head before extending an arm for Mainwaring to precede him through a narrow doorway into a room that was even more crowded than the card room.

When he reached the edge of the crowd nearest the table, he saw at once why Trent had brought him.

"It's a pretty little estate," the Earl of Upperton, Lady Hermione Upperton's father, said, running a finger beneath his cravat. "It's unentailed so it would be yours free and clear, Saintcrow. It's a valid stake."

Earlier that year Jasper and Lady Hermione had been thrown together thanks to the marriage of her dearest friend to his. Though they hadn't always dealt amicably with one another, Jasper had a great deal of admiration for the lady's spirit—and if he were honest, for her sharp wit and shiny dark curls that seemed always to be escaping their pins. He certainly had no wish to see her embarrassed or impoverished by her father's profligate time at the tables.

Before he could speak, however, Upperton's opponent, Lord Saintcrow, a man whom Jasper knew to be a skilled card player, cleared his throat. "I don't know . . ." he said, drawing out the last word.

It might have been a ploy to make Upperton add more to his wager, but it might also have been sincere discomfort at the stake the older man offered. Jasper didn't know Saintcrow well enough to say.

But clearly Upperton had been spooked by the other man's reluctance. When Jasper glanced at the pile of IOUs on the table before them, he saw why. The two men had been playing for some time apparently. And like many gamblers before him, at each loss, Upperton had reupped the stakes in order to win back what he'd lost. If he was offering up his unentailed property, the play had been deep indeed.

"My daughter's matched grays," Upperton said, his voice sharp with anxiety. "You know she's renowned for her appreciation of horseflesh. They are worth fifteen hundred at least."

Saintcrow, who had not seemed particularly interested before now, sat up straighter. "The ones I saw her driving in the park last week?"

It was well-known around town that Lord Saintcrow was in the market for a coaching pair, and had even applied to Tattersall's to search out a team for him. But it was an expensive way to acquire horses, and there was no denying that there was a certain allure in the idea of gaining a well-matched set of horses over the course of an evening for a few hundred quid instead of after months and a couple thousand pounds.

Upperton, however, was not so knowledgeable about horses as his daughter was. "I suppose they're the same ones," he said with a shrug. "I haven't seen them myself, but since she got them I've been approached by any number of chaps with offers to buy them."

I'll bet you have, Mainwaring thought with a grimace. Any man of sense would know Upperton was short of the ready and might be eager to sell off any valuable possessions. Even if they didn't, strictly speaking, belong to him. He recalled quite clearly that Hermione had purchased the pair with her own funds since her father—notorious for his objections to her fondness for driving—had refused to buy her a pair with his funds.

Saintcrow, however, had no notion of the horses' true ownership, and his eagerness was apparent in the way he leaned forward at the table. "I'll accept the pair as your wager, my lord. And the Lincolnshire estate."

Jasper exchanged a quick look with Trent. He could, knowing the truth about the horses, speak up, but to declare it openly in front of witnesses would be tantamount to calling Upperton a liar and men had been called out for less. Plus, the scandal would damage Hermione's reputation irrevocably. Something he'd avoid if he could help it.

Once the terms were set, the game itself was short and sweet—at least for Saintcrow, who at the end of play found himself the proud owner of a pair of finely matched grays, named as Jasper had heard Hermione say, Rosencrantz and Guildenstern, because their original owner had been fond of Shakespeare. He only hoped that the end of this particular drama was happier than that of *Hamlet*.

"You may collect the horses at your convenience, Saintcrow," Upperton said with a shrug, indicating that the loss of his daughter's prized possessions was not of particular interest to him. "Though I must insist you give me the opportunity to win back my losses sometime soon. That estate has been in my wife's family for generations."

"Clearly it is weighing heavily on you, my lord," Jasper said with irony as the earl rose from his place at the table.

He would have pulled Hermione's father aside to chastise him in private, but was forestalled by the appearance of Upperton's mistress, the widowed Countess of Amberly.

"Have you been a naughty boy, Upperton?" she purred, slipping an arm into the earl's.

"My dear lady," Upperton said blithely, "I have lost nothing that you will miss, I can assure you. And I always win back my losses. You will see."

And any chance Jasper might have had for discussing Upperton's losses with him was lost as the two lovers disappeared into another part of the house.

"That went well," Trent said dryly. "Though what we could have done to stop things short of leaping into the flames ourselves I have no idea."

"It's a damnable thing when a man can wager his daughter's belongings without a by-your-leave," Jasper groused as he and Trent stalked from the card room and toward the door to the street.

"True enough," Trent said. "But I have a feeling Lady Hermione will not take the news without a fight."

"Even Lady Hermione Upperton cannot interfere in a matter of honor like a wager," Jasper said, brushing a spare thread from the sleeve of his greatcoat. "Though I should like very much to see her try."

"You're sure Leonora and Freddy will be there?" asked Hermione as she negotiated her bright yellow curricle around a narrow turn.

Though Ophelia was not overly fond of riding in the fast carriage, she had agreed to do so that morning for the sake of the occasion. Today was Hermione's first outing as a full-fledged member of the Lords of Anarchy driving club.

"Yes," Ophelia answered sharply, gripping the side of the carriage with one hand and her pretty bonnet with the other. "Leonora promised me that they would be there to cheer you on. And if they are not I shall be quite put out since I planned to stand with them as we watch the procession."

It was with a sense of unreality that Hermione had had her beautiful matched grays harnessed to the curricle that morning. She had spent so long applying and being rejected by the most prestigious clubs in London that finally achieving her goal of membership was still a little unbelievable.

"Good," Hermione said with some relief. She wasn't sure why, but having her friends there to cheer her on was of the utmost importance to her. Perhaps it was because her only family to speak of was her father, and he had proved himself to be indifferent at the best of times. Much better to count on the affection of Leonora and Ophelia, who had on more than one occasion shown they were not as fickle as her father was. "I wonder if there will be a crowd. There are only twenty-four club members but I should like to think that a day as pretty as this will command a few onlookers at least."

"You only wish for the world to see your splendid carriage and even more glorious horses," Ophelia teased. Since Hermione had spoken nonstop about the pair since she'd acquired them a few months earlier there was little danger Ophelia would forget them. "Though I must again complain that you really ought to give them to me, considering that

Rosencrantz and Guildenstern were clearly destined to be mine."

"If you had the least inclination of what to do with them, my dear," Hermione said with a laugh, "then perhaps I would agree with you. As it is, you will have to content yourself with loving them from afar. Or at the very least, safely from the ground, for I am not convinced that you are not terrified now as they convey you through the streets of London."

Since Ophelia continued to grasp the side of the curricle like a shipwreck victim does a lifeboat, she did not disagree.

Fortunately for her, they were nearing the Queen's Gate of Hyde Park where club members had been instructed to muster.

To Hermione's pleasure, quite a number of on-lookers, on foot, by carriage, and on horseback had gathered around the gate to watch the splendidly col-ored carriages. The members of the Lords of Anar-chy were distinguished by the red and yellow striped waistcoats each driver wore. Hermione's driving cos-tume was a lovely fitted crimson and yellow striped spencer over a sturdy riding habit of light wool. She'd had it specially created for today's outing and was glad for it as soon as she saw how many curious looks she received as the only female member of the noto-rious club.

"Hermione!" she heard a familiar voice shout from a nearby open barouche. "Ophelia!"

A quick glance to the left revealed Leonora seated beside her husband and waving her handkerchief in the air in order to attract their attention.

Pulling alongside her friends' carriage, Hermione felt the scrutiny of the newcomers. "What?" she asked with a frown. "Have I got dirt on my face?" She lifted a gloved hand to brush her cheek.

"Nothing like that, you silly creature," Leonora said with a grin. "I was just taking in the sight of someone who is living out her greatest dream. How does it feel?"

Since her own thoughts hadn't been too far from her friend's on the matter, Hermione grinned, too. "It feels wonderful," she said, barely stopping herself from crying out a huzzah. "Better than I could have possibly expected."

"You'd better divest yourself of your passenger before you gallop off into the sunset," Freddy said wryly. "For I fear Miss Dauntry is not experiencing the same sort of bliss as you are at the moment."

Turning, Hermione saw with a start that Ophelia was indeed looking a bit like she wanted to leap from the curricle and never look back.

"Shall I give you a hand down, Miss Dauntry?" asked Lord Mainwaring, who had ridden up to their little party on a handsome bay, with the Duke of Trent not far behind on his own splendid midnight-black mount.

Before Ophelia could respond, Mainwaring was on the ground, and handing Ophelia down from Hermione's curricle and up into the Lisle barouche.

"You might have told me you were so desperate to get down, Ophelia," said Hermione with a frown.

Of course it had been Lord Mainwaring who came to her friend's rescue. He would consider Ophelia's reluctance to ride in such a fast vehicle as a mark of her true femininity. Whereas Hermione, with her taste for driving and fine horseflesh, was far too unladylike for such as him. She felt a pang of jealousy over the way he looked up at her friend before quickly stifling it. Today wasn't about attracting the notice of handsome gentlemen—at least not the sort who found the notion of a lady driving something akin to a dancing dog, she thought, paraphrasing Johnson, not that she did it well, but that she attempted it at all.

Today was about pleasing herself and herself alone. She was preparing to make her good-byes before driving to take her place in the crowd of other club members' carriages, when Mainwaring, back in the saddle, addressed her.

"I take it these are the remarkable grays I've heard so much about," he said, nodding toward where Rosencrantz and Guildenstern had begun to stamp their hooves in restlessness.

Hermione couldn't help but notice that Mainwaring's seat on his own horse was quite good. In buff breeches that outlined the strong muscles of his thighs and a bottle-green coat that looked as if it had been sewn onto his wide shoulders, he looked every bit the dashing nobleman. It didn't help that his keen blue eyes were watching her.

Shaking off her unwanted attraction to the man, she held his gaze. "They are, indeed. My pride and joy, and as much the reason for my presence here today as any skill on my part, I'd wager."

Her self-deprecation must have surprised him, for he frowned and said, "I sincerely doubt that. I've seen you drive, Lady Hermione, and while I might wish you had chosen a safer pastime, even a nondriver like myself has to admit that you are skilled with the reins."

The unexpected praise made her blink, and to her shame, she felt a blush creep into her cheeks. Since when did Mainwaring pay her compliments? "I . . . that is to say . . ."

Before she could finish stumbling through her awkward thanks, another rider approached to stop beside Mainwaring.

From the scowl on Mainwaring's face it was evident he was not pleased to see the newcomer.

"Lady Hermione," said the dark-haired man, who had intruded on their conversation. "We haven't been formally introduced. I am Saintcrow. And I'm afraid we've got a bit of a dilemma."

Hermione blinked. "I don't understand, Lord Saintcrow. We are not acquainted so I do not know how there might be any sort of trouble between us."

"Might you not wait until after the meeting of the club has finished?" Mainwaring asked the other man through clenched teeth. Clearly there was no love lost between the two men, but what had provoked such a response from Mainwaring? "There is no need to cause a scene."

"A scene about what?" Hermione asked, her stomach clenching at the possibilities as to what a public scene might pertain. "I assure you, gentlemen, I should rather know sooner than later."

"The long and short of it, dear lady," said Saintcrow with a shrug that seemed to convey he was not to blame, "is that your father wagered these splendid horses of yours at the gaming table last night and I was lucky enough to win them."

As if the crowd had been waiting with bated breath for the announcement, a gasp wafted through the assembled onlookers. For the second time that day Hermione felt a sense of unreality—though this time it was because the circumstances were so horrible that she could not believe them to be truly happening.

"I don't believe you," she said, her gloved hands clenching the reins, causing the horses in question to shake themselves as if in preparation for flight. "My father doesn't even own them. They are mine. Purchased with my own funds."

"My dear girl," Saintcrow said without much sympathy, "that is something you will need to work out between yourselves. I only know that he offered them to me as a fair wager and I accepted them. Though as your father, he doubtless does own everything you think of as your own. From that pretty confection of a hat to the gloves that you wear on those soft hands."

"Can this be true?" Hermione asked Mainwaring, who had moved his horse to stand alongside the curricle, a show of protection that she was grateful for despite her usual annoyance with that sort of high-handedness. "Does my father truly own them despite the fact that I purchased them with my own funds?"

"I don't know," Mainwaring said in a low voice. "But it is possible. We both know that the law is not particularly forgiving when it comes to ladies' property. Unless it is dispersed in marriage settlements or the like. And you did not inherit them from your mother's marriage portion, did you?"

Of course she hadn't, Hermione thought with frustration. She'd bought them from the funds she'd inherited from a distant aunt. But it was quite possible that her father could very well claim the funds for himself.

"You know I did not," she said, panic welling as she realized that this stranger—no matter whether he was in the right or not—would take Rosencrantz and Guildenstern from her on the basis of her father's word alone. "But they are mine."

"I'm afraid that's no longer true, Lady Hermione," said Saintcrow, who gave a gesture with his hand, and soon was giving orders to a trio of grooms to take possession of Hermione's curricle. "Now, be a good girl and let these men take your grays along with the curricle. I will see to it that the vehicle is returned to your mews as soon as the horses are deposited into my own stables. You would not wish them to come to harm without any sort of harness, would you?"

"She is Lady Hermione," said Mainwaring before Hermione could object, "and you will speak to her with the respect to which her rank and position entitle her." She could see from the way Saintcrow flinched that he did not much care for the tone the earl had taken with him, but that didn't stop him from offering an apology.

"Of course, my regrets, Lady Hermione," the viscount said, his dark eyes narrow with annoyance. Clearly he did not wish to make an enemy of Mainwaring, no matter how he might resent the other man's interference. "I am, of course, obliged for your grace during this difficult situation."

It was at this point that the members of the Lords of Anarchy seemed to notice the disturbance. Though she had never been particularly fond of Lord Payne, Hermione felt a stab of relief when the big man steered over to get a better look at the situation.

"Is there a problem, Lady Hermione?" the club president asked, his own highly polished black and red equipage shining in the sunlight. "Is this fellow bothering you?"

She might be the first female member of the Lords of Anarchy, but that did not mean she was any less a member. And the club took care of its own.

"It seems that there is some misunderstanding between my father and Lord Saintcrow," she said with what she hoped was enough of a damsel-in-distress look to earn more of Lord Payne's pity. She was not overly fond of manipulation as a form of getting things done, but her instinct was that Lord Payne would respond better to a soft word than bombast. "He thinks they belong to him now, which is patently false, since I purchased them myself with my own money."

"False or not," Saintcrow said showing his teeth, "I

have your father's vowel from last night here. Which I would have shown you, Lady Hermione, had you been patient enough to wait for it."

"Saintcrow," said Mainwaring before Lord Payne could respond. "I should think that in the circumstances a gentleman would give the lady the benefit of the doubt. One does not wish, after all, to be thought boorish."

Hermione waited with her heart in her throat to see if the combination of Lord Payne's brawn and Mainwaring's brains would convince Saintcrow to give up his claim.

But, it would appear, she was doomed to disappointment.

"Far be it for me to disagree with Mathematical Mainwaring," said Saintcrow silkily, "but even a man as skilled at the tables as yourself should be able to see the way this particular game will end. I have her father's IOU, which you yourself saw him give to me last night. The rest we will simply have to let the courts decide. In the meantime, I will take possession of my new horses."

"Perhaps it's best to do as the fellow says for now, Lady Hermione," Lord Payne said with a frown. "The drive is about to begin and this business has delayed our procession for long enough. I feel sure that as soon as this is sorted out, you'll be able to ride out with us at our next meeting."

All the good will Hermione had felt at having the club president by her side dissipated at his words. She might have known he'd abandon her at the first sign that her trouble would interrupt the club's revelry.

With a sigh, she handed the reins of her curricle to one of the burly grooms who'd accompanied Lord Saintcrow.

"Be sure to give them fresh oats," she instructed as

Mainwaring took her by the waist and lowered her to the ground beside her carriage. "And Rosencrantz is prone to strain in his left foreleg. A lineament of mint and rosemary can be made up without much trouble."

She was grateful for Mainwaring's strong arm as he ushered her over to the Lisle carriage, and when he lifted her up to sit beside Ophelia, she couldn't help but notice he smelled pleasantly of bay rum and man. She closed her eyes at her own foolishness. Leave it to her to be diverted from losing her beloved grays by an attraction to a man she found at most times to be more maddening than a thunderstorm at a picnic.

"I believe this situation calls for a fortifying cup of tea," said Leonora. "Let us repair to Craven House."

And before she could even glimpse the procession of curricles get under way, Hermione found herself being spirited away from what had begun the day as a happy occasion. And more importantly, in the opposite direction of her precious coaching pair.

She hoped Leonora intended to fortify the tea with something stronger than just boiling water.

She'd earned it.

Two

hat was a particularly painful scene," Trent muttered as he and Jasper rode alongside each other through Mayfair, en route to the Craven town house. "One might have thought Upperton would inform his daughter that he'd lost her prized horses in a game of cards before she was scheduled to drive said horses in the park."

Jasper, who was finding it difficult to forget the expression on Lady Hermione's face when she realized just how her father had betrayed her, swore. "I should have sent her a note as soon as we left Wallingford's last night. At the very least she would have known her time with the beasts was limited. It was badly done of Saintcrow to embarrass her in front of her peers like that."

"Peers?" Trent echoed with a frown. "Since when do you consider Lady Hermione—or any lady for that matter—as belonging in a club like the Lords of Anarchy? I thought you were dead set against ladies mixing with their ilk."

It was a fair question, Jasper reflected, considering only a few months ago he'd been rather vocal about his objection to ladies like Hermione rubbing shoulders with the sort of men who belonged to driving clubs. It wasn't that he didn't think women were good enough drivers, far from it. Instead, his objection rested on far more practical grounds. The men who belonged to such clubs were unlikely to curb their coarse habits before any lady who was so bold as to seek membership among their order. He wished only to shield ladies like Hermione from such behavior.

Sometime over the last few months, however, he'd had a change of heart. Perhaps because through her dedication, Lady Hermione had proved to him that she was strong enough to withstand the sort of rough manners she would be exposed to as a club member. And that it was her own choice to make and not his. Or her father's.

"Lady Hermione Upperton is as capable a female as I've ever met," he said now, to his skeptical friend. "And drives with more precision and care than any one of the men assembled today with the Lords of Anarchy. If anyone deserves to have their membership questioned, it's them, and not her."

Trent whistled. "I am glad to hear you are so willing to unbend your antiquated views about the role of the gentler sex, my friend." He laughed. "One might almost suspect you of having your views changed by repeated proximity to radical ladies like Lady Hermione, Miss Ophelia Dauntry, and Mrs. Frederick Lisle."

"It's not as if I were all that stiff-rumped before," Jasper said with a grimace. "I was simply persuaded by the evidence put before me. Like a mathematical proof, it was impossible not to note that one thing followed from the other."

But he knew in his heart of hearts that he had been exactly that unbending. Likely because his own mother—the lady he knew best—was quite opinionated about how ladies should behave. And though his father, who had died while Jasper was still a youth, was known to have been liberal in his views about such things, his mother was not. And since his father's death, she'd only grown more conservative.

"I am pleased to hear it," Trent said with a grin. "For I don't mind telling you I was beginning to wonder if you'd have done better as a vicar than a member of the peerage."

"My mother would love that," Jasper said with an answering grin. "Though I have a feeling she'd not take to the notion of giving up all the rights and privileges of being a countess with equanimity."

They were approaching the Craven town house when Jasper saw a familiar figure on horseback waiting nearby.

"You have a message for me?" he asked the young man in military dress who lingered just far enough away from the carriage carrying Freddy, Leonora, Hermione, and Ophelia so that their conversation would not be overheard.

With a nod, the messenger gave Jasper a document boasting a familiar wax seal.

Instead of giving the reins of his horse to the waiting groom, Jasper remained on horseback and steered his mount to where the occupants of the carriage had just disembarked.

"I'm afraid I won't be able to stay," he said with what he realized was real disappointment. He had wanted to explain what had happened last night with Hermione's father, and perhaps reassure her about what might be done to get her horses back. "I've just recalled a previous engagement."

Hermione, he noted, betrayed a flash of disappointment before it was quickly masked behind an expression of polite indifference.

Curious.

Aloud he said, "Perhaps I'll see you all at the Comerford ball tonight?"

"We will be there," Leonora said with a nod. "And I will do my best to persuade the rest of this motley crew to be there, as well. I fear we are sadly in need of a celebration after this morning's disappointments."

"I don't need a celebration," Hermione said grimly, her arms wrapped across her middle, almost as if she were trying to protect herself. "I need a few words with my father. Preferably with a guard close by so that I do not do him any lasting physical harm."

"Well, you will have to content yourself with a ball," Leonora said, giving Hermione a half hug. "And I know just what you should wear."

Jasper left them to their talk of fashion, feeling unaccountably annoyed at having to leave before he was sure Hermione was truly all right.

He found Sir Richard Lindsey seated behind a massive mahogany desk in a secluded corner of the Home Office. It was difficult to believe that many of the most sensitive investigations undertaken for the sake of the crown originated in such an unassuming locale. But Jasper had been a frequent enough visitor to the room that he no longer thought it odd.

"Mainwaring," the bespectacled baronet said with an expression of true pleasure. "I hadn't expected you so soon."

Standing, Sir Richard moved to the sideboard behind his desk and poured two glasses of brandy without bothering to ask if Jasper would like a drink.

Jasper had grown accustomed to his superior's odd hospitality, and wordlessly took the crystal glass from the other man. And after the scene in the park that morning, the alcohol was more than welcome.

Sir Richard inquired about Jasper's mother and

sisters and about the state of his estates. But the small talk was dispensed with quickly enough.

"I asked you here because I have a job I suspect you'll be especially well suited for," said Sir Richard, silently placing his glass down on the desk. "It's a rather delicate matter and I believe involves quite a few members of the *ton*."

During the war, Jasper had performed any number of offices for the crown using his position as a member of the beau monde as cover. With his help, a number of sympathizers with the Bonapartist cause had been quietly brought to justice. And since he'd been unable to serve his country in the military as Trent—who was then a mere younger son—had done, it had been something of which Jasper was quite proud. Despite the fact that he wasn't allowed to speak of his exploits openly.

But the war had been over for a few years now, and though Jasper knew that there were always those who intended the country harm who needed to be stopped, he hadn't considered that he could still be useful to the Home Office.

He said as much to Sir Richard, who laughed. "I can understand why you would think so, Mainwaring," the older man said. "But the truth of the matter is that enemies of the crown do not check if there is a war on before they begin their machinations. And in this case, the government would not even be involved in the investigation if the men in question were not using the gains from their crimes to fund a secret plot against the government."

"What is their purpose?" Jasper asked, curious. "I had hoped that Boney's followers had finally given up since his incarceration at St. Helena."

"I'm not at liberty to reveal their intent just now," Sir Richard said, his mouth twisted in a rueful smile.

"There are some things even our investigators are not allowed to know, and I'm afraid this is one of them. Suffice it to say that the threat is serious and we are certain that once they have the needed funds they will not hesitate to act against the government. Possibly with real violence."

Jasper had only worked on one other assignment where he was not privy to the intentions of those he investigated. It had turned out that the danger had been very real indeed, and as he had no reason to disbelieve his mentor now, he accepted the man's assertions without question.

"Who is it I'm meant to get close to?" he asked, a spark of excitement coursing through him at the challenge posed by the new task.

"How familiar are you with Viscount Saintcrow?" Sir Richard asked in response.

At the mention of Hermione's nemesis, Jasper blinked in surprise. He debated whether to reveal what had happened that morning, then decided the Home Office had little interest in Saintcrow's gambling winnings.

"A bit. We are acquainted," he said truthfully, "but not particularly close friends."

"That's fine," Sir Richard said, shuffling through a stack of papers before him on the desk. "I do not need you to become his dearest friend. I only wish for you to keep an eye on him. And a man named Fleetwood, whom we have reason to believe is involved with Saintcrow in a theft ring."

Finding the page he'd been looking for, Sir Richard gave Jasper a much-handled sheet of foolscap. On it was written a series of dates and names, like Wayfarer and Bonnie Jean and Nero.

"Ships, I take it?" Jasper asked curious.

"Horses," the other man corrected. "Over the past

year, horses have disappeared from some of the most prominent stables in England. Not only from the stock of breeders and trainers, but some out from under the noses of our most elite families. Like the Marquess of Kinsford, for instance."

Kinsford was several years older than Jasper, and spent most of his time racing horses and carriages and any vehicle he could get his hands on. So, the two men were not well acquainted. But even someone like Jasper, who spent more time at the card table than riding to hounds, knew of Kinsford's stables by reputation. He was said to have an uncanny ability to choose which horses would be best suited for coaching. And it was to him that many of London's coaching enthusiasts went for their horseflesh.

"And you suspect Saintcrow and Fleetwood are involved with the thefts?" Jasper asked, giving the page back.

"Yes." Sir Richard folded his hands before him on the desk. "Both men have been known to engage in some less than legal behavior when it comes to their business dealings. And even if they didn't spirit the steeds away themselves, they are likely to have had something to do with the thefts. Fleetwood in particular has been in the vicinity when several of the thefts took place. And we believe Saintcrow might be his associate in London."

"What is it you wish me to do exactly?" Jasper asked. After Saintcrow's behavior toward Hermione he was more than ready to make the man's life as difficult as possible. It was true that he'd been within his rights to take the horses back, but that didn't mean he'd gone about it in the most politic of manners.

"Pay attention to both men's habits while they're in town," Sir Richard said. "Attend the same social events that they do. Talk to their associates. And if you hear anything having to do with horses, let me know."

"I already know something about Saintcrow in that vein," Jasper said, quickly filling his superior in on what had happened between Saintcrow and the Uppertons.

"And what are the origins of these horses of Lady Hermione's?" Sir Richard asked, his brow furrowed in thought. "Could they be pilfered?"

"I hardly think that, sir," Jasper said with a shake of his head. "Hermione says her man of business purchased them for her through Tattersall's. And if Tatt's comes under suspicion then the whole of the English horse trade will collapse."

"Point taken," said Sir Richard. "But ask her if there was anything unusual about the purchase. It won't hurt. Though it's entirely possible that Saintcrow simply saw a chance to get his hands on a coaching pair without needing to do the work of stealing them and took it."

"I know where Saintcrow resides," Jasper said. "But where can I find Fleetwood?"

Sir Richard rattled off Fleetwood's address and Jasper swore.

"You are familiar with his direction?" the older man asked, brow raised.

Fleetwood's address was, in point of fact, just next door to the house where Lady Hermione Upperton and her father had moved at the beginning of the season—doubtless so that by renting out Upperton House, Lord Upperton would earn the cash needed to continue his gambling habit in the style to which he was accustomed.

"I am," he answered Sir Richard, hoping his expression did not convey his true feelings on the matter. He should probably tell the man that the suspect lived next door to Lady Hermione, but if he could he'd keep her out of this business. She'd gone through enough today. "It is near a friend."

"Capital," said Sir Richard with obvious enthusiasm. "Then you will be able to keep watch over the fellow without him suspecting anything. Especially if you are known to be friends with the neighbor chap."

"The friend is a lady," Jasper informed him, wanting desperately to remove his cravat which suddenly felt as if were tied far too tightly.

"Ah, even better. You can watch the man's house at all hours." He winked lasciviously—something Jasper hoped never, ever to see again. "Just keep your lady happy in the intervening hours and watch Fleetwood during your . . . ah . . . breaks."

"She's not that sort of lady," Jasper ground out.

If anything, Sir Richard looked crestfallen to hear his assumptions were wrong. Clearly the fellow had a more lurid imagination than Jasper had ever suspected.

"Ah, well then, you will have to limit yourself to respectable hours," he said with a shrug. "Unless the lady would be willing to keep an eye out during the rest of the time."

Jasper bit back a curse at the very idea.

"I do not think that is a good idea," he said finally, sure now that he could speak without insulting Sir Richard. "The lady is prone to recklessness and could possibly endanger the investigation."

Which, he thought, recalling the scene in the park, was not all that far from the truth.

Sir Richard's disappointment was palpable, but he seemed to trust Jasper's assessment of the situation. "Very well, then. It was only an idea. I will let you do as you see fit with the fellow. Just keep me informed of your actions."

"Of course, sir," Jasper said with barely disguised relief. He couldn't recall a more uncomfortable meeting with Sir Richard in their long association.

"If that's all," he said rising, "I'll be off."

Sir Richard also stood, and gave Jasper a slight bow. "It goes without saying that you should take great care for both your safety and that of your friend. One never knows what men like this will do if they feel threatened."

And with that warning ringing in his ears, Jasper hurried out of Whitehall.

He hadn't planned on it, but he needed to make a visit to Half-Moon Street to warn Hermione.

Three

When Hermione arrived home after several hours spent in the company of her sympathetic friends at Leonora's house, she freshened up a bit, then hurried out to the tiny mews behind the house in Half-Moon Street.

At the time she and her father had moved from Upperton House in Grosvenor Square to their rental house, she'd cringed at how much stable space they were giving up, but now that Rosencrantz and Guildenstern were gone, the small stable felt vast. Or at the very least empty.

Only her own riding mount was there now—her father having sold his own horses long ago, preferring to rely on hired carriages. Queen Mab was a pretty black mare whom Hermione had loved at first sight. "Hello, old thing," she crooned to the mare, who nuzzled Hermione's neck then sniffed the air for the scent of treats.

"Of course I didn't come empty-handed," she said, producing a shiny apple from the pocket of her coat. "See, I know what my girl likes."

"My lady," said a gruff voice from behind her. "If I might have a word."

Hermione sighed. She loved Jameson, but whenever he wanted to have a word it inevitably meant bad news.

Giving Mab one last scratch on the nose, she turned to the man who'd set her atop her first pony, and taught her everything she knew about horses.

"Of course, Jameson," she said with a smile. "I needed to speak to you, as well."

She'd not wanted to confess to him that Rosencrantz and Guildenstern would be gone—possibly forever—out of shame. It was unlikely that Jameson was unaware of her father's recklessness. He'd been with the family since she was a child, after all. And their removal from the comparatively palatial house in Grosvenor Square must have signaled to him that finances were not all that they could be. Still, it was with flushed cheeks and not quite meeting his eye that she told him of her coaching pair's repossession.

To his credit, Jameson didn't flinch at her tale. But when she chanced a look at his face, she saw that his lips were tight with anger. At her father she had little doubt. His family might have served the Upperton family for generations, but he was hardly required to like them. Especially the present earl, who had depleted the family stables to the point of near disappearance.

"I am that sorry to hear it, my lady," Jameson said gruffly. "I know how you loved that pair."

He could hardly have missed it considering she spent every spare moment fussing over them and ensuring they had every comfort. Still, it was soothing to her broken heart.

"Thank you, Jameson," she said sincerely. "I know you have endured much with this family, and I know it cannot be easy. But I am hopeful that their removal will only be temporary and we will get them back."

"Aye, my lady," he replied, giving no hint as to whether he believed her promise or not. "In the meantime, we'll do what we can to take care of what we have."

"Now, you wanted to speak to me of some other matter?" she asked, not daring to hope that it would be something good he intended to tell her.

Jameson nodded. "It's nothing to do with our stables, my lady." He lowered his voice and glanced left then right, as if ensuring they would not be overheard. "It's the fellow who has the one next door."

Hermione was shocked at his words. "What of him?" she asked in a low voice.

"He was poking his nose around here yesterday," Jameson said with a frown. "Made out how he was just being friendly like at first, but there was something about the way he asked questions that set my back up. Wanted to know just where you'd got the coaching pair in particular. Wasn't none of his business so I never said outright, but he was persistent, he was."

Since her father hadn't lost Rosencrantz and Guildenstern until last night, the man's curiosity the afternoon before was suspicious. Could Lord Saintcrow have targeted her horses with an eye toward persuading her father to offer them for wager? Of course it was possibly a mad coincidence that he'd lost them the very night that her neighbor inquired after them, but it seemed too convenient.

"What was this man's name?" she asked Jameson.

"Fleetwood, my lady," the groom said grimly. "He lives with his sister, he said. In that house there." He pointed to the house to the right of the Upperton back garden.

Hermione smiled. The fact that Fleetwood lived with his sister was a good thing, considering it would be highly improper for her to call upon an unmarried man. But calling upon a female neighbor would be unexceptionable.

"I shall simply have to pay a call upon this sister of his," she said with a grin. "In the spirit of being neighborly, of course."

But Jameson clearly did not think it as fine an idea as she did. "My lady, I don't like the notion of you visiting that house. I didn't like the fellow and make no mistake. There was something . . . not right about the man."

It was a rare break in protocol for Jameson to raise an objection to Hermione's actions. He'd not spoken so openly to her since she was a girl. And while she appreciated his concern on the one hand, on the other, she knew she had to make her own decisions. Especially if Mr. Fleetwood's curiosity had somehow influenced the loss of her beloved horses.

"I do not doubt you mean the best, Jameson," she said kindly, "but I promise I will be careful. And calling upon a neighbor lady is quite safe, no matter how untoward her brother might be. We are not in so elevated a neighborhood as we once were, but neither are we in the East End where thieves and the like run rampant."

"You must do as you think best, my lady," Jameson said stiffly, but it was clear he was not best pleased.

"Thank you," Hermione told him, suppressing the urge to hug him as she'd done as a child. In many ways, Jameson had been a better father to her than Lord Upperton had been. "I promise to be cautious."

And with that, he would have to make do.

Leaving Jameson to his work, Hermione stepped

out of the stables and into the narrow lane that ran behind the row of houses.

The back garden of the Fleetwoods' house was tidy enough, and had clearly once been someone's pride and joy, for though the flower beds looked to have long lain dormant, there were enough climbing vines and bushes scattered throughout to prove that someone with a taste for beauty had planted them.

It was, perhaps, not customary to pay a social call by knocking at the kitchen door of a home, but maybe she could learn more about the Fleetwoods by asking the cook for some cuttings from what looked to be a thriving kitchen garden. At least what little she could see of it from the fence line.

Stepping through the wooden gate, and onto the stone path that led through the garden, she was startled to hear a sharp cry from somewhere ahead of her.

Jameson's warnings still fresh in her mind, she debated whether it would be best to turn around and leave. But what if someone was hurt? And needed her help?

Her decision made, she continued forward in the direction from which she'd heard the cries.

"Hello?" she called out, wending her way through the overgrown shrubbery. "Is someone there? Are you hurt?"

There was no answer and as she pressed on, she came to a clearing, where a brick courtyard led up to the back of the house.

A courtyard that was currently deserted, with the exception of a black-and-white cat, who watched Hermione's approach with lazy interest.

"You're on private property," a loud male voice said sharply from behind her. Startled from its languor, the cat sprinted off.

Hermione wished she might do the same.

Turning to face her accuser, she saw an unfamiliar dark-haired gentleman, whose scowl made her wish she had listened to Jameson's warning.

"I'm terribly sorry," she said, hoping to placate him. "I was hoping to ask your cook for some cuttings from the garden." It had sounded like a good enough excuse at the time, but in the face of her neighbor's anger, she wasn't so sure.

She said nothing of the cry she'd heard. She wasn't sure why, but somehow she knew the man would not like knowing she'd heard it.

But despite her best attempt at pleasantries, he did not unbend.

"If you wish to speak to someone in the house, you can use the front door like any other lady of quality." His implication being that because she'd chosen the door at the back of the house she was not such a lady.

Before she could respond, he turned and gestured to the gate through which she'd come. "Let me see you to the gate, miss."

Hermione's sense of self-preservation warred with curiosity.

Curiosity won.

"It's 'lady,' actually," she said with unrelenting pleasantness. "Lady Hermione Upperton. Since we are neighbors, I don't think the tabbies will frown too terribly much on me for introducing myself. My father is the Earl of Upperton and we live, as you might already have deduced, in the house next door."

The man looked as if he were about to reply, when a shout from the lane behind them drew their attention.

"There you are!" said the Earl of Mainwaring, his

curly dark hair ruffling in the breeze. He hurried toward them, as if he and Hermione had been separated unexpectedly. "I've been searching all over for you, Lady Hermione."

What the devil was he doing here?

"Won't you introduce me to your friend?" he asked pointedly, as if they were in a ballroom rather than the back garden of her "friend's" house. His expression was bland, but Hermione could feel the annoyance coming off him in waves.

"We've not been introduced," Hermione said stiffly. "I was just about to ask his name when you arrived so unexpectedly."

"Mainwaring," said the interloper, holding out his hand to Hermione's neighbor, ignoring the way she glared at him. "I like this courtyard very much, indeed. I've been thinking of doing something on a similar scale at my own house, though it's difficult to convince the mater to make any changes at all. You know how mothers can be, eh?"

To Hermione's surprise, the man seemed to relax in the face of Mainwaring's chatter and gave a grudging nod. Clearly he took the earl's upper-class-twit act at face value.

"I do indeed understand," he said with a smile. Giving a slight bow, he said, "Robert Fleetwood at your service. I'm afraid I must have seemed unwelcoming to your lady, here. It's just that I worry about my sister. She suffers from nerves and I fear that she will be overset by the sight of unfamiliar people in the garden, which she considers to be her private domain."

Annoyed that the man had revealed to Mainwaring what he'd been so reluctant to tell her, Hermione wondered if his tale about his sister was truthful. He seemed sincere, but she could not trust him in light of what Jameson had told her.

"I am sorry to hear of your sister's illness," she said despite her misgivings. Then, deciding to test Mr. Fleetwood now that Mainwaring was there to offer her protection, she continued. "I hope it wasn't she I heard crying out earlier. It was definitely a female voice and she sounded quite overset."

Was it her imagination or was that a flash of anger in Fleetwood's eyes? She'd have to ask Mainwaring about it later.

Still, he seemed unruffled enough when he spoke a few seconds later.

"Indeed," Fleetwood said with a frown. "It was very likely Mariah. She suffers from nerves and is unable to contain herself at times. Which is why I chose this house with its very private garden."

Hermione felt a blush rise at the man's pointed look. But Mainwaring saved her from further apologies by speaking up. "I do hope she'll be feeling more the thing soon," he said, all sympathy. "Lady Hermione and I will leave now so that you may go to her at once."

And though she would have liked to remain for a bit longer to question Mr. Fleetwood about his sister and perhaps to question whether he was acquainted with Lord Saintcrow, Mainwaring linked her arm with his and with a wave in Fleetwood's direction led her back through the garden and to the lane beyond.

She waited until they were safely out of earshot before turning on him.

"What on earth was that? You had no business interrupting my conversation and behaving as if we had some prearranged meeting." She opened the gate to her own garden with more vehemence than necessary and it whipped backward on its hinges. "What business could you possibly have in the lane behind my house?"

Following her at a leisurely pace, Mainwaring shut the gate calmly behind him as he trailed her to a little sitting area in the corner of the garden. On the side opposite that of Fleetwood's house.

She had no intention of inviting him into the house. Especially not after he'd spoiled her encounter with Mr. Fleetwood.

"It's all very innocent, I assure you," Mainwaring said, leaning a broad shoulder against a sturdy wooden arch covered with climbing roses. His coat of blue superfine was without so much as a speck of dust, but he seemed unworried about the possibility of picking up pollen from the blooms. "I called to speak with your father, and when I learned he was out, I asked for you. I was told you were in the stables, and picked up your trail there."

His words brought her up sharp.

"Why were you here to see Papa?" she asked in a tight voice, though she had a very good idea.

Mainwaring's look of discomfort only confirmed it.

"It is not your responsibility to confront him over my horses," she said firmly. "I appreciate your concern, but there is no need for you to fight my battles for me."

"I was there when he lost them," Mainwaring said quietly, and she felt a sting of betrayal at the confession. "There was nothing I could do to stop him, but I did witness the game with Saintcrow."

The reminder that Mainwaring was just as addicted to the tables as her father was came as a timely warning lest she succumb to the new amity between them.

"And you didn't think to tell me this morning before I took them to the park?" she demanded.

"I assumed your father would let you know," he said calmly. "Of course I know now that was wishful thinking at best."

"Yes, well, I've come to expect such things from my father," she said bitterly. "But I had hoped that my friends would act with my best interests in mind."

"I didn't realize they were your only coaching pair, Lady Hermione," he said with what seemed like sincere remorse. "If I had I might have acted differently. I knew of course that you would be upset at their loss, but I thought at the very least you'd be able to drive another pair for your first outing with the Lords of Anarchy."

"You were against me joining a driving club at all," she reminded him, recalling just how he'd opposed the notion when they'd first met. "I had thought you'd changed your mind, but now I begin to wonder."

He stepped closer, and she was reminded of how much taller than her he was. This close she could smell the scent of his cologne and something else that was peculiar to him alone.

"It's been a long time since I felt you should be excluded from the membership of the competitive driving clubs," he said softly. "I admire you for your determination. And I truly did not refrain from informing you about your father's loss last evening in order to ruin your first outing with the Lords of Anarchy."

She lowered her lashes in the face of his intense gaze. Despite her misgivings about his gambling, she was beginning to find him irresistibly attractive. Something she needed to fight against if she wished to avoid the sort of life she now lived with her father.

"I suppose it's not your fault that my father chose to wager with my horses," she said finally. "He has been doing things like this for years now. Likely long before you or I were even born."

"It's an unpleasant situation," Mainwaring finally said, stepping back a little. As if he sensed her inner turmoil. "But it might be possible to convince Saint-crow to drop his claim on them, if it can be proved you were the true owner and not your father. Do you perhaps have the original paperwork from when your man of business purchased them?"

"I do," Hermione said, grateful for his interest, though not sure that it would help. "I will ask Mr. Wingate to send it round. But speaking of my horses . . ."

Quickly, she related what the groom had told her about Fleetwood's strange appearance in the Upper-ton mews.

If anything, Mainwaring looked more troubled. "Thank you for trusting me enough to tell me about this," he said, his blue eyes intense. "Now, I am go-ing to ask you to do something for me. And you are quite likely to tell me to go hang."

Since she was not known for her reticence when it came to speaking her mind, she did not dispute his assessment.

"Do not have anything else to do with Fleetwood," Mainwaring warned. "Or his sister. If she even exists."

"Why wouldn't she exist?" Hermione asked, mo-mentarily diverted by the idea. "It's hardly the sort of thing he'd choose to make up."

"I didn't say it was the truth," he explained, "just a possibility. There is definitely something havey-cavey about the fellow. I cannot tell you what precisely, but please trust me in this."

Just then, a female cry sounded from the direction of the Fleetwood house.

"That was not the sound of a ghost," Hermione said firmly, her gaze on the wall separating her own garden from her neighbor's. "It was a human woman. And if there is something I can do to help, then surely I must do it. If it is Mr. Fleetwood's sister, then she doesn't necessarily know anything about his oddities."

But rather than offer a similar condolence for Fleetwood's sister, Mainwaring's generous mouth tightened. "No! You must promise me that you will not venture next door again, Hermione. I must have your word."

She was very tempted to do as he'd said before and tell him to go hang—especially at his demanding tone. Who was he to tell her what to do, after all?

And yet, there had been something about Mr. Fleetwood that set her nerves on edge—especially considering what Jameson had said about him. So, staying away from the man was not something she found particularly bothersome. Yes, she did have sympathy for the woman—whoever she might be—who lived in the house, but she was not so deaf to her own instincts that she'd ignore them to put herself in danger.

"Fine," she said with what she hoped sounded like grudging acceptance. It would not do for Mainwaring to take it into his head that he had the power to stop her from doing whatever she wished.

"I realize it goes against your very nature to consider something that I might say to be remotely worthy of notice," he said with obvious relief, "but pray believe me when I say that I have very good reasons for wishing you to leave both Mr. Fleetwood and his sister—mythological or otherwise—alone."

"You didn't just happen upon me in Fleetwood's back garden, did you?" she asked suspiciously.

"I did not," he said, pinching the bridge of his

nose, as if he very suddenly felt a sharp pain there. "But I can tell you no more than that."

Noting the tension in his angelic features, Hermione considered, for perhaps the first time, that there might be more to Mainwaring than she'd originally thought. Despite his demurral, she wanted to ask him more about the reasons behind his warning. Not only because it seemed possible that there was a connection between her mysterious neighbor and Lord Saintcrow, but also because it promised to offer her a diversion from her current woes.

But in the face of his obvious reluctance, she did not press him.

Four

When she went back inside, after bidding Mainwaring a hasty good-bye, it was to find that her father had come and gone while she was in the mews.

Either he was reluctant to face her in light of his reprehensible actions, or to her mind, worse, he hadn't any notion that what he'd done was so very wrong.

"Thank you, Greentree," she said to the butler who had delivered the news about her father's whereabouts with his customarily dour expression.

Taking in the shabby entryway of their rented house on the edge of Mayfair, Hermione sighed, then made her way upstairs with the beginnings of a headache gathering between her eyes.

After a hot bath and a brief nap, she felt much more the thing, and later that evening as she descended the steps to where Leonora and Freddy's carriage waited, she did so with a spring in her step.

"You're looking well this evening," Freddy said with an appreciative smile as he moved to the backward-facing seat so that Hermione could take the one next to Leonora.

"You are indeed, dearest," Leonora said, kissing

her friend on the cheek. "That shade of vermilion is particularly nice with your dark hair."

The gown was one that Hermione had been saving for a special occasion. Especially since its vibrant color was not particularly appropriate for a young unmarried lady. But as with her quest to join a driving club, her choices when it came to her wardrobe were hardly made with an eye to toeing the line of good behavior. She was finished with blind obedience to the strictures society imposed upon her. Especially since her father seemed so unconcerned with his own actions.

She knew she looked more than presentable in the high-waisted gown, with its low-cut neckline and puffed sleeves. Every time she took a step, she felt the swish of its silk against her chemise and stays beneath. And the cashmere wrap she'd chosen to go with it was achingly soft against her bare arms.

In short, the gown made her feel confident.

And after the debacle she'd suffered earlier in the day, she needed the added bolster the attire provided her.

When they were announced at the Comerford town house an hour later, she was glad of her decision to look her best. Because from the moment she stepped over the threshold, she became aware of fans being lifted to hide conversations and speculative looks from every gentleman who crossed her path.

It was only after she'd followed Leonora and Freddy into the ballroom proper, however, that the true onslaught began.

"Lady Hermione," said Mrs. Charity Glendenning, whom Hermione had known since they were both in the nursery, in a breathless voice as she rushed forward. "You are so brave to come here tonight. I told Felicity that any lady bold enough to join the

Lords of Anarchy would most certainly not be ashamed to show her face at a ball. And I was right."

She was shadowed by her dear friend, and sometime partner in crime, Lady Felicity Fremont, whose expression was frozen in a perpetual frown. Both ladies had married shortly after their first season and had not hesitated to use their matronhood as a blunt instrument with which to batter the other ladies who had not been so lucky.

Since neither had married gentlemen whom Hermione found at all tolerable, she was not so much jealous of the pair, as annoyed by their continuous attempts to shame her for remaining unwed. If her only choices were eternal celibacy and marriage to a man cut from the same cloth as Peter Glendenning and Lord Charles Fremont, then celibacy it would be.

"I'm not sure what you're speaking of, Charity," Hermione lied with a bright smile. "You don't mean that business at the park this morning, surely?"

"Of course that's what I mean, silly," said Charity with a shake of her guinea-gold curls. "It's all anyone is talking about, my dear," she continued sotto voce. "You must have been utterly mortified. Bad enough for your father to lose your horses, but for Lord Saintcrow to demand them from you in the middle of the park. . . ."

As she spoke, Charity's fan moved faster and faster. As if it were propelled by the power of her anticipation of Hermione's embarrassment.

"I heard you were forced to walk home," said Lady Felicity in a low voice. "That you hadn't even brought your purse so you could take a hackney."

"What nonsense is this?" Leonora demanded, moving to stand by Hermione's side. "Of course she didn't walk home. We took her up in our carriage with us."

Because Leonora was a celebrated poet, and as such was still a bit of a novelty in most *ton* circles, the two women's eyes widened at her championship of her friend.

"I'm sure we don't mean anything untoward, Miss Craven," Charity said, her face flushed. "Of course we didn't."

"It's Mrs. Lisle," said Hermione with a brittle smile. "You do remember that Leonora is married to Lord Frederick Lisle, now don't you?"

Since both ladies had been overheard wondering aloud why an eligible *parti* like Freddy Lisle would ally himself to a poetess of all things, Hermione was fairly certain they did remember, but it felt good to call attention to the mistake given how gleeful Charity had been upon seeing Hermione enter the room.

"Of course, we remember," said Felicity, blinking owlishly. "And of course we meant no disrespect to you, my dear Lady Hermione. Naturally, we wished to offer you our sympathies after all you endured earlier today. Especially given our long acquaintance."

At that moment, Hermione saw Charity's eyes widen, and her fan, which had begun to slow while Felicity spoke, began to beat furiously.

Turning, she saw that Freddy, who had gone off in search of Mainwaring and Trent as soon as they arrived, had been successful in his quest, and the two men flanked him on either side, like guards of a sort.

She took a moment to survey the three men, each handsome in his own way. Freddy, his burnished curls a little longer than was fashionable, was the tallest, and wore his evening dress like a second skin. The Duke of Trent, on the other hand, was every inch the military man for all that he'd left off his gold braid and scarlet coat for the understated elegance of an evening coat and an elegantly tied cravat.

But it was to Mainwaring that her eye was drawn. By any reasonable measure he was handsome, offering a darkly beautiful contrast to Freddy's golden good looks. A little shorter than his friend, the earl even so held himself with the poise of a man who had known from an early age that he stood to inherit a peerage, and all that it entailed. There was no question of his authority, and despite her natural aversion to masculine power, Hermione felt herself shiver a little in the face of it.

When he bowed over her hand, she couldn't help the stab of satisfaction at Charity and Felicity's consternation in the face of his singling her out.

"Lady Hermione," he said, holding her hand for a shade longer than was proper. "You are looking lovely this evening."

Though she knew it was only Mainwaring, Hermione felt a blush steal into her cheeks. Clearly she was spending too much time in the man's company if he was able to stir such a response from her.

Neither of them made mention of their encounter that afternoon in Half-Moon Street.

"Thank you, my lord," she said when she'd recovered her breath. "That is kind of you. If I may say so you're looking quite well yourself."

With a smile that indicated he had guessed the direction of her thoughts, Mainwaring thanked her. "I hope you will save a waltz for me," he said, pointing to the dance card dangling from her wrist. "As well as the supper dance. If they haven't already been claimed, of course."

Seeing that they would get no more of a reaction from Hermione or her friends, Charity and Felicity excused themselves and slunk away to share whatever rumor and innuendo they could with their fellow guests.

"What did those two have to say for themselves?" Trent asked once the gossips were out of earshot. "I could almost feel the enmity radiating from them."

"I've never been a great fan of either lady," Leonora said with a frown, "but I admit I had no idea they'd be so bloodthirsty in the face of potential prey."

"Thank God we were here," Freddy said, bowing slightly to Hermione. "Else who knows what they might have got up to."

Hermione found herself wanting to object to being made out to be such a poor-spirited creature when Mainwaring surprised her by speaking up.

"I have little doubt that Lady Hermione would be able to hold her own against those two, or any other harpies who might decide to go after her." At Hermione's gasp, he winked at her. "This is, you must recall, the same lady who persisted in her quest to join a driving club until one finally invited her in. That is no small feat."

"Oh yes," she said, reminded of just why she might need the others' protection, "I am such a force of nature that my own father thought nothing of wagering my personal property over a game of cards. Clearly, I am to be feared by all."

"That was not your fault, dearest," said Leonora, squeezing her shoulder. "In truth, I cannot think your father would have behaved any differently if you were Lord Herman Upperton instead of Lady Hermione. Your sex had nothing to do with it."

"So it was merely a bad coincidence that his loss of my horses happened the night before I was to parade them through Hyde Park?" she asked with raised brows. "If so, it was a case of wretched bad luck on my part."

"Trent and I were there at the gaming hell where he lost them," Mainwaring said with a kindness that made Hermione's gut clench. "And he spoke of your horses as if they were his own. In truth, I think he only thought of them as a means for him to keep playing."

"I suppose that's true enough," she said glumly. "But I no longer have my horses all the same."

"We came here tonight to get your mind off your loss," Leonora said with a pointed glance at Mainwaring, who shrugged. "Now, I believe I saw Ophelia standing near the punch table. Shall we go in search of her?"

And before Hermione could object, she found herself being escorted across the ballroom.

"What was that for?" she demanded of her friend once they were a little ways away from the gentlemen. "I was enjoying Mainwaring's company for a change."

"I am sorry for that," Leonora said in a low voice, "but something just occurred to me. And I thought it best not to speak of it within earshot of Freddy, for I feel sure he'd do his best to dissuade you from it."

"From what?" Hermione whispered. She couldn't imagine what sort of scheme her friend was concocting. Unbidden, the memory of her hand grasped in Mainwaring's rushed back to her.

"Remember what I said about your father not paying any attention to whether you were a son or a daughter when he gambled away your horses?" Leonora asked as she pulled Hermione into a small alcove on the other side of the ballroom.

Wordlessly, Hermione nodded.

"What if you *were* a son?" Leonora asked, her eyes bright with excitement.

Clearly, her friend had lost her mind.

"But I am *not* a son, dearest," said Hermione patiently. As if the fact that she was a female was something she needed to share with Leonora.

"But what if you were to pretend to be your father's son?" the poetess explained. "To confront Lord Saintcrow?"

"But my father has no son." Hermione wondered if she should fetch Freddy so that he could take Leonora home to rest. "Only me."

"I don't mean you should call yourself his son. Just that you should visit Lord Saintcrow at his home. In a disguise of some sort. So that your reputation doesn't become any more tainted. After all, it would be a scandal of the first order if you were to go to Lord Saintcrow's home dressed as yourself. But if you were in disguise, then no one would know it was you."

Hermione blinked. "But why would I visit Lord Saintcrow in the first place? His agreement with my father has already been made. And I hardly think he will change his mind based on my paying a highly improper call upon him."

"Those are not the words of the same lady who convinced London's most notorious driving club to let her become a member," Leonora said, setting her fists on her hips. "What happened to that lady?"

"She was humiliated before all of London in the middle of Hyde Park," Hermione said wryly. "Surely you don't think that compounding that scandal with another will save me."

"I think it could get you your horses back," Leonora said firmly. "And the sooner you have them back, the sooner you can take your rightful place as a member of the Lords of Anarchy."

"What are the two of you discussing in such heated tones?" Ophelia asked, stepping forward into their little enclosure. "Your father hasn't done something else, has he?"

It was just like Ophelia to worry over her, Hermione thought with a warm heart. She really did have wonderful friends. Even if at the moment, Leonora seemed to have lost her wits.

But when Leonora explained her proposal to Ophelia, the other girl clapped her hands. "It's perfect," she said with a grin. "It's been ages since we had an adventure. And if the three of us beard the lion in his den, then Lord Saintcrow will have no choice but to give your horses back."

"The three of us?" Hermione echoed. "Are you mad? The three of us cannot descend upon Lord Saintcrow's town house en masse!" She was not accustomed to playing the role of the voice of reason in their little group, but it was clear someone needed to.

"Oh, don't be such a spoilsport, Hermione," said Leonora, who now that she had someone to agree to her mad plan was only more enthusiastic about it. "It will be fun."

"If you say so," Hermione said with a sense of impending doom. "Though I draw the line at dressing like a man."

If she'd learned one thing about her friends, it was that once they had the bit between their teeth, there was no way of getting them to change their minds. And if she were truly honest with herself, it had been a long time since the three of them had got up to any sort of adventure.

"Very well then, we'll all three wear heavy veils," Leonora said. "And we'll simply convince Lord Saintcrow that your father was mistaken about the true ownership of the horses. I'm sure once it's explained to him, he'll see reason."

"You saw him this morning," Hermione said with a shake of her head. "I explained it to him very succinctly."

"Yes, dearest," Ophelia said softly. "But you said it to him in front of other men."

Would Lord Saintcrow be more reasonable when confronted alone? When there was an opportunity for him to do the right thing and save his precious *amour propre*? Thinking back on the man's behavior that morning, she thought it was possible.

Very well.

"Let's do it," she said, placing her hand in the center of their little circle, so that the other two ladies could place their own hands on top of hers.

"If nothing else, we'll get an adventure out of it," Leonora said with a grin.

Hermione certainly hoped so. And if truth be told, it could hardly be any worse than that morning's debacle had been.

Five

*W*hen Jasper searched out Hermione for their waltz, he found her in deep conversation with Lord Payne, the current president of the Lords of Anarchy.

"I feel sure we can work something out, Lady Hermione," Payne was saying with what to Jasper's eye looked to be an overabundance of solicitude. Payne was married, so there was no question that his intentions, whatever they might be, were honorable. And despite the fact that the fellow had so far as he knew done nothing to disrespect Hermione, Jasper did not like the man.

"Thank you so much, Lord Payne," Hermione said with a bright smile, her eyes shining with real excitement. "I hope there will be a way for me to retrieve my horses from Lord Saintcrow's possession, but until then I will be very grateful for the loan of your bays."

It had not gone without Jasper's notice that she was looking exceptionally well this evening. For someone who had experienced a very difficult morning, she seemed in good spirits. If his mother or sisters had endured such a setback they'd have taken to their beds. Possibly for a week. Of course none of them would have considered joining a driving club in the first place, but that was beside the point.

Her gown, which was some shade between red and orange—he was no connoisseur of color—made a striking contrast against her dark hair, which was arranged with a series of wispy curls framing her face. A coiffure that fairly begged a man to brush them away from her cheek for a kiss.

Seeing the direction of Payne's gaze, he observed that the other man had not failed to notice the way her gown set off Hermione's very generous bosom. Time to cut this interview short, he thought with a frown.

"My apologies for the interruption," he lied with a slight bow to Lord Payne, "but I must claim Lady Hermione for our waltz. You understand don't you, old chap?"

Hermione's lips pursed at the intrusion, but Lord Payne didn't seem to mind. "Not at all, Mainwaring," he said with a nod. "We were just finishing up. Club business, you understand."

"One might have thought the club could have done something earlier today to stand up for its newest member," Jasper said blandly. He did not care for the way Payne had implied that he had some sort of private matter to discuss with Hermione. "I feel sure Saintcrow might have backed down if he'd been faced with the whole of the Lords of Anarchy rather than a single defenseless lady."

"I wasn't defenseless," Hermione said sharply, looking as if he'd betrayed her in some way. "I am quite able to take care of myself, thank you, Mainwaring. And it had nothing to do with the club."

Jasper felt her frown like a stinging pinch, but he did not back down. "If that were the case then you would have been able to keep your horses, Lady Hermione."

Lord Payne looked from one to the other with

something like amusement. Which annoyed Jasper further. "We did not intervene, Mainwaring, because it looked to us like she already had champions in yourself and Lord Frederick. If you were not strong enough to stop Saintcrow from taking possession of her horses, then that is no fault of ours."

Before Jasper could respond, Lord Payne gave a short bow. "I shall see you later in the week, then, Lady Hermione. Enjoy your dance." And then he was gone.

The bastard hadn't even stayed behind long enough to be contradicted.

"That was entirely unnecessary," Hermione said with a glower. "Especially since you yourself have admitted that there was little anyone could have done to dissuade Saintcrow from taking my horses."

The opening notes of a waltz sounded then, and in a strangely possessive mood, Jasper maneuvered Hermione onto the dance floor.

"I could have refused to take the floor with you, you know," she continued pettishly. "With anyone else I would have done."

"Then I am heartily glad you did not," Jasper said, breathing in the soft floral scent of her. "And I did not mean to offend you. I was merely taking your side. It seems to me that your fellow club members have not shown you the sort of support to which you are entitled."

"So you truly believe Lord Saintcrow would have been convinced to abandon his intent to take my horses if the Lords of Anarchy had intervened?" she asked, her brow furrowed.

"Well, perhaps not," Jasper admitted. Affairs of honor, like wagers, were not something that a gentleman typically interfered with. If Saintcrow said he'd won the horses from Hermione's father, then that was all that most men needed to give the fellow wide latitude. "But they might have tried. What good is it for you to belong to a driving club if they do not advocate on your behalf?"

"Oh, I don't know," Hermione said with a roll of her eyes. "Perhaps because I wish to test my driving skills against those of the best drivers in England? I didn't join the Lords of Anarchy for the fellowship. Or even the safety of numbers. It was strictly about the driving."

"And I suppose Payne lending a pair of his own horses is about the driving, as well?" Jasper asked, applying slight pressure at her waist as they moved with the dance.

"As a matter of fact," she responded with a smile, "it is. I cannot drive without horses, and he has more than one pair. Thus I will take loan of his."

He wanted to object on the basis that it was highly improper for a lady to accept such a gift from a gentleman, but since it was a loan, and therefore not precisely a gift, Jasper kept his mouth shut. And in his gut he knew his objection had nothing to do with the impropriety of the situation and everything to do with his growing possessiveness when it came to Hermione. If anyone was going to loan her a coaching pair, it should be him.

Unfortunately, he didn't own a coaching pair and, given his lack of enthusiasm for driving, was unlikely to in the near future.

"Since this subject is so unpleasant for both of us," Hermione continued, "let us speak of something else. Why don't you tell me how your family go on?"

They finished the waltz engaged in polite chatter about his mother and sisters and her wardrobe discussions with Leonora and Ophelia.

When he brought her back to the edge of the ballroom once the dance was ended, he was about to make an excuse and flee when she gasped.

"My father," she said through clenched teeth, as she stared at the door leading into the ballroom. "I have a few words to say to him."

Before Jasper could respond, she was wending her way through the throng of guests. Suspecting that she might do something she'd regret, he hurried after her.

Lord Upperton, when they reached him, was in conversation with one of his cronies, Viscount Lindhurst, whom Jasper knew to be just as devoted to the gaming tables as Upperton. He didn't notice his daughter was standing behind him until she tapped him on the shoulder.

The flash of fear in his eyes before he masked it with ennui was almost comical.

"My dear daughter," Hermione's father said languidly, "I didn't know you'd be here this evening. What a delightful surprise."

If the man thought his daughter would give him a reprieve because they were in a public location, he'd underestimated the degree of her annoyance.

"I cannot imagine you are nearly as surprised as I was this morning when Lord Saintcrow informed me that he had won my grays from you at the gaming tables, Papa," she said with a smile that did not reach her eyes.

Upperton's eyes widened and he said with a jovial laugh, "Ah, my dear, you mustn't bore my friends with our private family matters. I pray you will excuse us, Lindhurst. My daughter is having a fit of the vapors, don't you know?"

When Upperton grasped her upper arm in an attempt to pull her from the room, Jasper intervened. "You'd better unhand her, my lord," he said quietly, his own hand gripped tight on the older man's forearm.

"Why don't we retire to one of Comerford's less crowded rooms."

At Jasper's grip, Upperton scowled, but let Hermione go. Wordlessly, he allowed Jasper to lead them into the hallway beyond and into an empty parlor.

When the door was closed firmly behind them, Hermione glared at him.

"This is between Papa and me," she said firmly. "I appreciate your help, but it is not necessary."

"Oh, let the man stay, Hermione," Lord Upperton said wearily. "If for no other reason than to protect me from you."

Hermione's expression darkened. "Then you admit that I have reason to be angry with you?"

Lord Upperton moved farther into the room, which was clearly some sort of little-used antechamber—perhaps for keeping unwanted guests in suspense while the butler took their cards to the mistress of the house. With a sigh, he stared into the fire which burned merrily despite the tension in the room.

"I did nothing wrong," Upperton said, his back still turned, as if facing his daughter while he said it was too much even for his powers of mendacity.

"Nothing wrong?" Hermione almost shouted. "You lost my grays at the gaming table! My grays. Which belong to me. Not you. Do you not acknowledge that at the very least it was untoward?"

Jasper wanted nothing more than to make this right for her, but as a mere bystander he could not. He could see to it that her father faced her with his explanations, but he could hardly force the man to admit his guilt.

When Upperton turned around, it was with an expression of paternal indulgence that even he found condescending. And the man wasn't his father.

"My dear daughter," Upperton said with a fatuous smile, "I know you are unfamiliar with men's business, so you will simply have to believe me when I say it could not be helped. I owed a debt to Lord Saintcrow, and he very kindly agreed to take the horses in exchange for it. It really could not be helped. And I must tell you how grateful I am to you for your forbearance in the matter."

Jasper had been there, and knew that Upperton was lying through his teeth. But this was one of those cases where the truth of the matter would do no good. Since Saintcrow had the horses in his possession now, it would take nothing short of a legal proceeding or some very strong persuasion to get them back.

"My forbearance?" Hermione echoed, her voice softer now. As her father had spoken, she had slowly seemed to lose whatever strength her anger had given her. And in its place was a resignation that was far more difficult to see. "Papa, I am not a fool. And I do not admit that what you did was right. By law you might be entitled to my belongings, but ethically, what you did was a betrayal. And I'm not sure I shall ever be able to forgive you."

The silence that fell upon the little room was near deafening. Jasper wanted to speak, simply to relieve the tension. But he held his tongue. He was here to see that they didn't kill each other. But the discussion was between Hermione and her father.

Then, as if from long years of practice, Upperton stepped forward and touched his daughter on the shoulder. If her flinch upset him, he didn't show it. Merely held on tight and said, "I understand you're angry, daughter, but as I said, it was men's business. Now, if you'll excuse me, I said I'd meet some friends in the card room."

Hermione bit her lip, but said nothing. Just waited silently for her father to leave the room.

When the door closed behind him, Jasper moved to stand in front of her. "All right?" he asked quietly. He wanted to take her in his arms, but they were not at that stage yet. If they ever would be. He was all too aware that his own frequent appearances at the gaming tables—no matter how he might think himself far more controlled than Upperton—could pose a problem for someone who had lost so much because of them. As Hermione had.

Almost as if she'd overheard his thoughts, she said, "You were there last night, weren't you?"

At his nod, she turned away from him and moved to stand before the fire, where Lord Upperton had so lately stood.

"Did you know that the reason we let the London town house and moved to Half-Moon Street was because he needed the money to pay back his debts?" she asked without turning. "My father has lost everything that isn't entailed. And the estate is in such disrepair that the tenants whose families have lived on Upperton land for centuries live in squalor while he goes about his business as usual. Plays every night, convinced that he will finally win enough so that we can move back into the Upperton town house."

"I did not know it," Jasper said softly, stepping forward to stand just a breath away from her. "But I am not surprised. With men like your father, it is almost a sickness. They cannot stop playing no matter how much they lose."

She turned. But didn't seem surprised to find him so much closer. Instead she looked up, and lifted her hand to finger the diamond stickpin winking from the center of his neck cloth.

"And do you also have this sickness?" she asked,

not looking up. "Do you feel a compulsion to throw away your family's money over the turn of a card?"

"It's not like that with me," he said, though he knew that was exactly what a man who could not turn away from the tables would say. "It is something I enjoy. Something I am good at. That is all."

At last she looked up, and he saw skepticism mixed with some other emotion in her eyes. "Are you good at it?" she asked softly. And he wondered if they were still speaking about gambling.

In the soft light of the little room, her skin was luminous, and Jasper found himself counting the tiny freckles ranged out over the bridge of her nose. "I'm very good," he said, and knew that he, at least, didn't mean gambling.

Almost as if they were being pulled together by a magnetic force, he lowered his head and took her lips in a kiss as soft as a whisper.

His lips were softer than she'd imagined.

That was the first thing that ran though Hermione's mind as Jasper kissed her. The second was that she wanted more. And when she opened her mouth under his, she got it.

Almost as if he were asking a question, his tongue slipped once, twice between her lips before she opened wider and welcomed him in. Then there was no hesitation. This was a man who knew exactly what he was doing, and as Jasper's hands slid up her hips to rest at her waist, Hermione leaned in closer until her breasts were pressed firmly against his hard chest.

The soft heat of his mouth on hers was utterly delicious, and as she learned to stroke her own tongue against his in a rhythm that felt familiar somehow, she gave herself up to the mindless pleasure of it. And when she felt his hand stroke up over her ribs to cup her breast, she gasped with surprise.

"Easy," he whispered against her mouth, even as he stroked his thumb over the awakening peak of her nipple. "Easy."

The sensation sent a shiver through her, and a flash of awareness down lower, where only her own hand had ever stroked. When her hips gave an involuntary jolt upward, she felt a hard reminder of just what this mindless passion could lead to.

It must have broken the spell for Jasper as well, for he pulled back from her. And for a moment they stood with only a small space between them, breathless, Hermione's hand at her mouth, as if checking to see that it was still her own.

The sound of voices in the hall severed the connection completely.

She had thought it unexceptional that her father had left her alone in a room with Mainwaring, but only because she felt so safe with him. He might be maddening at times, but she'd never been concerned that he would take liberties with her—not like she was with Lord Payne, for instance. But the sound of people outside the door—people who might very well discover them alone here, and thus compromise Hermione beyond repair—was enough to provoke her into panic.

"We cannot be found here," she hissed, seeing in relief that Jasper looked as concerned as she was.

He glanced around the room, and she saw his eyes settle on a decorative screen in the corner. "Behind there," he said firmly. And without having to be prodded, she hurried to where the screen stood behind a large fern, and slipped wordlessly behind it.

She had thought Jasper would remain in the room at large, perhaps seated on the settee or with his back to the fire, but instead he crowded in behind her until she moved over to allow him to stand beside her. Thankfully, the fern in front of the screen would hide their feet, and the screen itself was tall enough to hide a man of Jasper's height.

They had no sooner made it into hiding than the door to the room opened with a snap, the newcomers' conversation in progress.

"I don't see what business it is of ours," Lord Atherton was saying, his slightly nasal tone more peevish than usual. He was a member of the Lords of Anarchy whom Hermione had not been particularly pleased to meet. "If the silly chit cannot keep her father from wagering with her horses it's no concern of ours."

"I agree," Mr. Leighton-Fox, another club member said, his voice disturbingly close to where Hermione and Jasper hid. "Why can we not take this opportunity to simply be rid of her? You thought it would be a point in the club's favor to have a lady member, Payne, and it didn't work out. There's no reason why the club cannot simply revert to what it was before you became president. Without the criminality, of course."

Hermione stiffened at their dismissal and would have stepped out and given them a piece of her mind, were it not for Jasper's hand clamping firmly over her mouth. She glared at him over his hand and tried to convey to him with her eyes that she was not best pleased with him at the moment. But he did not relent, and held a silencing finger up over his lips, and when his eyes seemed to ask if she would remain quiet, she scowled but nodded.

Men were not her favorite people at the moment.

"I quite understand your wish to let Lady Hermione go, chaps," said Lord Payne in a placating tone that put Hermione's back up even more. She had thought the club president was her champion if not her friend. "But we cannot simply revoke her membership because of her father's behavior. He's done nothing that any one of us wouldn't have done if we found ourselves in the same situation. Besides, she is a fiery little thing and I have no doubt there'd be hell to pay if we were so unwise as to do something to cross her."

"You don't mean to tell me you're afraid of a lady, Payne," said Mr. Leighton-Fox with a laugh. "Please say it's not true."

He was right to be afraid of her, Hermione thought with a satisfied smile. She would not take kindly to being ousted from the club. Especially not after she'd worked so hard to get her membership.

Lord Atherton clearly thought the same. "Woman scorned and all that, Leighton-Fox," he said with a laugh. "Though I do wish we could get rid of her. But I don't think we can revoke her membership. What I object to is having the club offer her the loan of a coaching pair. We might not have to revoke her membership if she cannot drive with us. It's the perfect solution."

"I offered her the pair because the Lords of Anarchy take care of their own," Lord Payne said sharply. "As was pointed out to me in rather annoying thoroughness by Lord Mainwaring this evening. And I do not take kindly to having the club's loyalty questioned. Which is why we will see to it that Lady Hermione is able to drive out with us at the next possible opportunity."

"Mainwaring?" said Leighton-Fox with a scoffing tone. "He can't even drive."

"Chooses not to," Lord Payne said. "There is a difference."

"Why the devil would a man choose not to drive?" asked Lord Atherton, as if the very notion offended his sensibilities.

"Father died in a carriage accident," said Lord Payne tersely.

At his words, Hermione glanced over at Mainwaring, whose stony expression was enough to tell her that the man's words were true. She'd known his father was dead, of course. He was the earl, and had been the head of his family from a young age. But she hadn't known his father had been killed in a driving accident. It clarified much. Like Lord Atherton, she'd thought it decidedly odd that Mainwaring didn't drive, but it made sense now.

"Mainwaring is beside the point, anyway," continued Lord Payne. "I simply wanted the two of you to know that I expect Lady Hermione to be treated with every courtesy by the club members. No matter how you might resent the fact that she is a member. Am I understood?"

The two men muttered their assent, and despite her earlier pique with Lord Payne, Hermione found herself feeling quite charitably toward him.

"But what of the other horses?" Mr. Leighton-Fox inquired. "If you give her the bays, what are we to deliver to Canningham?"

"Damn you, Leighton-Fox," Lord Payne hissed. "No names. And the buyer can bloody well wait for delivery. He said he would not kick up a fuss if it took a while to find exactly what he wanted. And as he's safely up north, he won't know that we've taken possession of a pair he might like."

"Besides that, there's nothing to say that we won't get another pair that will do in the meantime," said Lord Atherton. "Too bad S . . . Mr. S. got hold of the grays before we could get them back."

At the mention of grays, Hermione's eyes widened. She felt Jasper's hand on her shoulder and she was utterly still as she listened for Lord Payne's response.

"We've talked this to death, lads," he said, much to Hermione's disappointment. "Let's just concentrate on ensuring Lady Hermione is happy as a club member. And we'll figure out what to do about the other pair later."

The other two men murmured an assent and soon they were leaving the room.

When the sound of the door closing behind them echoed through the tiny room, Hermione and Jasper slipped out from behind the screen and into the now empty chamber.

"They were talking about my grays," Hermione hissed, as if Lord Payne and his cohorts would be able to hear them through the four walls. "I'm sure of it."

But Jasper didn't seem so sure. "They said Mr. S., though. Not Lord S."

"Do not be pedantic. It matters not if they said Mr. or Lord," she said firmly. "They were talking about grays and this S. person getting them before the club could get them back."

Instead of agreeing with her, however, Jasper looked rather like her father when he was trying to placate her. "We can't be sure what they were talking about. And even if they were talking about your horses, they very clearly think they are out of their reach."

Hermione stared at him. How could one go from feeling so very close to someone to feeling as if he were a complete stranger?

"Why are you being this way?" she demanded. "You heard exactly what I did. And you aren't stupid. Why are you pretending to be?"

She watched as an expression of exasperation crossed his face, and Jasper ran a hand over his face.

"Fine," he said, "I heard what you heard. And yes, they very likely were talking about your horses. But this is not something that I wish you to become entangled in. For one thing it could be dangerous, and for another thing, as long as Lord Payne is protective of you, then you will remain relatively safe."

"Who are you to decide what I can and cannot become entangled in?" she demanded, her fists resting on her hips. "You are nothing to me."

As soon as the words left her mouth, she regretted them. It was rather like challenging her father to a game of cards—there was no way Jasper would back down now. Which she realized as she watched his eyes darken.

"I am very far from nothing to you," he said, stepping closer, so that her bosom almost touched his chest. "Which I think I proved quite admirably before we were interrupted."

She quaked inside but refused to let him see it. "A few kisses don't give you the right to order me around," she said haughtily.

"Don't they?" he asked in a low voice, his gaze on her mouth. "I rather thought they did."

"Then you are sadly mistaken," she said, oddly breathless.

They stood there like that for the space of a few breaths before another sound outside the room reminded Hermione that they'd been out of the ballroom for some time now. If she didn't wish to find herself in the position of being ordered about by Mainwaring for a lifetime, she'd better get out of this room, and fast.

"I'm going to leave this room," she said, stepping

back from him with a glare. "You wait in here for a few moments so that we aren't seen leaving together."

Her managing tone prompted a smile on his lips. "Yes, ma'am."

A little disappointed that he hadn't objected, she turned and slipped out of the room. If she wasn't mistaken, she heard him laughing as she went.

Six

Later that evening, after a few fruitless searches for Upperton in the lesser-known gaming houses of London, Jasper, accompanied by the Duke of Trent, finally ran him to ground in the back room of one of the more exclusive hells where only the most skilled of players were allowed in.

He'd been restless after his encounter with Hermione, and as he watched her dance through the Comerford ballroom with other men, he found himself thinking back to their conversation with her father. He'd been completely unrepentant about losing her horses.

Setting aside what he'd heard Lord Payne and his henchmen discussing with regard to Hermione's grays, and the possibility that the horses might have been taken from her whether Lord Upperton gambled them away or not, there was still the fact that her father had taken something that didn't belong to him and all but given them away.

It was bad cricket. And though he was not in any way tied to Lady Hermione Upperton, Jasper felt a need to see her father pay. And the easiest way he had to do that was to engage the man in a game of cards. It was, after all, something that Jasper was better at than anyone he'd ever met. And he'd met a lot of cardplayers in his day.

Lord Upperton was playing four-handed whist with three men Jasper knew from around town. Not wanting to alert their quarry to their hunt for him, Jasper and Trent took up positions at a nearby vingt-et-un table where they could keep an eye on Hermione's father from afar while appearing to watch the play at their own table.

When it looked as if the play at the whist table was winding down, Jasper exchanged a meaningful glance with Trent and wandered over to where Upperton was counting his winnings.

"Having a run of luck, Upperton?" he asked the older man, infusing his tone with only mild curiosity, not wanting to scare him off.

He'd thought Upperton might take against him thanks to the fact that he'd come to Hermione's defense earlier that evening, but to his surprise, the older man did not appear to remember it.

Hermione's father grinned, thumbing through the stack of coins and vowels before him. "Indeed I am. Indeed I am. Can I interest you in a game?"

"I'm not here to play, Upperton," said Jasper sharply. "I'm here to discuss your daughter."

At that, the other man looked wary. "Why? Don't think I didn't see you sniffing around her skirts tonight. If you want her it will cost you."

Jasper hadn't thought Upperton could compound his other faults with further crimes against his daughter, but he'd been wrong. Not one to let a chance to get some extra funds pass him by, Hermione's father clearly saw Jasper's interest in her as the potential for engineering a windfall.

But, as much as the notion of playing into Upperton's slimy hands bothered him, it was the thought of emancipating Hermione from that grip that gave Jasper pause.

What *if* he were to offer for her? She'd no longer be beholden to the whims of a man who had no compunction about gaming away her belongings. And God knew he'd be a more benevolent husband than Upperton was a father.

Trent, who up till now had merely stood behind Jasper like a bodyguard, spoke up. "I really think you should consider speaking of this matter in private, my lord. For your daughter's reputation if not your own."

It was clear that Upperton didn't want to lose his place at the table, but in the face of two younger, stronger men scowling at him, he did the smart thing and shoved his winnings into his purse and rose to follow them.

Once they were in a small room reserved for private games, he found a bottle of claret on a sideboard and poured himself a generous glass, not bothering to offer any to his interlocutors. "Well, what is it, then? What's she done now? The chit has caused me nothing but grief ever since her mother died when she was a child. I should have sent her to live at the estate in the country but foolishly thought she'd be happier in town."

Disgusted by the man's attitude toward his own daughter, Jasper folded his arms across his chest in an attempt to keep from putting hands on him. "It's going to be difficult to convince me that you had anything but your own best interests in mind when you made the decision to keep her in London, my lord."

"Oh, come, boy," said Lord Upperton with a flash of annoyance. "You know nothing of what it is to care for a daughter. Especially one as headstrong as my Hermione. I daresay half of what she's told you about me is lies. You know how ladies are."

"No," Jasper said, his tone quiet with menace. "How are they?"

At that, Upperton blanched. "Now see here. I won't be lectured to about how I care for my own daughter by the likes of you. So say your piece and leave me be."

"You've a game to play, do you?" Trent asked conversationally.

"I do," said Upperton haughtily. "So, if you'll excuse me."

Jasper gripped the other man by the arm before he could leave. "I have a proposition for you, Upperton."

He felt Trent's questioning gaze on him, but ignored it.

"I will play one hand with you. Winner takes all."

He couldn't fail to note the gleam of avarice in Upperton's blue eyes, so like his daughter's with that small exception.

"I saw you staring at my winnings the moment you entered the room," the older man said with a grin.

"It's not your purse I'm interested in," Jasper said sharply, even as he moved to open the door and usher his opponent into the card room beyond.

As they took their seats at an empty table, Upperton called for a new deck, and took a great gulp of his claret. "Just the game you're interested in, eh?" he asked, upending his pouch of coins onto the surface of the table.

"Not exactly," Jasper said in a low voice. He leaned across the table so that only Upperton and Trent, who had taken another seat at the table, could hear. "I would like to play for your daughter's hand."

He watched with amusement as disbelief shone from Upperton's gaze. Trent was silent, but looked troubled.

"You're joking," Upperton said with a shake of his head. "I'll give her to you, boy, for the right price."

"I have no wish to *purchase* her," Jasper said through clenched teeth. "But I find myself of the opinion that you should no longer be in a position to control her life. And since you seem to be of the opinion that you are quite good at the tables, I should like to see if you are so good that you can keep from losing the last thing of value you possess."

He watched as Lord Upperton's nostrils flared at his words. He had little doubt that if the time came when Hermione's father found himself without another penny to wager with, he'd barely flinch at placing her hand in marriage upon the table. Indeed, he was very likely saving Hermione from marriage to any one of the other men who sat at other tables in this room, their eyes bloodshot, concentration on the cards they held before them.

"You think you're so high-and-mighty, Mainwaring," said Upperton through clenched teeth. "I'd like to see you try to win against me. You might be good at amateur play, but I've been at the tables since long before you were even born. And I'll not be beaten by the likes of you. I'll sell her to the highest bidder, too, just to spite you."

If there had been any doubt that Lord Upperton was a venal, heartless man, his threat to auction off his daughter put paid to it.

Any hesitation Jasper felt about his course of action evaporated. "Then by all means," he said with a grim smile. "Let us play."

"Mainwaring," hissed Trent, "do you know what you're doing?"

Jasper saw the concern in his friend's gaze, but ignored it. "I'm certain, old fellow. Quite certain."

It looked as if Trent might want to argue, but to Mainwaring's relief, he didn't. Just as well, because Jasper wasn't certain he'd be able to withstand a voice of reason. And somewhere deep in his primitive brain, he didn't want to be dissuaded from this course of action.

The naked truth of it was that he wanted Hermione, and as he'd suspected, her father would not hesitate to wager her hand should he feel it necessary. And Jasper was damned if he'd allow the whims of that madman to endanger his own ability to have her.

The game itself was laughably brief. Two-handed whist, which concluded with Jasper winning by the comfortable margin of four tricks.

And as he might have expected, Upperton was sanguine about his loss.

"I thought for sure I'd be able to do it, but damned if you aren't as good as they say," said Hermione's father with something like admiration. "You'll have to teach me how you do it."

"It's not something that can be taught, I'm afraid," Jasper said with a shake of his head.

"Even so," Upperton said with a laugh, "you're a member of the family now. So I'll be able to watch you at play any time I like."

At the mention of family, Jasper blinked. As he often did, he'd gone so far into the zone of play that he'd not even remembered what it was they were playing for.

Trent, however, had not forgot. He clapped Jasper on the shoulder. "Congratulations, old fellow," he said with a grin. "I believe you've just won yourself a bride."

And as he looked around, Jasper realized that they

had not been so inconspicuous as he'd at first thought. One by one the other gamblers in the room came forward to offer their congratulations.

Damn it, he thought to himself. Hermione was going to be furious.

"I am all for the occasional bit of convention-flouting, Hermione," Miss Ophelia Dauntry said the next morning as she climbed into the closed Lisle carriage where Hermione and Leonora waited for her, "but are you quite sure this is the way to go about getting your horses back?"

"Do not be missish, Ophelia," said Hermione firmly. "We all agreed last evening that a conversation with Lord Saintcrow is the only way to convince him to give my grays back. And if there are three of us to persuade him that will only mean the odds are in our favor."

She had not told her friends about the conversation she'd overheard last evening between Lord Payne and his lieutenants in the Lords of Anarchy, but that was partly because she didn't wish to reveal that she'd been with Mainwaring when it had happened. They'd quickly pounce on the fact that she'd been in a closed chamber with a handsome man and completely ignore the fact that Lord Payne had all but admitted that he was intent upon getting her horses from Lord Saintcrow.

It was an odd situation, to be sure, but one that would be quickly rectified once she got the horses back from Lord Saintcrow. Horses changing hands one time was unobjectionable, but the same pair being stolen from their owner twice in the space of a week would be far too suspicious for a man as sensible as Lord Payne to risk.

"One prying eye could ruin us," Ophelia said with

a shake of her head. "Do you understand that? You might not care about your marriageability, but I care about mine."

Hermione knew that her friend dreamed of a love match—something that would be the polar opposite of her parents' marriage, which was acrimonious to say the least. And a love match could only be achieved if she were able to meet as many eligible gentlemen as possible. Something she could not do if she were removed from the marriage mart by scandal.

"I will understand if you wish to go back," Hermione said turning to face her. "I asked you solely because I knew if I didn't you'd rip up at me. But there is no need for us both to ruin our reputations. I haven't a care for mine. With the exception of the fact that it might harm my membership in the Lords of Anarchy. But that will make little difference if I haven't got horses to drive."

"And I'm an old married lady now," Leonora interjected, "so I cannot be ruined. Not in that way, at any rate."

"You know I would not have come if I didn't wish it," Ophelia said, waving off their concerns. "I was merely pointing out the gravity of our mission. Though I do wonder if it might be easier to simply have your man of business who purchased the horses for you show Lord Saintcrow the bill of sale. It will say nothing about your father, which will prove that they belong to you."

But Hermione had already considered that. "If I thought he would simply take Mr. Wingate's word, I would have done exactly as you suggest. But Lord Saintcrow made it perfectly clear in the park yesterday that he doesn't care who the horses belonged to—me or Papa. He was determined to believe that they are now his, Fee. He was unbending. He won the game with my father and in his mind that's the end of it."

"Men are such irrational creatures, are they not?" Leonora asked with a sigh. "Even when what you tell them is eminently logical, they behave as if because we're ladies we must of a necessity be speaking rubbish. It really is most annoying."

"Are you speaking of Freddy?" Hermione asked, momentarily diverted. "I thought he was one of the good ones!"

Leonora laughed. "Oh, he is. But that doesn't mean he's not just as foolish as the rest of them from time to time. He is convinced that simply because I am with child that—"

The interior of the carriage exploded with squeals.

"My ears!" Leonora said, clapping her hands over her wounded appendages.

"You're going to have a baby!" Ophelia said, hugging her friend. "That's marvelous news!"

"Why didn't you tell us first thing?" Hermione demanded. "And more importantly, why on earth are you here with us on this fool's errand? If anything happens to you Freddy will kill us all."

"I should hope he would refrain from killing me at the very least," Leonora said wryly. "I am after all carrying his child."

Ophelia and Hermione grinned at their friend. It was the best news Hermione had heard in a long time. She was aware that Leonora had been afraid that she might not be able to conceive, so she knew how much of a relief it was to learn she'd been wrong.

"Besides," Leonora continued, "I wouldn't miss this for the world. Once the baby comes we will be sorely lacking in opportunity for adventure."

"A baby will be an adventure in itself," Ophelia said with a misty smile.

The carriage rolled to a stop then, breaking the festive mood.

"We're here," Hermione said with relish. If truth were told she was looking forward to confronting Lord Saintcrow. He'd been quite unpleasant to take possession of her horses in the park for all to see. And though she was rather afraid he'd not be easily persuaded as she hoped, she had to try at the very least.

Taking the hat and dark veil that sat on the seat opposite, she plopped it atop her head and pulled the black netting down over her face. "Well, how do I look?"

"Like a lady in deep mourning," said Leonora with a grin as she took her own hat and veil from the seat.

All three ladies had donned their darkest gowns for the outing. And Hermione was pleased to note that Leonora, too, looked like a woman in deep mourning.

"Now me," Ophelia said, donning her own headgear. "Well? Can you see who I am?"

"I can assure you that even your mama would not be able to recognize you beneath your veil," Hermione said, adjusting her own veil.

It was perhaps unusual for three ladies wearing such headdress to walk about together, but they had already decided to explain that they were sisters in mourning for their recently deceased father. And no one with any sort of decency would press them for more information in the face of such an explanation. At least that was their hope.

"Here we go," she said to Ophelia as the door of the carriage opened and the coachman handed them down.

Lord Saintcrow's home was in an older, if still respectable, neighborhood and there was nothing to distinguish the front entrance of his house from any of the others on this row.

Wordlessly the ladies ascended the few steps leading to the door, and taking a deep breath, Hermione lifted the brass knocker and rapped. But almost as soon as she came into contact with the door, it swung forward.

"What is it?" Ophelia asked in puzzlement as Hermione gasped.

"The door is already open," said Hermione, giving the door a gentle push and watching as it swung inward.

Ophelia lifted her veil, as if it had deceived her eyes. But it was clear from her alarmed expression that she saw the same thing as her friend.

"I do not like this," Leonora said.

Hermione didn't like it either, but she stepped into the gap between the door and the frame.

"Hello?" she called, pushing the door open wider. "Hello? Is anyone there?"

Seven

I don't like this," Ophelia said, echoing Leonora as she followed Hermione, who stepped into the entranceway.

"Nor do I," said Hermione. "But it's possible that Lord Saintcrow's servants have the day off. Or perhaps he hasn't got any. After all, he is a notorious gambler. I know well enough what it is for a nobleman to be forced to retrench."

"Even so," Ophelia said, stepping inside, followed by Leonora, "it is not sensible to enter the man's house entirely unannounced. He is a man and you know what sorts of things they get up to." She lowered her voice and whispered, "Mistresses and the like."

At her friend's words Hermione paused. "Hm. I hadn't thought of that. But it's broad daylight. You know very well nobody gets up to that sort of thing during the day."

"Patently false," Leonora said, lifting her veil and securing it so that her face was free. "Men like to engage in that sort of thing at any time of day. Ladies do too, if we're being honest."

For a moment Hermione and Ophelia forgot that they were in Lord Saintcrow's house, and stared at their friend.

"It's true," Leonora said defensively. "But I don't hear anything so it's unlikely Lord Saintcrow is entertaining his mistress right now."

"What if Lord Saintcrow is lying injured somewhere?" Hermione asked. "I don't know about you, but I would feel quite bad if I were to learn we were here and might have helped while his lordship was in need of assistance."

"But the person who injured him could still be here," Ophelia argued. "Waiting to harm us as well."

"Where is your concern for your fellow man, Ophelia?" asked Leonora, moving closer to the staircase.

"Oh, I have plenty of concern," Ophelia answered wryly. "But I have more concern for my skin should Lord Saintcrow find us here bickering in his front entrance hall. He's not the most understanding of gentlemen by all accounts. And I do not think he would care overmuch that we were worried for his well-being. In fact, it now occurs to me that he might think that Hermione is here to steal her horses back."

"From inside his house?" Hermione asked ironically. "The man is odd but even he is not so foolish as to keep horses in his guest bedchamber."

"That's not what I meant," Ophelia said in a huff.

"Ladies," Leonora said sharply. "We need to make a decision. I, for one, think we should go upstairs and see if Lord Saintcrow is injured. It is highly unusual for his door to be open as we found it. And if you will listen, the house is as quiet as a tomb."

"I say we go upstairs," Hermione said, turning to see what Ophelia's vote would be.

Ophelia looked from one of her friends to the other before sighing. "Fine. I vote we go upstairs, too. But if I get killed I will haunt you both with every fiber of my undead being."

Silently the ladies made their way up the stairs and

into the upper hall. "Lord Saintcrow," Hermione called out as they made their way to the first door. "Are you here?"

But the house was silent. So silent that she felt a little chill run through her. A nervous sweat broke out on her brow, and she used the handkerchief she'd clutched in her hand to complete her mourning disguise to delicately dab at it. She steeled herself as she opened the door, but it was merely a storage closet. Her sigh of relief was loud to her own ears.

"I don't like this one bit," Ophelia hissed even as she opened the next door and peered inside. "Just an empty parlor."

"We will only look in this hallway and if he's not here, we'll leave," Hermione assured her friend. "I admit now that I am simply curious to see if there is anything unusual here. So far it has been depressingly conventional. I thought perhaps a gentleman of Lord Saintcrow's reputation would have a more interesting house than this."

"He's hardly going to have a gaming hall hidden away in a corner of his house," Leonora said with a nervous laugh.

"I know," Hermione said as she turned the knob of the next door. "But . . . oh, this is his study."

To her surprise, there was a lamp burning in this room. "Lord Saintcrow," she called as she stepped inside. But a quick scan of the room revealed it to be empty.

"He's not here," Ophelia said from behind her. "I must confess, however, that I do love a good library. Something about the smell of books."

"There is another odor in here as well," Leonora said with a frown from the doorway. "If you don't mind I'll just stay out here. My stomach cannot take foul odors at the moment."

"It's quite unpleasant," Hermione agreed, stepping farther into the room. "I wonder he doesn't do something about—"

She broke off with a little scream as she looked down at the carpet on the far side of the massive desk. "Dear God!" She brought her hand up to cover her gaping mouth.

"What?" Ophelia asked sharply from where she'd been perusing the shelves. "What is it?"

"We have to get out of here," Hermione said, hurrying forward to tow Ophelia from the room with her, almost knocking down Leonora who was standing just outside the room "Come on!"

Neither of the other ladies argued as they hurried down the stairs and to the floor below.

They'd just reached the ground floor when the creak of the front door made them all look up in alarm.

Her heart beating a sharp tattoo in her breast, Hermione nearly cried out in relief to see that it was Lord Mainwaring.

"Hermione!" he said sharply as he saw her. "What the devil are you doing here?"

"There's no time to argue just now," she said, pulling him into the entrance hall and out of sight of the door. "We must leave without being seen. Which means we'll need to go one at a time."

"Mrs. Lisle," Mainwaring said, with a slight bow for Leonora before turning to Ophelia. "Miss Dauntry."

"I am glad to see you have a chaperone at least," he said to Hermione, "but what the devil are the three of you doing here? Especially since it would appear there are no servants around."

But Hermione had no time for his scold. "I don't give a hang about the proprieties, Mainwaring," she snapped. "Lord Saintcrow is dead and we have to leave before someone suspects we had something to do with it!"

When Jasper arrived at Hermione's house that morning, it was to learn that rather than waiting to hear his proposal as he'd hoped her father would have instructed her to do—which, thinking about it now, was indeed a foolish pipedream on his part—she was instead off somewhere with Leonora and Ophelia. At least that is what Greentree, the Upperton butler, told him.

Thanking the man, he climbed back onto his horse, Hector, and set him in the direction of Lord Saintcrow's town house.

The conversation he and Hermione had overheard last night between Lord Payne and his fellow Lords of Anarchy had been unusual to say the least. It was clear from what Payne had said that there had been some sort of understanding that Hermione's two horses were to go to some other buyer. But somehow—perhaps by mistake—they'd been sold to Hermione's man of business, and before Payne could get them back Lord Upperton had lost them to Saintcrow.

The Home Office had known about a ring of horse thieves. But these weren't ordinary horses. They were expensive enough to merit the sort of payoff that men like Payne and his ilk would demand before they became embroiled in illegality.

And it was clear from what the men had said last night that Saintcrow wasn't an innocent bystander in this.

When he got to Saintcrow's town house, however, it was to find the door ajar. And when he stepped inside, who should he see but Hermione with Ophelia on one side and Leonora on the other.

He wasn't sure what he'd been expecting from her, but the declaration that Lord Saintcrow was dead had certainly not been among the possibilities.

"Are you sure?" he demanded, taking her by the shoulders so that he could look her full in the face. "How do you know?"

But Hermione wasn't going to be manhandled by anyone. "I am not blind, my lord," she said, pulling herself from his grip. "He . . . his . . ."

For the first time in his acquaintance with her, Lady Hermione Upperton was speechless.

Guessing that her reticence meant that there was some sort of fatal wound that was visible, Jasper nodded, and this time when he touched her shoulder it was to comfort. "You needn't explain. I get the idea. But why were you here in the first place? I needn't tell you that visiting a gentleman's home is highly unusual behavior even if you are accompanied by another young lady and a matron."

"Do not bother her with details," Ophelia said fiercely, linking her arm with Hermione's and glaring at him. Jasper, who had previously found Miss Dauntry to be rather bland, was surprised by the vehemence in her tone. "She had her reasons, and since Leonora and I were with her, there can be no objection. But now we must leave here at once."

"I have little doubt she had her reasons, Miss Dauntry," said Jasper with a trace of annoyance. Hermione would always have some reason or other for going her own way. But this time she'd put herself and her friends in danger. "Let me go see Saintcrow for myself and then I will see you three safely home."

For once, Hermione did not argue. She swallowed and gestured for him to go upstairs. "He is in the study. Second door on the left. Behind the desk."

With a brief glance at her distraught expression, Jasper took the stairs two at a time. He smelled the foul odor of death as soon as he reached the hallway. He hadn't been to war as his friend the Duke of Trent had, but he'd seen plenty of death in his time working behind the scenes for the Home Office. The sort of things that concerned the government were by their nature dangerous, and faced with the choice between a traitor's death and death by their own hand many of those who worked against king and country chose the latter.

When he stepped into the library, he saw that just as Hermione had said, the body of Saintcrow was on the floor behind the desk, so that it wasn't visible when one first entered the room. Kneeling, he saw that the man's throat had been cut. Not the sort of injury that could be mistaken for a suicide. And there was no sign of a weapon on the floor around him. He would have lifted the body to see if it was perhaps beneath him, but it would not do to muddle the scene overmuch. The authorities would already be alarmed at the fact a peer had been killed in his own home, and any sign that someone else had been here before them would only raise their suspicions further.

A quick glance through the papers on the man's desk showed that they were a mess as well. Whether that was from Saintcrow's lack of tidiness, however, or the killer's search for something was difficult to determine.

He strode around the other side of the desk when a flash of white near the leg of a nearby chair caught his eye. Leaning down to pick it up, he saw that it was a ladies' handkerchief. Lady Hermione's if one were to go by the delicately embroidered initials. Sending up a brief prayer of thanks that he'd been the one to find it instead of the authorities, he hurried back down the stairs and found the three ladies waiting where he'd left them.

"Put your veils on and let's go," he said without preamble. Wordlessly the three ladies waited for him to scan outside the door to ensure there were no passers-by, and when he gestured for them to follow, they did.

It was the most subdued he'd ever seen Hermione and he wondered what sort of thoughts were going through her head. It was difficult to face death for the first time. He'd lost the contents of his stomach upon seeing his first corpse. And was rather shocked that a lady, even one as hardy as Hermione, had been able to keep hers.

When they reached the street outside, the urchin he'd had watching his horse while he went inside stepped forward, reins in hand.

Tossing a coin the boy's way, he said, "There's another half crown for you if you will wait a few more moments while I see these ladies off."

With a grunt of assent, the boy pocketed the coin and led Hector back down the street.

"I take it that was your carriage at the end of the street, Mrs. Lisle?" he asked, with a nod toward where the coachman waited for them.

At Leonora's assent, he said, "Walk as if you are merely on a quiet stroll, ladies. You are sisters in mourning and as such are subdued."

"What will you do?" Hermione asked in a low voice as he followed behind them. "It cannot be known that I was here. He took my horses from me yesterday. The authorities will almost certainly suspect me if they learn I was inside the house."

"I have no intention of informing them that you were anywhere in the vicinity," Jasper responded, understanding well why she was worried. "If no one else saw the three mysterious ladies entering Lord Saintcrow's home, then you will be safe from scrutiny. But it wasn't wise of you to come here. Even disguised as you were. It will hardly take a great leap of imagination to guess that at least one of the heavily veiled ladies who visited him today was the same lady from whom he wrested her prize coaching pair the day before."

"If I had known he'd be dead I would not have done so," Hermione said in a low hiss, turning slightly to glare at him from beneath her veil. At least, he thought she'd be glaring given her tone of voice. "But I can hardly go back in time and undo it."

He considered pointing out that if she'd behaved with propriety in the first place, there would be no need for her to undo anything, but decided it was not the time.

"No, you cannot. I simply wished to point out that there is a good chance you'll be suspected of having visited him at least, and murdered him at worst." When he heard his own words, he winced a little at the harshness of them. But it was nothing more than the truth. And Hermione did have a preference for plain speaking, if nothing else.

"I am well aware of that, my lord," she bit out. "But the fact remains that I had nothing to do with the man's death, and Leonora, Ophelia, and I were well within the bounds of propriety by calling upon him together. We might have been a little forward, but hardly beyond the pale."

By that time they'd reached the end of the street where the Lisle carriage waited.

Not bothering to argue with Hermione, Jasper handed first Leonora, then Ophelia, and finally Hermione into the vehicle. Leaning inside before he shut the door, he said in a low voice, "Remain home until you get word from me. You should both go about your normal business, to keep yourselves from suspicion."

"What will you do about . . . his lordship?" Hermione's voice broke before she said the words, and the reminder of her vulnerability made Jasper wince at his earlier harsh words.

"I'll get word to the right people," he said softly. "I know it was frightening, what you saw. But there was nothing you could have done. He was gone before you arrived. Now I suggest the three of you get some rest and try to forget about what you saw."

"Easier said than done, my lord," said Hermione with a shake of her head. "But we will try."

Having to content himself with that, Jasper shut the carriage door and nodded to the coachman that he could depart.

Eight

*W*ith assurances to Leonora and Ophelia that she would inform them if she learned anything further about Saintcrow's death, Hermione closed the door of the rented Upperton town house and hurried upstairs to scrub away the memory of the afternoon's horror in a steaming bath.

She was staring sightlessly out her bedchamber window toward the back garden when she heard a shout from the direction of the neighboring yard.

The Fleetwoods' garden.

Mindful of her promise to Mainwaring not to go near her neighbors, she was, however, grateful for the distraction from the events of the morning. So she watched with interest as a lady and a gentleman stood arguing near the gate of the neighboring yard. It was too far away to tell if the gentleman was Mr. Fleetwood, though the build looked right. His hair was obscured by his hat, however, and as she hadn't ever met Miss Fleetwood there was no way to know if it was her neighbor's sister she saw now.

She knew they argued because of the vehement gesticulations on the part of the lady, and something about the way the man held himself. It wasn't a happy conversation—that was certain. And Hermione, wondering if their enmity had something to do with Mainwaring's warnings against the Fleetwoods, watched fascinated and horrified as the gentleman took the lady by the shoulders and shook her.

And, as she watched, the man in the garden pulled his companion closer and, to Hermione's surprise, dipped his head and appeared to kiss her.

Yes, she thought, watching wordlessly as the lady's arms wrapped around the gentleman's shoulders and seemed to pull him closer, they were most definitely embracing. Either that man wasn't Mr. Fleetwood or the lady was not his sister.

"Your bath's ready, my lady."

Hermione leaped up in alarm at her maid's voice. Her cheeks reddened at being caught spying on her neighbors. And reluctantly, she turned away from the scene below. "Yes, thank you, Minnie."

Determined not to look down again, she pulled the curtain closed and hurried into the dressing room where she allowed Minnie to help her undress and sank into the fragrant hot water.

But once she was alone with her thoughts, it wasn't the embracing couple next door she remembered, but the face of the deceased Lord Saintcrow. Despite her anger with him yesterday morning, she had not wished the man dead. And certainly not in such a violent manner.

He'd seemed so vital. So alive. It was shocking to think all that vigor had been snuffed out in the space of a day.

Had it been simply a thief who'd killed him? Someone who was caught in the act of robbing his lordship and panicked?

Recalling the gaping wound in Saintcrow's throat,

Hermione doubted it. One didn't slit someone's throat out of surprise. Indeed, she thought, turning her mind to the puzzle of it, one would need to get behind the victim to do such a thing. It was possible that the killer had heard Saintcrow coming and hid somewhere, only leaping out once the man's back was turned to inflict the wound. But somehow she didn't think it had happened that way.

There hadn't seemed to be any sign of struggle. Perhaps the killer had been known to his lordship. Had seemed innocuous enough for poor Lord Saintcrow to turn his back on him. And then when he wasn't looking, the killer had made his move.

Despite the heat of the bath, Hermione shivered. It would take a great deal of anger to make someone want to kill another in such a personal way. She'd been as angry at the man as she had ever been at another human being—with the exception of her father, of course—and yet, she'd never considered doing such a thing. Stealing her grays back, yes. Murder? Absolutely not.

Recalling her grays, she sat up in the tub. What would happen to them now that Lord Saintcrow was dead?

Not waiting for Minnie to return to help her out, she stood and wrapped herself in the toweling the maid had left beside the tub. On bare feet, she padded across the thick carpets into her bedchamber and the small writing desk there.

When her note was finished she rang for Minnie, asking her to give the note to a footman and have him deliver it posthaste.

Mindful that she shouldn't let on that she knew what had happened to Saintcrow lest for some reason the note were intercepted, she'd only requested that Lord Mainwaring do what he could about her poor horses. He had already done so much for her—unbidden, but even so—that she felt slightly guilty asking for one more favor. But she rather supposed he'd prefer that she follow his orders to stay home instead of going to see about the horses on her own.

When had her life become so complicated?

Only yesterday she'd been pleased to begin her tenure as a member of one of London's foremost driving clubs. And now she was without her precious horses, she'd seen the man who won them dead, and spied on one or (shudder) both of her neighbors engaged in an illicit embrace. And to top it all off, she had kissed the Earl of Mainwaring.

It really was not to be borne.

After reporting Saintcrow's death to the magistrate, Jasper went to Brooks's in search of Trent and Freddy.

Since Lord Upperton had so recently lost an estate as well as his daughter's horses to Saintcrow, it was likely that suspicion would fall upon him. Or, worse, upon Hermione.

And, since he knew Hermione hadn't killed the man, he needed to speak to his future father-in-law to determine whether he'd been the culprit. Given Saintcrow's involvement in the theft ring, it seemed unlikely, but he needed to question Upperton all the same. Before the magistrate's investigators did if at all possible.

Trent and Freddy he wanted for moral support. It wasn't every day one questioned one's prospective in-laws about murder.

"Thank God!" Trent said as Mainwaring approached the table where the duke and Freddy were reading the papers. "This fellow has been boring me to death with his constant praise of married life. I suppose I should expect something similar from you any day now, but you can't be there yet since you only won your bride last evening, so you'll do for a diversion."

"I hear congratulations are in order," Freddy said with a grin as Jasper took a seat at their table. "It's not every day a man wins his bride's hand in a game of cards, Mainwaring. Well done! Though I have a feeling Lady Hermione is not going to be best pleased with the news."

"An understatement," Jasper said grimly, indicating to the hovering waiter that he'd like a glass of claret. "I haven't told her yet, but then she was busy this morning stumbling over dead bodies and the like."

Quickly, he told the other two about what had gone on at Saintcrow's house that morning, being sure to tell Freddy that Leonora had been there but was well enough when he'd sent them on their way.

Even so, Freddy was not best pleased to hear his wife had been involved. "She is not feeling her best at the moment," he said. "I would have thought that now of all times she'd choose to avoid madcap stunts like this."

Jasper and Trent exchanged speaking looks.

"In the family way, is she?" Trent drawled, as Freddy stood.

Biting back a laugh as his friend's expression warred between worry and pride, Jasper said, "Congratulations, old man!"

Giving himself over to self-satisfaction, Freddy grinned. "Indeed she is," he said proudly. "But she'd been devilishly ill. Which is why I'm so angry she allowed the other two to persuade her to go to that scoundrel's house. I realize Hermione wants her horses back, but was it really necessary to involve Leonora in her schemes?"

Jasper rather thought that Leonora would take exception to her husband's assessment of her ability to make her own decisions, but forbore from pointing it out given Freddy's understandable protectiveness.

"I suspect Leonora would have had her guts for garters if she'd tried to embark on the errand without her," Trent said, having no such compunction.

To his credit, Freddy didn't disagree. "You're likely right. She's scolded me more than once about trying to wrap her in cotton wool. But it's damned difficult to keep from doing so when she's so damned vulnerable."

Knowing how he'd felt that morning when he'd learned Hermione had been in Saintcrow's house, Jasper didn't doubt how Freddy felt. It was difficult to put into words just how terrified he'd been to imagine what might have happened if Saintcrow's killer had still been there when Hermione and her friends barged in.

"Go look after your lady," he said, clapping Freddy on the back, "She seemed well when I sent them off in the carriage, but I have little doubt you'll not be content until you see for yourself."

"Thanks, old man," Freddy said with relief, rising. "We'll drink a toast to your own betrothal just as soon as you've had a chance to talk it over with Hermione."

"You haven't told her yet?" Trent asked, once Freddy was gone. "What the devil?"

"I was going to," Jasper explained, taking a swig of his wine, "but when I arrived at her house, it was to learn she'd gone off with Leonora and Ophelia. So, I thought to seek out Saintcrow to see if he could be persuaded to give up her horses. Imagine my surprise when I found Hermione and her two best friends terrified in the front entry hall of Saintcrow's house."

"I might have expected it of Lady Hermione," Trent said, "but I thought Leonora and Ophelia had more sense than that."

At Jasper's pointed look, he shrugged. "You have to admit that she's a dashed headstrong filly. Once she takes a notion in her head it's impossible to change it."

"Might I remind you that you are speaking of my future bride?" Jasper said mildly. He could take umbrage at what Trent was saying about Hermione, but even he had to admit that she was not the meekest of creatures.

"Oh, you know as well as I do what she's like," Trent said, unrepentant. "The only question is, what will you do to protect her from suspicion?"

"At the moment, it's her father I need to speak to," Jasper said, explaining why he'd run his friends to ground in Brooks's in the first place. "I sent Hermione home to await further instructions from me, and before you ask, she was shaken up enough by finding Saintcrow's body that I believe she will not venture out for the rest of the day at least."

"And you want to see if Upperton knows anything about Saintcrow's demise?" Trent guessed.

"Precisely," Jasper said, rising. "So, let's go."

They ran Lord Upperton to ground at White's, where he'd somehow managed to keep up his membership.

"My lord," said Jasper to Hermione's father, where he slumped in a dark corner with a cup of strong coffee—obviously nursing a headache from overindulgence the evening before. "Might we have a few words?"

Without waiting for an invitation he and Trent took chairs on either side of the older man.

"What do you want?" Upperton said indignantly. "Didn't you get what you wanted from me last night? I would have thought you'd be off celebrating your impending nuptials."

"Is that any way to speak to your future son-in-law?" Jasper asked, noting the nervous way that Upperton beat his fingers on the table before him. "I would have thought you'd welcome me with open arms. Especially if you're hoping for any sort of beneficial marriage settlements."

That woke Upperton from his malaise. Sitting up straighter, he said, "But I thought because you won her at cards there would be no settlements."

It was really too disgusting that the man would let his daughter go into a marriage thinking there would be nothing put in place to protect her interests, Jasper thought. "Of course there will be settlements," he said, biting back the scold he longed to give the man. It would do no good, and since he knew that he would provide adequately for Hermione and any children they might have, even if her father would not, it was beside the point.

"That's a relief," said Upperton with a grin. "I look forward to meeting with you, Mainwaring."

"We're not here to speak of settlements, however," said Jasper, exchanging a glance with Trent who was looking at Upperton as if he were a toad. "We're here to ask you about Lord Saintcrow."

At the mention of Saintcrow, Lord Upperton frowned. "What of him? He hasn't found some fault with those damned horses, has he? If so, it's too late. The fellow won them fair and square and I haven't got the blunt to pay him the amount they're worth."

"Nothing like that," Jasper assured him, suppressing his annoyance at the ease with which Upperton discussed his daughter's horses. "Indeed, he won't be able to find fault with anything ever again."

"What's that supposed to mean?" Upperton demanded.

"He's dead, man," Trent informed Hermione's father, who blanched at the bold announcement.

"Well, don't look at me!" he said, throwing up his hands as if to ward off an accusation. "I had no reason to see the fellow dead. We'd completed our business. I was finished with him."

"But what of Hermione's anger over how you lost her horses," Jasper asked, watching the older man carefully. "Did you perhaps try to get them back, and argue with Saintcrow over the matter?"

Upperton's look of puzzlement was reassuring on the one hand—that he did indeed have nothing to do with Saintcrow's murder—but on the other, it was highly angry-making. Because it was clear from his expression that asking for his daughter's horses back was so far from the realm of his possible motivations as to be unthinkable.

What a delightful man he would have as a father-in-law, Jasper thought with sarcasm.

"It was finished," Upperton said with a shake of his head. "My daughter might not understand the whys and wherefores of gentlemanly behavior, but I thought you would, Mainwaring. A gentleman does not renege on a deal. No matter how angry one's daughter might be over it. I would no more ask for those horses back than I would cheat at the tables."

At the very least, Jasper was glad to know that neither of the Uppertons was responsible for Saintcrow's murder. He might despise the way Hermione's father dismissed her wishes out of hand, but he was relieved not to need to defend the man against a murder charge.

"Very well," he said aloud. "Now, I must ask you to return home and inform your daughter about what passed between us last night. Because I mean to ask for her hand this afternoon, and it would be better if she knows about it beforehand from you."

Upperton looked as if he would like to object, but on seeing just how serious Jasper was, he bit back his protest.

"Very well," he said with a nod. "I'll just finish up this drink and—"

"Better to go now," Trent said with pleasant menace.

"I agree," Jasper said, equally persuasive.

Upperton sighed. "Very well. I'll go now."

When he was gone, Jasper gave a sigh of his own. "And that's the man to whom I have pledged to tie my family for the rest of my life."

"Look at it this way," Trent said, ordering a glass of ale. "If nothing else, it will make a charming story to tell your grandchildren."

But Jasper was rather skeptical whether Lady Hermione would allow there to be any issue from their marriage at all. Especially when she heard how he'd happened to go about winning her father's consent to the match.

Nine

"What is it, Papa?" Hermione asked once she'd taken a seat.

She'd spent many an unpleasant session standing before her father's desk in the library back in the Upperton town house in Grosvenor Square, but this was the first occasion on which she'd done so in their rental house in Half-Moon Street. But no matter the locale, there was an eerie similarity to the feelings of frustration such meetings engendered. Especially when whatever infraction he called her to task for seemed to pale in comparison to his own actions—whether it was losing the money meant to pay the butcher at the races, or her coaching pair at the card table.

This time, however, something was different.

For one thing, he looked guilty. Something she'd never, ever, seen her father do.

That he might well feel guilty given the fact that he'd lost her horses, she didn't consider. He'd not shown any sort of remorse at the ball last night. Indeed, he'd been as unrepentant as ever. Even if, by some miracle, the error of his ways had been pointed out to him, she didn't think he'd be easy to convince. A man didn't change his entire outlook on life in the space of an evening. And her father had never been one to alter his behavior even an iota at another's behest.

Could it be that he'd learned of Lord Saintcrow's death? she wondered. It was possible. Maybe even probable. But he would hardly look guilty about that. Unless of course he'd had something to do with it. But she had her doubts about that possibility as well. He had no reason to want Lord Saintcrow dead. Certainly not over the loss of her horses.

"There is something I must tell you, my dear," he said, breaking into her reverie.

"You'd better just tell me, Papa," she said when he didn't speak up at once. "Clearly your news is bad."

She only prayed he hadn't wagered Queen Mab this time.

"Do not speak to me as if I am one of your grooms, daughter." Lord Upperton bristled. "I may be a disappointment to you but I am still your father."

Knowing that argument was futile, and wanting him to get to the point, she sighed. "I meant no disrespect, Papa. I simply wish to know what you have to tell me. And my apprehension lent sharpness to my tone. My apologies."

He made a noise of disbelief, but did not press the matter.

"I have been making preparations to wed the Countess of Amberly," her father said.

Since she knew that the countess was his lover, and wealthy enough to make a marriage to her advantageous to her father, Hermione was hardly shocked by the news.

"To further that aim," her father continued, toying with a bit of dried sealing wax on the surface of his desk, "I was engaging in some business dealings last evening that would make it possible for me to court Lady Amberly in the style to which she has become accustomed."

Translation: he had been gambling to earn enough of the ready to convince his creditors not to reveal his degree of debt to the lady before he could manage to wed her.

"I see." Hermione wondered idly just how naïve her father thought her. Surely he didn't think she believed this nonsense about business dealings. He'd lost her horses. And only a simpleton would miss the disappearance of bits and pieces of valuable furnishings from the house.

"Yes," he continued, staring at a spot just over her left ear. "I have sold the Lincolnshire property for a tidy sum. You know how difficult it sometimes is to get monies from our estates, and as we've never visited it since your mama died, I thought it time to part with it."

An outright lie, she guessed. The likelihood was that he'd lost it at the tables. And despite her determination to remain calm, she said, "That property was in Mama's family for generations."

Not to mention that it had been promised to Hermione upon her marriage. Which would not be happening anytime soon, she admitted, but she'd liked the idea of having something of her mother's when she wed.

But her father had already moved past that, waving his hand in the air as if her objection were a mere trifle.

"I will purchase something handsomer once I'm wed to Lady Amberly," he promised her. "And do not think I've forgot it was to go to you on your marriage. I will simply have to give you something else. And sooner than you might have guessed."

His words sent a frisson of unease through her.

"What do you mean?" she demanded, tired of his innuendo and evasions.

But instead of looking cowed by her tone, Lord Upperton seemed pleased with himself. Clearly his earlier trepidation had been replaced with sangfroid now that the news of the property loss had been given.

"It is high time you were married," Lord Upperton said in a tone that made her grip the arms of her chair as if it were in danger of tossing her out onto the Aubusson carpet. "Don't you think, my dear?"

No, no, no, no.

"What have you done, Papa?" she asked, not daring to stand up lest her legs give out beneath her. "What have you done?"

"Nothing awful, I assure you," Lord Upperton said with a shrug. "I've been thinking about what would become of you if something untoward were to happen to me. I cannot countenance the thought of you playing poor relation to my nephew Charles in the event of my death. Why, you'd be tossed out on your ear within a week of his assuming title."

That he was likely right considering that Hermione and her cousin Charles had been at loggerheads since their first meeting as children was beside the point.

"Why this sudden fear for my future?" she asked with a frown. "Are you ill?"

He had been looking paler of late, she considered, and his skin was looking quite gray now. Maybe his late nights at the tables were taking a toll.

"Certainly not," Lord Upperton said with the indignation most men of middle years reserved for questions of their own immortality. "I am fit as a fiddle."

That was a relief at least. He was a trial, but she loved her father despite his sins.

"Then what . . . ?" she began, before the answer came to her in a blinding revelation.

"Lady Amberly wants me out," she said flatly.

The widowed countess was well-known throughout the *ton* for being the highest of sticklers—though if that were the case then her interest in Lord Upperton was hardly in keeping with her previous patterns. Even so, she had made it plain on her one and only meeting with Hermione that she disapproved greatly of the younger lady's practice of so masculine a pursuit as driving, and had even suggested that if Hermione wished to spend time in her company then she should turn her attention to something more suitable to her station and sex.

Her father's flush at her assertion told Hermione all she needed to know.

"Lady Amberly's opinion of me notwithstanding, Papa," Hermione said through clenched teeth, "I believe I am capable of deciding when and whom I shall marry. And I certainly do not need you making arrangements in back rooms of gaming hells to see me settled. If it comes to pass that you do marry Lady Amberly, then I shall simply seek shelter from one of my friends."

At least she hoped she might. Leonora was newly wed, but she would surely allow Hermione to stay in the guest room of Craven House for a short time until she could make other arrangements.

"This has nothing to do with the countess," Lord Upperton said haughtily. "I simply thought it time for you to wed and I made arrangements to that end."

"Who is it?" she asked, unable to keep the tension from her voice. Please let it not be some crony of his from the tables, she prayed silently. Marriage to a gamester would be like jumping from the frying pan into the fire.

"I've promised him to let him break the news himself, my dear." Her father's gentle tone was even more difficult to endure than his bluster. "Do not worry. I think you'll be quite pleased. He's accounted to be a handsome fellow. And I feel sure you'll rub along well enough together."

One rubbed along well enough with an acquaintance one didn't find particularly entertaining. One rubbed along well enough with the anonymous maid provided by an inn for an overnight stay.

A husband—the very word made Hermione's gut clench in objection—the man who would be able to forbid her from keeping horses at all if he chose; who might decide to deposit her in some country backwater to molder; who had the right to use her body whenever the mood struck him . . .

This last sent a shot of fear through her so strong she had to keep from crying out.

"I promise you I would not have agreed to the match if I thought he would mistreat you, Hermione," Lord Upperton said, as if the very idea that she thought him capable of marrying her off to a monster were painful to him.

A brisk knock on the study door heralded the arrival of a guest. Her prospective bridegroom, no doubt.

"Lord Mainwaring to see you, my lord," said Greentree with a bow.

Mainwaring? What was he doing here?

She'd been expecting her future husband.

Not Mainwaring.

But he might have some news of Saintcrow's murder, she thought with a gasp. Maybe he even knew what had become of Rosencrantz and Guildenstern.

"Send him in," her father said with a nod.

Which reminded her that Greentree had said Mainwaring was there to see her father.

He likely had some questions to ask about Papa's dealings with Saintcrow.

She stood. "If you don't mind, Father," she said with a brisk nod, "I'll just leave now before your guest—"

But the sound of the doorknob behind her said she was already too late.

"Lady Hermione." Mainwaring said, stepping into the room. "I hope you are well."

He didn't mention her shock earlier in the day, which was just as well since she'd not mentioned finding Saintcrow's body to her father.

"I am well enough, thank you, my lord," she said, unable to meet his gaze. For some reason she found herself feeling nervous with him. Which was foolish since they'd seen each other just that morning.

"I'll just leave the two of you to chat," Lord Upperton said, stepping out from behind his desk and making a hasty retreat.

Hermione stared at the door, which her father had closed behind him. Why had he left her here alone with . . .

Suddenly the reason was all too apparent.

"You!" she said, pointing rudely at Mainwaring. "It's you?"

"I had asked your father to let me tell you," Mainwaring said with a shrug. "Though it would appear he told you about the betrothal but not the identity of the prospective groom."

"No, he most certainly did not," she said harshly. Her heart was beating with a speed that made her fear it would burst from her chest. "How could you do this to me? I thought we were friends."

"We are friends," he said, thrusting a hand through his untidy curls. "At least, I think we are. And I don't think you quite understand how this came about."

She was angry, but not too angry to miss the import of his words.

"What do you mean?" she asked, a premonition of dread making her spine tingle.

"Did your father not tell you the circumstances in which our agreement was made?" he asked softly, as if speaking too loudly would frighten her off.

It was just like him to spare her feelings when what she wanted was the unvarnished truth.

"I'm sure you know by now that he did not," she said tartly.

He looked as if he would like to be anywhere but in her father's library at the moment. Still, he pressed on. "I won you in a game of cards," he told her baldly.

Hermione felt her stomach drop, and as if she could stop the scream trapped in her throat, she clasped her hand over her mouth.

When her knees threatened to buckle, she collapsed into the chair she'd so recently vacated.

Mainwaring crouched beside her, and pressed a crystal glass into her hand. "Drink this," he said firmly.

She hadn't even been aware of him searching out the decanter, she realized with a start. Taking the glass, she sipped the whisky.

"Drink it all," he ordered, and she found herself obeying, though some part of her brain knew that in any other circumstances she'd reject his demand.

Something about the alcohol brought her back to awareness. Like a sharp noise, or a slap in the face.

"Better?" Mainwaring asked, taking the empty glass from her. There was concern in his dark blue eyes, and something else. Shame?

He might well be ashamed for accepting her father's bet.

To know Lord Upperton had been so far gone at the tables that he'd wagered his own daughter's hand in marriage was as abhorrent to her as if he'd sold her to the highest bidder. She'd known her father was not overly fond of her. He thought her mannish because she enjoyed driving and horses and eschewed the gentler pursuits of most other ladies of her class. But she'd never considered that he might be so lost to paternal concern that he would do a thing like this.

Even when he'd wagered with her horses, it hadn't occurred to her that there was a degree further he might go.

And what was worse, he'd given her hand to a man who spent just as much time at the gaming tables as he did. She wasn't sure what she'd wanted in a husband but it certainly wasn't someone just like her father. Even a man as kind and handsome as Mainwaring.

To her horror, she felt the sharp sting of tears behind her eyes.

"Here," Mainwaring said, handing her a pristine white handkerchief. "I know it's a shock. It was certainly not what I anticipated of an evening of cards."

Wordlessly she dried her eyes and blew her nose.

"Nor was this how I anticipated passing the afternoon," she said once she'd regained her composure. "First he loses my mother's estate in Lincolnshire and now my hand. I suppose I should be thankful that the Upperton estates are entailed."

"I might have a bit of good news regarding the Lincolnshire property," Mainwaring said, rising. "My man of business has contacted Saintcrow's heir with an offer. And if all goes well I'll make a wedding gift of it to you."

"There's that, I suppose," she said wryly. "But honestly, Mainwaring, do you not think that we might find some way out of this? After all, you weren't intending to marry me. Much better that we should simply agree to let this matter drop and go on with our lives."

If he was offended by her dismissal, he didn't show it. Instead, if anything, he looked even kinder.

"That's impossible, I'm afraid. You see, it's a point of honor. Your father cannot renege on his agreement. And I certainly won't agree to give up my . . ." He paused, as if searching for the right word. "That is to say, it would be unthinkable for me not to accept the things your father wagered. It's simply not done."

"Then make it done," she said haughtily.

"I'm afraid it's not that simple," said Mainwaring. "There were witnesses. There's nothing for it but for us to marry. And the sooner the better."

She made a noise of impatience. "Will you not see reason? I don't wish to marry you! And I very much doubt you wish to marry me. Look at the scrape from which you had to rescue me this morning!"

Hermione stood up from her chair and began to pace.

Jasper supposed he should be pleased she hadn't tossed the whisky in his face.

Well aware of the uphill battle he faced, he stood up from where he'd crouched beside Hermione's chair and watched as she strode over to stare out the window.

"It is true that I was not best pleased to find you in a dead man's house this morning," he said reasonably, "but that has little bearing on the agreement between your father and me. I know you find it difficult to accept right now, but make no mistake. We will be married. There will be no 'way out of this' as you put it. And the sooner you accept that, the sooner we can begin to move past this."

"It's easy for you to say," she said, turning to glare at him. "You haven't had your entire world upended by the turn of a card."

He raised a brow and stared at her until she looked up, and realizing what she'd said, blushed.

"Perhaps you have," she said heatedly, "but you will be able to go about your life in much the same way as you've done before. It's different for men."

Something he was heartily glad of, though he would not say it aloud at the present moment.

"I do understand it is quite a lot to take in," he sympathized. "Truly I do. But given your father's propensity to wager away the things you value, do you not think it will perhaps be a bit more . . . stable in my household instead of his?"

That was clearly not something that had occurred to her, and he watched as she mulled the prospect over.

"You are at the tables almost as frequently as he is," she said thoughtfully. "How am I to know you won't do the same thing? Won't wager away my belongings, my horses?"

"I am not the same sort of player as your father," he said reasonably. It hadn't occurred to him that her objections might spring from what she perceived as his similarity to her father. He supposed from the outside they did seem to be cut from the same cloth. "I am not compelled by some inner need to play, for one thing. I do so merely for the competition. In much the same way you drive your curricle."

Clearly she had never considered that one might play cards for the sport of it. Which was not surprising since she'd lived her whole life with a man who was as addicted to the tables as some men were to whisky.

"What is the most you've ever lost in one night?" she asked, as if the answer would tell her something about his character.

"Two thousand pounds," he said without hesitation. It was not a small amount, he knew. And it wasn't something he was proud of. The fact that he'd won that back and more afterward was beside the point, he knew. She wanted to know and he'd told her. He would make no excuses for himself.

She blanched, and lowered herself to the settee, as if in shock. Still, she didn't hesitate to ask another question. "Have you ever wagered something belonging to someone else? That didn't belong to you?"

No secret where that one came from.

"No," he said firmly. "I do not wager with things that are not mine. In fact, I do not wager with things at all. I play for money only. And I win more than I lose, though that is likely not what you want to know."

Something about what he'd said had reassured her, however. At least that's what he thought as he watched some of the tension fade from her eyes.

"Why do you not drive?" she asked suddenly, her brow furrowed as if she were trying to understand so foreign a concept.

Not wanting to tower over her, but not quite sure it was safe to sit beside her again, Jasper folded himself into the small chair next to the settee.

"It's no great secret," he said with a shrug. "But my father died in an accident while he was driving a high-perch phaeton. I was with him."

"Oh." Her hand covered her lips, as if to keep further exclamations of horror from spilling out. "Lord

Mainwaring, I am so sorry. I should not have asked, please excuse—"

"Do you not think we've moved beyond titles at this point?" he asked in a low voice. "Why do you not call me Jasper?"

Was it his imagination or did her eyes darken a bit?

"Only if you will call me Hermione," she said, a raised brow daring him to argue with her.

"Very well," he said with a nod. "Hermione."

He liked the way it felt on his tongue. Like a little song. Or a poem.

Now he was being a sentimental fool, he thought to himself with an inward groan.

"Were you injured, Jasper?" she asked, not deterred from their earlier subject of conversation.

"Not really," he said with a shrug. "A few bumps and bruises. I don't remember any of it. My memory of that day stops just after breakfast. Almost as if my mind is shielding me from the pain."

"Thank goodness for that," she said with a shake of her head. "I cannot imagine such a thing. I must confess that I feel some degree of guilt over my assumptions for your choice not to take up the reins."

"You were not alone in assuming it was because of some cowardice on my part," he said, rubbing the back of his neck. "It's more because I wonder if my own skills or lack thereof would be as dangerous as my father's were. I know of course that such things are hardly inherited, but I must confess that I am not eager to tempt fate by trying. And as an earl it has not been difficult to manage not to drive myself. Indeed, with a few exceptions I've never wanted or needed it."

"It certainly puts your dislike of my own driving

in perspective," she said with pursed lips. "And here I thought you were simply being a typical male."

"Oh, there is a bit of that, I'm afraid," he admitted. "It does seem to me that ladies should not be so eager to ape masculine pursuits. But it has been a long while since I considered your skills with the ribbon as something to be hidden under a bushel. You are quite good. Even one as unskilled as I can admit as much."

"At least you're honest about it." She shrugged.

"So," he said, bringing them back to the matter that should be foremost in their thoughts. At least insofar as his body was concerned. "What do you say to this marriage business? Would it be so bad to be married to an earl with no driving skills? I cannot promise you a lifetime of bliss, but at the very least you will no longer be your father's pawn to move about as he pleases."

"I am still quite unhappy with the way you went about this," she said, rising to face him.

Taking her movement as a sign that she was coming around, he moved to stand before her. Close enough that he could see the way her dark lashes fanned across her cheeks.

As if she sensed his gaze, she lifted her lids and locked eyes with him. "Why did you accept his wager?" she asked softly.

Unable to look away, he stepped into her, liking the way she held her own with him. "The truth is, I was afraid he'd lose you to someone else," he admitted. "And I couldn't have endured knowing you belonged to anyone else."

Her eyes widened in surprise, and unable to stop himself, Jasper covered her mouth with his.

Ten

This time when Jasper kissed her, Hermione thought with surprise, it felt inevitable. Gone was the tentative nature of last night's kiss and in its place was something more primal. A claiming of sorts, and despite her objections to her father's deal with Mainwaring, she found his kiss as intoxicating as the whisky he'd made her drink.

Opening her mouth beneath his, she welcomed his tongue with a soft stroke of her own. Something he liked very much indeed, if his groan of approval were any indication. And when she slipped her arms around his neck and slid her fingers up into the hair at the back of his neck, he responded by pulling her tighter against him. So that she felt the press of his arousal against her stomach.

He was demanding, this man who maddened her so. But somehow she knew that if she were to say the word, he'd stop. And that knowledge gave her permission to experiment by slipping her hand beneath his waistcoat to palm the warm skin beneath his lawn shirt, even as she thrust her tongue against his in an instinctive dance that she'd never tried with anyone but him.

She gave herself up to sensation as he kissed his way

down her chin, over her throat, and down to where her bosom peeked out of her bodice. And when he slid the sleeve of her gown down over her shoulder, he followed the path of the seam as it slid down to bare her nipple.

The heat of his tongue against the taut bud of her breast almost was her undoing. With a mewl of desire she clasped his head to her, pressing herself forward as he suckled her. It was just as unthinkably arousing as it had been the night before, only this time, there was no one to disturb them.

When he lifted his head and pulled her to sit astride him in the chair before her father's desk, she almost wept with relief that he hadn't done so to stop.

This time, he pulled the other sleeve down and put his mouth on one breast while he stroked the other with his hand. With one knee on either side of his waist, she lifted up to give him better access to her, and discovered she was at the perfect angle to assuage some of the ache between her legs against the bulge in his breeches.

"Let me," he said against her as he slid a hand down over her leg and pulled her gown up to where her garters held her stockings in place. With a gasp of anticipation, she lifted up and felt his hand slide over her hip and to the spot where her body ached to be filled.

And when he stroked his finger over the center of her, where she wept for him, she gave a sigh that was part relief and part excitement.

Wordlessly, Jasper returned his mouth to her nipple, and the combination of the pull of his lips and the stroke of his finger over her wet center was almost too much to bear. Unable to control herself, she moved her hips against his hand. Once, twice, she brushed against him, and when he pressed a finger inside her, she almost cried out with relief.

As she moved restlessly against his hand, he began to use his teeth on her nipple, and she felt herself hurtling toward something. Another finger joined the first, and she felt a pleasant fullness as he stroked his thumb up over her most sensitive part and Hermione was no longer able to control herself. With a cry of rapture she let herself go and bucked her hips against Jasper's hand in a frenzy of ecstasy, unwilling and unable to curb her movements against the tide of her orgasm.

When she came back to herself, Hermione was collapsed against Jasper's chest, his hand stroking over her back.

She made to pull away, but he held her fast.

"I'm so mortified," she said against his neck cloth, hiding her face there lest he see the truth of her words in her eyes.

"No need for mortification on my account," he said in a low voice, that she could feel where their chests met. "That was, I think, the most beautiful thing I've ever seen."

She pulled back to see if he was telling the truth.

He met her gaze with a raised brow. "I would never lie about a thing like that," he said, kissing her lightly.

Men were strange creatures, she thought, shaking her head. "If you say so," she said.

"I hope that your enthusiasm means you've decided that we should, indeed, be wed," he said when she sat back on her haunches to look at him fully.

She would have responded, but a loud knock on the front door reminded her that they were in her father's office. And worse, the door was unlocked.

With a gasp, she turned in his lap, ignoring the strangled noise Jasper made when she sat a bit more firmly than necessary on his groin, and leaped to her feet.

Pulling the sleeves of her gown up over her shoulders, she glared as Jasper rose and pulled his waistcoat down and flipped the tails of his coat out. His cravat, she feared, would never be the same again.

"I think we'll do," Jasper said with a nod.

Hermione hurried over to the chair by the window where she picked up a book on animal husbandry and began to read. Jasper stood before the bookcase and scanned them as if searching for the map to a long-lost treasure.

"And I tell you that his lordship is not home and I will not disturb Lady Hermione, sir," they heard Greentree say to the unwanted visitor in his most condescending of tones.

"I know what you're saying, sir," the visitor said in a thick East End accent, "but I'm going to see her ladyship whether you like it or not."

They heard the butler mutter something, but soon enough a knock sounded on the door of the library.

"I beg your pardon, my lady," said Greentree from the other side of the door—which doubtless meant he knew very well what had gone on behind the unlocked door earlier—"but there's a man here to see you and he won't be turned away."

"Send him in, Greentree," Jasper said in his loftiest tones.

When Hermione glared at him he shrugged, unrepentant. She would give him a piece of her mind over his heavy-handed manner later, she vowed silently.

"I'm from Bow Street, my lady," said the man who stepped into the room, his belly preceding him. "I only need a moment of your time, if you please."

At the mention of Bow Street, Hermione's heart raced. Could he be here about Saintcrow? She glanced at Jasper but he kept his gaze on the runner.

Swallowing, she schooled her features into a mask of calm. "Very well, sir. Greentree, please have a tray of tea and biscuits brought to us."

"Yes, my lady."

Her stomach in knots, Hermione gestured for the runner to have a seat.

"Now, sir," she said once she'd taken a seat in an armchair near the fire. "What may I do to help you?"

"Mr. Isaiah Rosewood, my lady," said the man with a low bow. "At your service."

"And I'm the Earl of Mainwaring," said Jasper from where he'd stood silently as the man from Bow Street got his bearings. "I was just here visiting my fiancée when you arrived."

She saw now why Jasper had taken the opportunity to give orders to Greentree for the runner to be admitted. It wasn't because he wished to overrule her, but instead had been a chance to show the Bow Street runner that he was in charge here.

It was perhaps a sad commentary on the status of ladies in their present society, but still, she was more than happy to have Jasper's protection when she felt the runner's speculative gaze upon her.

Something she felt even more strongly when he said, "I am here seeking information, Lady Hermione, about a gentleman of your acquaintance. Lord Saintcrow. I understand you were involved in an altercation with the fellow yesterday?"

Again she looked to Jasper and this time found him smiling reassuringly. Bolstered by his support, she spoke up.

"Indeed, sir," she said with what she hoped was calm. "I discovered yesterday that my coaching pair had been lost in a card game to Lord Saintcrow. Unfortunately I didn't learn of it until he arrived just before my first procession with my driving club. As such, I was a bit less than pleased, shall we say?"

"You were quite angry, isn't that the case, my lady?" The runner's keen blue eyes were fixed on her as if waiting for a slipup.

"As could be expected, sir. I learned that my father lost horses that I believed were mine in a game of cards. Though you have only to ask anyone who was present at the time that I relinquished them with what I consider to be rather good grace in the circumstances."

"Indeed, my lady," the man said with a nod. "I did hear that you gave them over to him without much fuss. Perhaps too little fuss?"

"What do you mean by that?" Jasper asked, moving to stand beside Hermione, his hand resting on her shoulder protectively.

"Why, just that you seemed to be rather unruffled by the matter once you decided to give them over to the fellow." He tilted his head in a questioning gesture. "Could that have been because you planned to confront the fellow later on?"

"Of course not!" she snapped. "If I planned to confront anyone it was my father, who had lost the horses I purchased with my own funds without so much as a by-your-leave."

"Then it would surprise you to learn that Lord Saintcrow was found dead this morning? Only a day after he took your horses?"

"I . . . that is to say, I don't . . ."

"In point of fact, Rosewood," Jasper said with asperity, "I was the one who found Saintcrow's body. I went to speak to him about a private matter and found the poor fellow dead. I'm quite certain Lady Hermione wasn't even in the vicinity."

It was clear from Rosewood's lack of surprise that he'd known about Jasper's role in the report. "And can you tell me what it was that you went to speak to him about, my lord?"

"If you must know," Mainwaring said with unruffled calm, "I went to ask him to sell me the grays he had off Lord Upperton. They were Lady Hermione's, you understand, and I wished to make a gift of them to her."

Hermione wasn't sure if this was the truth of why he'd showed up at Saintcrow's or something concocted on the spur of the moment to confound the runner.

Rosewood, however, took it at face value. "That's quite an expensive gift, my lord."

"Well, I suppose the surprise is ruined now, but I meant to make them a betrothal gift to Lady Hermione," Jasper said with just the right degree of sheepishness.

"Sorry, old thing," he continued with another squeeze of her hand. "I meant to make a surprise of it, but this is the matter of a chap's life. Of course I had to spill the beans."

"And how long have you two been betrothed?" Mr. Rosewood asked, without giving a hint as to whether he found the situation at all suspicious.

Deciding that Jasper had some sort of plan regarding all of this, Hermione waited for him to speak.

"Only for a few weeks," he said with a fatuous grin. "We've kept it a secret from the public, you know. What with her father being reluctant to grant his permission and all."

"Indeed," Rosewood said with a nod. "And where

is Lord Upperton this afternoon? Your butler only informed me that he was out, Lady Hermione. Not where he was."

"I don't know, Mr. Rosewood," she said with a smile. "He often leaves the house without telling me his destination. Off at his club, I would imagine. Or some other place where gentlemen go. I really don't know, since I am not one of them, you understand."

"No, you aren't," said Jasper with an appreciative grin.

"And have you had a chance to speak to him about his loss of your horses, Lady Hermione?" The investigator's eyes were sharp, as if trying to see through to what her true feelings about the sale of horses had been.

"No, as it happens, I have not," she answered truthfully.

"So it is fair to say that your father might not have come home at all and you would not know it?" the runner asked.

"I said I hadn't spoken to him about the horses, not that I hadn't seen him at all," she said sharply. "But I do not make it a habit to keep watch on my father's comings and goings. He is a busy man."

"Certainly, playing cards with men like Lord Saintcrow," Mr. Rosewood said. "You must have been furious with him about the horses. I know I would be."

"I'm not sure how Lady Hermione's feelings toward her father have anything to do with the murder of Saintcrow," Mainwaring interjected. "That is neither here nor there."

"I simply thought it might have made Lord Upperton regret his sale of the horses to Lord Saintcrow. A daughter's disappointment can be a powerful motivator, my lord."

"What are you saying, Mr. Rosewood?" Hermione asked, realizing that he suspected her father of the murder.

"But, then again," said Rosewood, ignoring her question, "a lady's anger can also be a powerful motivator when she is the one who thinks she's been wronged. Did you perhaps pay a visit to Lord Saintcrow this morning, my lady? Before your fiancé here did so, that is?"

"I don't like your tone, Rosewood." Mainwaring's voice was as cold as ice. He was every inch the nobleman and Hermione couldn't help but be grateful that he was on her side.

"I'm sorry to hear that, my lord," said the man from Bow Street, "but I'm investigating a man's murder and that sometimes means I have to ask unpleasant questions. Now, my lady, did you visit Lord Saintcrow today? For I've heard from a couple of the man's neighbors that a trio of ladies in mourning veils were seen entering his house. Could one of them have been you?"

Before she could speak, Mainwaring stood. "This interview is over, Mr. Rosewood. I will thank you to take yourself off and find another line of inquiry."

Rather than argue, the Bow Street runner stood as well. He sketched a bow to Hermione, saying, "I thank you for your time, my lady. And I hope if you think of answers to my questions you'll send word to me by way of Bow Street."

"I'll make sure you get any information the lady is willing to give," Mainwaring said, escorting the other man to the front door.

As soon as it was shut behind the runner, he hurried

forward and took Hermione by the arm and led her back into her father's office. He shut the door firmly behind them.

"No matter what you do, no matter how he tries to intimidate you," Jasper said firmly, "do not under any circumstances speak to that man again without having me with you."

"I thought I did rather well," she said, surprised by his vehemence. "It was you who raised his suspicions when you all but threw him out."

"Hermione," Jasper said, grasping her by the shoulders, "that man was suspicious the moment he stepped in here. Otherwise he wouldn't have come to pay you a call in the first place. He knows that three ladies called on Saintcrow this morning and he knows that I called on him. That's four possible suspects. And since I reported the murder he's likely to think I'm innocent."

"And because we three were in disguise he'll think it more likely that we killed him?" Hermione asked, not liking the genuine worry in his eyes. "Is that it?"

"Precisely," Jasper said with a nod. "And though he won't like to consider the notion that ladies might be capable of committing murder, he's not from our world. In the seedier parts of London mothers kill their babies. Prostitutes kill their customers. Women committing murder is not as uncommon as it is in our world. So he's already predisposed to consider you're capable of it."

At his description of what happened outside Mayfair, Hermione shivered. She was all too ready to think that her own world—despite the unpleasantness her father's gambling brought into her life from time to time—was the same as everyone else's. She knew well enough that there were parts of London where people fought tooth and nail for every morsel of food or ray of light. But it had taken Jasper reminding her of that to recall that it was only thanks to divine providence that she lived in the comfort of Half-Moon Street.

"And I complained about having to retrench enough to let this house," she said with a shake of her head. "What a fool I've been."

But Jasper hugged her to him. "Don't say that. You are a remarkable lady. And just because you haven't experienced the horrors of life in Whitechapel doesn't mean you're a terrible person. You have dealt admirably with your father's excesses. And now you will deal with this. But I will admit that I think we should marry as quickly as possible now."

"Because you think that if we marry, Mr. Rosewood will look elsewhere for the killer?" she asked, grateful for his strong arms around her.

"In part," he said, resting his chin on her head. "And also because you let me put my hand up your skirt a little earlier."

When she gasped in outrage, he kissed her. "There's my girl."

"Beast," she said, punching him lightly in the chest.

"And don't you forget it," he said with a grin.

Eleven

$\mathcal{M}$indful of the multiple errands he would need to take care of himself before a wedding with Hermione could happen, Jasper chose to do the most difficult of those before word of the fateful card game made it to Grosvenor Square.

Unfortunately he was too late for that.

When he arrived at the Mainwaring town house after leaving Half-Moon Street, he'd only just handed his hat and coat to the butler when a screech sounded from somewhere on one of the upper floors.

Ah, he thought. Mama has heard, then.

"Her ladyship has been rather overset this morning, my lord," said the butler, Greaves, in a vast understatement. "I believe she had a note earlier from your aunt Agatha."

"Just so, Greaves," said Jasper, squaring his shoulders. "Are my sisters at home, do you know?"

"I believe I heard them in conversation with her earlier, my lord," the sober-faced retainer said. "Though I do not make it a habit to follow their movements, of course."

"Of course, Greaves," Jasper said, even as he headed up the thickly carpeted staircase.

It was just as well if his mother and sisters were

together, for then he'd need only tell his story once. And, he thought with a mental roll of his eyes, he'd need only to deal with one long session of weeping.

Why did Hermione's tears seem infinitely preferable to those of his own blood relations? Perhaps because he'd come to realize that his mother and sisters used them as a means of controlling him rather than as a genuine expression of emotion.

He stepped into his mother's small sitting room to find his sisters huddled together on the sofa looking miserable in their post-tearful puffiness. His mother, on the other hand, sat bolt upright in the chair beside them, her pale face showing signs of earlier tears, but bearing a mulish set to her jaw that Jasper could not like.

"Good afternoon, ladies," he said with more cheer than he felt, "I take it you have heard my good news."

"How can you possibly call your betrothal to that . . . that hoyden good news, Jasper?" cried Evelina, the elder of his sisters at nineteen. "Lady Hermione Upperton is as unfashionable as any lady in the *ton*. Did you know that she has only recently gained admittance into a driving club? I expect next she will file down her teeth to make spitting tobacco juice easier!"

"You will speak of Lady Hermione with respect, Evelina, or I will send you to spend the rest of the season in the country where you can learn some manners," he said sharply. He was willing to endure any sort of whining and insults hurled at his own head. But he would not stand to hear Hermione spoken of thusly. Her world had been turned upside down through no fault of her own and he was damned if he'd allow his own sisters to make it worse. "Do you understand?"

Unaccustomed to such harsh words from her normally indulgent older brother, Evelina's rosebud mouth formed a shocked O. She was too surprised, it seemed, even to cry.

"So I see you're taking her side over that of your own sister, Jasper," his mother said with cold calm. "I must confess I find myself disappointed that a son of mine would behave so rashly. Especially given how much your father set store by family."

"If my father set such great importance on family," Jasper said sharply, "then he would have done better not to drink a bottle of wine before he took to the road, don't you think, Mama?"

Perhaps because of his earlier conversation with Hermione, the accident was fresh on his mind. And he'd been reminded of just how culpable the late earl had been in his own demise. He had loved his father, of course, but it was hardly the action of a man whose family's well-being was foremost on his mind to get himself killed by driving while intoxicated.

"So, that's how this will be, is it?" his mother asked, not even blinking at Jasper's slander of his father. She could hardly fault him for the words since he'd heard them often enough from her own mouth, after all.

"This can be as pleasant or as unpleasant as the three of you make it," Jasper said, leaning his shoulders against the mantelpiece. "I will tell you that, as you have likely already heard, I engaged in a card game last evening with the Earl of Upperton in which his lordship offered a small property in Lincolnshire and the hand of his daughter, Lady Hermione, as his bet. Lord Upperton lost and I, as a gentleman, could not refuse his proffer. Thus, Lady Hermione and I are to be married by special license before the end of the week."

"This will ruin any chances we might have to make a good match," the younger of his sisters, Celeste, said. "I daresay we will all need to retire to the country to avoid the gossip. This season is a complete ruin."

"If that is what you wish to do, of course," Jasper said, inclining his head. "Then you are all three welcome to do so. I daresay Lady Hermione would prefer to settle in to the household without having a resentful trio of in-laws underfoot while she does so."

"You would throw us out of our own home?" Lady Mainwaring asked, her lips tight with anger.

"Of course I'm not throwing you out," he said in kinder tones than he felt. "You are all, of course, welcome to remain here. But I do think it best if you consider perhaps removing to a house of your own if you feel you will be unable to behave with civility to my bride. And if you do not make that choice, in the event that you are indeed uncivil, I will make it for you."

"You never used to be so hard, Jasper," Evelina complained. "I think you have become callous thanks to your friendship with the Duke of Trent. He might be a duke but it is not as if he was born to the title."

"Since Trent and I have been acquainted since Eton I do not think that you can lay the blame for my so-called callous nature at his door," Jasper responded with a raised brow. "And he might not have been born to the title, but I must say that I find his manners entirely more agreeable than your own have been today."

"That is because my heart is breaking," Evelina cried, raising her handkerchief to her mouth and fleeing the room.

"She was about to bring Viscount Fordham up to scratch," Celeste said hotly. "She's convinced he will drop her acquaintance once he gets word of your scandalous behavior."

Jasper just barely stopped himself from sighing aloud. "Since Fordham can hardly be said to hold a spotless reputation himself," he said, "I do not think it likely he will run for the hills at the unusual circumstances of my betrothal. And if he does, then he is hardly the sort of fellow I should wish for Evelina to marry."

"That's easy for you to say when you aren't the one who will have to listen to the other ladies of the *ton* laugh gleefully over poor Ev's broken heart," Celeste retorted. She rose, shaking her head in disappointment, though whether it was over Fordham's hypothetical perfidy or Jasper's actual, he could not be sure.

"There is still time for you to flounce off, if you are so inclined, Mama," Jasper said, pinching the bridge of his nose between his thumb and forefinger. Had he had the beginnings of a headache when he entered the room?

"Your sisters are right, you know," Lady Mainwaring said with resignation. "No one will come near them this season now. This is what you are sacrificing with your foolishness."

"Honor is not foolish, Mama," he said without backing down. It would not do to show her the slightest bit of weakness for his mother was skilled at exploiting any bit of a dent in his armor. "I have given my word to Lady Hermione now and I will abide by it. I do regret the disappointment that has ensued for you and the girls, but it's not to be helped."

"I only hope that you will not find yourself regretting your actions, Jasper," she said with the air of one could not wait to say she'd told him so. "Marriage

is a serious business and one that is best not undertaken lightly."

"Yes, Mama," he said, biting back a grin at her of-
ficiousness, "I have heard the marriage liturgy before.
And I do not undertake this lightly. Lady Hermione
and I have been somewhat acquainted through mutual friends. And I believe we will be able to make a
good match, if not at first a conventional one."

"You know your own heart best," she said, at last
sounding resigned. "Now, if you will be so kind as
to take yourself off, I have a headache and I wish to
have a lie-down."

Watching as the last of his female relatives swept
out of the room, Jasper couldn't help but feel relieved
that the worst of it was over.

His mother and sisters might not be happy about
his marriage, but at the very least they knew he would
tolerate no disrespect for Hermione.

He had a sneaking suspicion, however, that Lady
Hermione would be quite able to take care of herself
if necessary.

Was it thoroughly wrong of him to anticipate seeing her rout the Mainwaring ladies at the first possible moment?

Perhaps, but he was willing to take his punishment
for it.

Sometime later that afternoon, Hermione was staring at her closet in an attempt to determine whether
any of her current wardrobe was worthy of being
worn by the Countess of Mainwaring, when she
heard a scratch on her door.

Ophelia poked her head round, and seeing Hermione was awake and alert, stepped in, shutting the
door firmly behind her.

"I just thought I'd stop in to see if you'd learned

anything more about Lord Saintcrow," she said diffidently. But Hermione wasn't fooled.

"Mainwaring sent you, didn't he?"

Her friend colored. "Perhaps," she said with a shrug. "I must admit I was more intrigued by the fact that he was the one who summoned me than the actual fact of the summons."

She waited, then. One brow raised in an imitation of Leonora at her most inquisitive.

"When did you become so nosy?" Hermione asked without rancor. "I expect it from Leonora but you are supposed to be the prim and proper one!"

"Someone has to press you for information while she's indisposed," Ophelia said, pursing her lips. "You are quite forthcoming about your plans for world domination, but anything having to do with gentlemen or feelings you lock away without giving anyone the key."

"I'm not that bad," Hermione said, gesturing her friend toward the conversation nook in the corner of her dressing room. "You make me sound like some sort of vault."

"A vault to which I begin to suspect the Earl of Mainwaring has somehow got the key."

Hermione rolled her eyes. "Do not make the mistake of thinking this is a love match, Ophelia. Leonora might be the poet but you've got the soul of a romantic lurking behind that practical exterior."

"Aha!" There was no disguising the triumph in the other lady's shout. "So it is a match, then! I knew it. From the moment you first argued over the suitability of ladies in driving clubs, I knew there was something between you."

"Do not be silly," Hermione said with more affection than heat. "We are to be wed, but it's not through the fault of either of us."

"What do you mean, 'fault'?"

"Just that," she said, pulling her stocking feet beneath her as she got comfortable on the settee. "My father had the temerity to gamble away my hand in marriage last night."

Quickly, she explained what Mainwaring had told her earlier about his encounter with her father in the gambling hell. She made no mention of what had transpired between herself and Mainwaring that afternoon in the drawing room. Some things even her friends could not be privy to.

Ophelia's eyes grew wide with astonishment.

"And what has your father to say for himself?" she demanded, angered on Hermione's behalf. Ophelia was nothing if not loyal. "I hope he groveled at your feet."

"Oh, he thinks he's well within his rights," Hermione said with a scowl. "And at this point, I'm not sure I'm not pleased with his loss of this particular wager. He's left me to clean up any number of messes this week. And none of them has exactly caused me a great deal of happiness. This one will, at the very least, put me under the care of someone who has a sensible head on his shoulders. I wasn't on the lookout for a husband, but as they go I could have done worse than Mainwaring."

"That's a relief at least," Ophelia said with a twist of her lips. "If you were thoroughly opposed to the match I'd have done what I could to ensure you were well out of it. But this means that we can end the week with our encounter with poor Lord Saintcrow as our biggest scandal."

"I suppose it will be a relief if there is no mention of a trio of veiled ladies leaving Lord Saintcrow's town house in tomorrow's papers." Hermione said with a wry smile.

"If that happens I will need to flee the country," Ophelia said with a speaking look. "As it is, I am often stuck at home listening to Mama tell me that the reason I haven't taken is that I've not been making myself agreeable to the right gentlemen. I can only imagine her response to this morning's adventure."

"I should think it's more a case of the right gentlemen not making themselves agreeable to you," Hermione said with a frown. "I vow, I don't think I've seen one man with the least bit of sense approach you at a ball all season. And you know that I am the soul of forgiveness when it comes to male stupidity."

This made Ophelia laugh, as Hermione had intended it. She didn't like to see her friend brought low by her mother's harping. Ophelia was a smart, sensible lady whose beauty was not immediately apparent to those who didn't bother to look. But she was a dear friend and Hermione didn't wish to see her spirit broken by a parent with little understanding of her daughter.

"Oh, yes," Ophelia agreed with a snort, "as forgiving as can be. When I think of how many men you've allowed to live rather than cutting them down with the single word it would take, I cannot help but consider you as the soul of kindness."

"So, your mama is beginning to turn her attention to you now that Mariah has become betrothed?" Hermione said after they'd stopped giggling.

"Indeed," Ophelia said with scowl. "I had hoped she'd take a well-deserved holiday from such matters now that her life's ambition has been realized."

Mariah Dauntry had become engaged to a marquess only one month earlier, and seeing her eldest daughter happily settled had been Mrs. Duantry's main purpose in life. Unfortunately, now that one daughter was taken care of, she wanted to do the same for the next eldest, Ophelia.

"Well, I shall be sure to introduce you to any number of handsome gentlemen once Mainwaring and I begin to host social events," Hermione said, thinking it sounded odd to mention herself in the same sentence as Mainwaring. And yet, there was a certain rightness to it.

"When will you wed?" asked Ophelia with interest. "I presume it will be by special license. Will you have any guests, do you think? May I attend?"

"So many questions," Hermione said mildly. "I don't quite know the answer to all of them. Though he did say he'd like to do the thing by the end of the week. So definitely special license, and I daresay you might come if you wish. I shall need someone to stand up with me. And though I suppose one of his sisters would be happy to do the honors, I should prefer it to be someone I know and love."

Ophelia clapped her hands. "I should be delighted to attend. Have you considered what you will wear?"

They spent a pleasant two hours discussing nothing more pressing than fashion, and Hermione found she was able to relax for the first time in two days.

And, to her relief, she even found something acceptable to wear to her wedding.

If only she could think of the wedding itself with such calm.

Twelve

The next morning, after another night spent in sleeplessness, Hermione went downstairs to find, to her surprise, her father seated at the breakfast table as if nothing much had happened in the last few days.

Staring for a moment at him, or rather at the papers which he was skillfully employing to hide his face from her, she was struck by just how detached from him she now felt.

They'd never been particularly close. Even when the death of her mother might have brought them together. But she'd never realized just how unreliable Lord Upperton was until these last couple of years. She had made her debut from her aunt's house, along with a cousin the same age. And when the cousin had married and moved away, Hermione had gone back to live at Upperton House with her father.

They'd managed to get along well enough, she supposed, but then Lord Upperton had begun to behave with the recklessness that had characterized his actions of the last few days. He gambled frequently, was drunk more often than not, and as evidenced by his loss of her grays, in his desperation for the next game, he'd grown callous. He would do whatever it took to ensure his continued access to the gaming tables.

Even betray his only child.

"I am surprised to find you here," she said, before crossing to the sideboard and filling a plate with more food than she could possibly eat. "I thought perhaps you had chosen to take rooms elsewhere."

When she turned to take a seat, he lowered the paper to the table.

Hermione bit back a gasp. Lord Upperton looked dreadful. His eyes were shadowed by dark circles, his skin tone was sallow, and he looked as if he'd not slept in weeks.

Taking a seat in the chair the footman held out for her, Hermione glanced down at her plate unseeing. She was unable to look back in her father's direction for a moment, so she took a deep breath.

"Why would I take rooms elsewhere when I've only just leased this place?" he asked querulously. "Doesn't make any sense, daughter."

Finally able to school her features, Hermione looked up at him again. This time noting the details she'd missed earlier. The burst blood vessel on his nose, the spot where his valet had missed with that morning's shave. She wished she could feel some sort of affection for him. But all she felt now was a sickly cocktail of disappointment, sadness, and nostalgia for the days when he'd been her beloved Papa.

"I suppose not," she said, taking a piece of toast from the rack just to have something to do. "I suppose you've learned about what happened to Lord Saintcrow?"

For a moment the question hung in the air between them like the sickly sweet perfume of an aging beauty.

"I don't know what you would have to say about it," he said finally, taking a slurping sip of tea. "An unmarried chit like you should have no dealings with a man like that."

Hermione sighed. "Cut line, Papa. I know it's to him you lost my grays. He told me as much when he came to collect them just before my first promenade with the Lords of Anarchy."

Lord Upperton winced. "I told the fellow to talk to me before he took the horses. He wasn't supposed to take possession of them until after you'd done your bit of folderol with that damned driving club."

She knew she shouldn't be touched by the knowledge that he'd not deliberately set out to humiliate her, but she was. At the very least it meant he had some feeling for her. And that was better than nothing.

Even so . . .

"The point is not when he arrived to take possession, Papa," she said, remaining firm despite her angst, "but that he came to collect my horses at all. You know full well that they belonged to me, outright."

But he waved that objection away. "You know as well as I do, daughter, that what's yours is mine. A father must be able to dispose of a daughter's belongings. Especially if they are leading her into activities that could endanger her."

"My horses weren't leading me into anything," she said, her voice rising with indignance. "If anything they were keeping me sane. I certainly would have run mad if all I had to occupy my time with was listening to other ladies prose on about needlework, or the latest fashion. And besides that, I purchased them with my own money. I believe that makes them my personal belongings."

"We won't quibble about technicalities, Hermione," her father said coolly. "What's done is done. What I wish to know is if you've settled things with Lord Mainwaring yet."

And just like that she went from being mildly annoyed to angry.

"If by that you mean to inquire whether he has told me about the card game you lost to him, thereby giving him my hand in marriage," she said through gritted teeth, "then, yes, I have settled things with Lord Mainwaring."

"But what's this?" he asked, looking as disappointed as child whose ice has melted. "I thought you'd be pleased. Fine, strapping man like that? You couldn't have done better yourself. And I do know how you dislike parading around the marriage mart. This way you don't have to!"

"That's not the point, Papa," she nearly shouted. "You might as well have offered me up to the highest bidder! I am well aware that you're within your rights to give my hand to whomever you wish, but did you have to do it in such a blatant spectacle?"

"Do not raise your voice to me, Hermione," Lord Upperton said sharply, all traces of childishness gone. "I did what I thought best for you. As your father that is my right. If you do not like the way I went about it, well then, you will simply need to get past that. I feel sure Lord Mainwaring will be more than adept at polishing away the tarnish of how the betrothal happened."

"It's not a betrothal, Papa," she said, pressing her fingers over her eyes to keep the tears that threatened from falling, "it is a marriage, which we will undertake at the end of the week at the very latest. I suspect Mainwaring will come here today to discuss the settlements."

Instead of looking chagrined at her disappointment, he singled out the thing that would most impact him and his plans. "Oh, I cannot possibly meet with the fellow today. My head is aching like mad.

And I promised the Countess of Amberley that I'd take her for a drive in the park this afternoon."

He would have gone on further, but a footman appeared and announced that his lordship had a visitor in his study.

"That is likely him now," she said, crossing her arms over her chest. She would have liked to be a fly on the wall during these marriage negotiations. For she had little doubt that her father would do what was best for himself and that Mainwaring would instead try to do what was fair. "I'll come say hello."

If her father thought it odd that she wished to see the fiancé she'd just upbraided him for securing for her, he didn't say anything about it. Instead, with a groan of unhappiness, he stood up from his chair and followed Hermione into the hallway in the direction of his study.

But when Hermione stepped over the threshold, it wasn't Mainwaring who lounged comfortably in the chair before Lord Upperton's desk, it was instead Mr. Rosewood.

Removing his hat, which he clearly had not given to Waverly upon his entrance, Mr. Rosewood said, "Lady Hermione, it is a pleasure. I hope I find you well."

"As well as I could be after two consecutive visits from the authorities," she said without heat. "I do not believe you've met my father, the Earl of Upperton?"

As her father stepped farther into the room, she noticed that he had a bruise on his upper cheek. Perhaps Mainwaring had not been able to keep his cool with him after all. For some reason, the notion buoyed her.

"Lord Upperton," said Rosewood, bowing deeply to her father. "I cannot tell you how happy I am to find you here. I feel as if I've been searching all over London for you."

"As you can see, sir," Lord Upperton said with an unreadable expression, "I am here in my own home."

"I can see that, my lord, but you weren't here yesterday. Or at any of the other places where I tried to search you out." Rosewood shrugged. "Any other man I'd have suspected of absconding. But no, you're here. Which will make my job so much easier, let me tell you."

"I'm sure I am as interested as the next man to see your job made easier," Lord Upperton said sarcastically, "but why don't you tell me why you were looking for me. Then you can be on your way."

"Ah, of course," said the Bow Street runner with a smile that didn't meet his eyes. "I came to ask you a few questions about Lord Saintcrow. I'm sure by now your daughter has told you all about it."

Taking a seat behind his massive desk, Lord Upperton nodded. "She made some mention of it, yes."

"Then you are also aware that Lord Saintcrow's death has been deemed suspicious. I know you will do your best to help us learn what truly happened to his lordship."

Hermione took a seat in the far corner of the room, wanting to hear what was said, but not wishing to be seen.

"What can I possibly do?" Lord Upperton's tone made it clear that he thought an investigation into the death of Saintcrow was a waste of time. "I only met with the fellow once and that was before his murder. I don't like to speak ill of the dead, but he was involved in any number of business dealings with less than scrupulous men who would not think twice about murder."

"But you see, your lordship, I have heard from more than one source that you were involved in some rather nasty business with Lord Saintcrow only days before he died." The big man's brow furrowed. "I don't mean to say that you killed the man, just that you might know who did."

Relaxing slightly, Lord Upperton pulled a bottle of brandy from his desk drawer and poured a hefty glass. Then glancing up, he offered Mr. Rosewood a glass. But the other man declined.

"I know nothing of who killed Saintcrow," said the earl once he'd downed the entire glass. "We completed our business and that was the last time I saw him. I wish I could help you."

"Oh, do not be too hard on yourself," Rosewood said with a smile. "I think you've helped me quite a bit."

Rising, he gave a brief nod to Hermione, and just before he reached the door, he turned. "One more thing, Lord Upperton. Can you tell me whether Lord Saintcrow won anything from you besides the coaching pair?"

Lord Upperton nodded. "Yes, he did. A small estate in Lincolnshire. Is there a problem with that?" Hermione noted that he had the good grace to look guilty at having his earlier lie about the estate revealed.

Rosewood looked thoughtful. "No problem at all. I thank you both for your time."

And with that, the runner left father and daughter alone.

Having finally secured a special license thanks to an uncle who was a bishop, Jasper turned Hector in the direction of Whitehall. He'd known the summons from Sir Richard Lindsey would come but was slightly vexed to have to face his mentor so soon after his unpleasant audience with his mother and sisters.

For he had little doubt that the spymaster would

find Jasper's entanglement with Hermione problematic at best.

When he strode into the older man's office some time later, it was to find Sir Richard, scribbling notes as he read through a stack of documents. No doubt different ones from the ones that had littered his desk when last Jasper was there.

There was no mistaking the sharp glance the man gave Jasper when he entered the room. Clearly he was in for a dressing-down of proportions in keeping with the desk he now stood before.

"I am pleased to see you didn't ignore my request for an accounting," Sir Richard said with a raised brow as he removed the spectacles he used for reading. "I thought perhaps you would wait until after the deed was done so that I would be unable to persuade you against your chosen course of action."

"Not at all, sir," said Jasper with a slight bow before he lowered himself into a wing chair opposite. "I have been busy, of course, but naturally my work for the crown is of the utmost importance."

"I am glad to hear you say it, lad," Sir Richard said, the slight burr of his native Scotland revealing itself as it always did when he was incensed. "For I did wonder for a moment whether your work for us was uppermost in your mind when you chose to sit down to a game with Lord Upperton. Especially considering that his home's proximity to the Fleetwoods was one of the reasons for you to further your friendship with Lady Hermione. I hardly need to tell you how difficult it will be to watch the Fleetwoods' comings and goings if Lady Hermione lives with you in Grosvenor Square."

"Logistics aside, sir," Jasper said with the plain-speaking he knew his mentor valued from him, "I could not, as a gentleman, allow her father to marry her off to someone else, either. At least I am acquainted with the lady, and despite my misgivings about her strong opinions, I am rather fond of her. Marriage to another man would not only lead her to a great deal of unhappiness, but might also remove our only connection to Fleetwood.

"And," he continued, knowing that this was his true trump card, "she is a member of the Lords of Anarchy. Which will be quite useful if we are to discover whether there is some link between the club and the ring of thieves."

"If, that is," Sir Richard said with a frown, "your suspicions about Fleetwood's dealings with the Lords of Anarchy are correct. We have not, to date, seen the man attend any of the meetings or ride out with the club."

"That is because he works with them not as a member, but behind the scenes." Jasper leaned forward, his elbows on his knees. "I do not know what it is that Fleetwood has to do with the club, but my gut says it's important. And I am quite sure now that the club itself is dealing in stolen horses. I overheard Lord Payne admit as much at the Comerford ball when he thought he wouldn't be heard."

Jasper told him about the conversation among Lord Payne and his cohorts, putting special emphasis on the bit where they discussed orders and deliveries. "My gut says that Fleetwood wasn't just a curious horse enthusiast the day he visited Hermione's stables, either. He was looking to see which horses she had there. Perhaps because the horses in question had originated with their ring of thieves."

"Your gut," Sir Richard said with a shake of his head. "I know your famous gut hasn't let me down before, Mainwaring, but I must tell you that I am far more comfortable when it's your head for calculations and figures that you ask me to trust. I can see the numbers and calculate them in my own, slow, way. Your gut I must take on faith. And that, I do not mind telling you, is something that I have a bit of trouble with."

It was an argument of long standing between the two men. Though Mainwaring's nearly incredible ability to speed through calculations was one of the reasons Sir Richard had sought him out in the first place, he had his own doubts about the bone-deep convictions that led him to conclusions that might in other circumstances seem mad. But Jasper lived with both abilities for so long that he had learned to trust himself. He could not explain how he knew there was a connection between Fleetwood and the driving club, but he was damned sure it was there.

"I realize that my marriage to Lady Hermione might present a divergence from our initial plans for surveilling the Fleetwoods," he said now, "but it's a matter of honor, sir, and I will not leave the lady in the lurch for you or the crown."

"Well," Sir Richard said with a frown. "That is a fine speech, but I would like to know how you intend to continue the investigation once you are wed to a lady who seems damned close to the suspects in this inquiry and might even be guilty of Saintcrow's murder."

"That's not fair, sir." Jasper was willing to listen to Sir Richard's chastisement of him, but he was damned if he'd let the man accuse Hermione of murder. "She had nothing to do with it. I know. I was there."

"What do you mean, you were there?" Sir Richard's eyes blazed. "Explain yourself!"

Jasper told him about how Hermione and her friends had descended upon Saintcrow's residence the day of the murder and found him already dead.

"So you do not know, in fact, that the three ladies are innocent of the crime," Sir Richard said. "Just that when you arrived they were upset from seeing it."

"You don't really believe that three gently reared ladies are capable of slitting a man's throat over a pair of contested horses?" Jasper asked, aghast.

Sir Richard tilted his head. "I do not, as it happens. I think it rather more likely that he was killed by one of his confederates. But I am not the only one you need to convince of it."

"No," Jasper agreed. "There is a runner who has been questioning Hermione and her father over the matter. He isn't positive that she was one of the three veiled ladies that were seen coming from Saintcrow's house on the day of the murder, but he has his suspicions, I think. And I do not think he will be dissuaded by our marriage. If anything, he seems like the sort who will work harder to prove she did it because of her elevated rank."

"Then do what you can to protect your lady, man," Sir Richard said with a vehemence that startled Jasper. "I am content with what you've learned so far about the theft ring. Just continue to watch Fleetwood and maybe look further into his possible connections to the Lords of Anarchy. It cannot be a coincidence that a club of driving aficionados has such close ties to a horse-theft ring. If I were horse mad and wanted access to the best carriage horses I could find without paying full price for them, I might not look too closely at where my steeds came from."

"It has crossed my mind that Lady Hermione's horses, Rosencrantz and Guildenstern, might not have the most pristine ownership records." Jasper hated the thought, especially given how heartbroken Hermione had been when she lost them. But it was a possibility he had to look into. "She's asked her man of business to send copies of the bill of sale and we're still waiting on that. In the meantime, I've purchased them from Saintcrow's heir, so if they do turn out to be stolen we can see that they are returned to their rightful owner."

"Good man," Sir Richard said with approval. "I hope for your lady's sake that they turn out to be what they purport to be."

Thirteen

$\mathcal{H}$ermione was seated in the drawing room in Half-Moon Street, debating whether to send a note to Jasper about Mr. Rosewood's interview with her father, when she heard the knocker on the front door strike a tattoo.

What if Rosewood had come back? she wondered, nervous energy coursing through her. Lord Upperton had left for his club, and Jasper's warnings that she wasn't to speak to Rosewood alone again rang in her ears.

She would simply tell Greentree that she was not receiving callers at the moment. That should be enough to send the fellow away. He couldn't expect everyone to welcome him into their homes with open arms.

But when Greentree presented the caller's card to her, it was not whom she'd expected.

Curiosity and a shade of trepidation ran through her even as she said, "Send her up, Greentree. And please have cook send up some refreshments."

"The Countess of Mainwaring," intoned Greentree before the lady stepped into the chamber.

For the barest moment, the two ladies surveyed each other.

Lady Mainwaring was very obviously Jasper's mother. He'd inherited his blue eyes and fine features from her. As well as the curls in his hair, though hers was a much lighter shade of brown. And whereas he was nearly six feet tall, his mother was shorter than Hermione. But it was evident from the way she held herself that she was accustomed to deference from everyone she met.

"Lady Mainwaring," Hermione said, stepping forward to offer the other woman her hand. "What a pleasure to meet you. I hope you will come in and make yourself comfortable."

The chilly smile the other lady gave her did not bode well for their future relationship. "Thank you, Lady Hermione," said the countess with a strained smile. "I hope that you do not find my visit overly intrusive."

She gave Hermione's hand a limp squeeze before lowering herself gracefully to one of the armchairs separated by a small table. "What a pretty little room this is. I am quite surprised to see it so well furnished. I had heard your father had chosen to let the Upperton town house, and thus supposed your rented rooms would be quite gauche. How pleasant it must be for you to reside here."

Hermione blinked at Lady Mainwaring's rudeness. "Indeed," she said when she found her voice. "Quite pleasant." Clearly Jasper's mother had come with a purpose in mind. She wished most heartily that the lady would reveal that purpose as soon as possible.

"My son informs me that he has made you an offer of marriage and that you have accepted," the countess said without preamble. "I must request that you withdraw your consent immediately. Before too many people hear of it. I realize that it came about because of some silly card game, but it will be much easier to play that off as a foolish male mistake than rumors of promises made between the two of you."

If Hermione had been expecting to be welcomed into the Mainwaring family with open arms, she saw now that she had been horribly mistaken. Which was a shame considering that she had no mother of her own now. She had hoped that she and Jasper's mother would develop the same kind of rapport that Leonora enjoyed with her mother-in-law, but it was clear that it was not to be.

She was saved from immediate reply by the arrival of the tea tray. Taking comfort in the ritual of pouring for them both, she was calmer when she responded to Lady Mainwaring.

"I realize that the suddenness of our match must have come as something of a shock to both you and Lord Mainwaring's sisters," she said coolly. "But I'm afraid that both our minds are quite firm on the matter. It took some convincing for me to see the wisdom of it at first," she continued, "but I am quite convinced that it is the best choice for both of us. Though I do take your objection quite seriously."

Lady Mainwaring set her teacup down on the table with a rattle. "If you took my objection seriously, Lady Hermione," she said with pursed lips, "then you would do me the honor of respecting my wishes. It's clear to me that both you and my son are determined to rain as much scandal down upon our family as possible. Which you, no doubt, are accustomed to considering who your father is, but despite my son's propensity for cards, we are not yet as notorious as the house of Upperton, and I should like to keep it that way."

Hermione had to bite her tongue to stop from telling her future mother-in-law just what she thought about that lady's assessment of her notorious family.

Instead, mindful that for a little while anyway, she would need to live under the same roof as Lady Mainwaring, she took a fortifying sip of tea.

"I am sorry to hear you feel this way, Lady Mainwaring," she said with more deference than she felt. "But I am afraid that though your displeasure is evident, it was not you but your son who asked me to join your family, and unless I am vastly mistaken *he* is the Earl of Mainwaring, and therefore the one to make such a decision. I do thank you for stopping by and I hope that you were not too inconvenienced by having to journey all the way to Half-Moon Street."

She rose, watching in amusement as Lady Mainwaring's face grew pinched in light of Hermione's little speech. Finally, seeing that her hostess was not going to apologize, the countess got to her feet.

"I had hoped that you would listen to reason," she said haughtily, "but it is clear to me now that you are just as headstrong as the gossips say. Do not think that this is the last you will hear of this."

And with her head held high, the Countess of Mainwaring swept from the room like an empress flouncing away from her court.

Hermione did not sit back down until she heard the door close behind her. At which point she collapsed into her chair.

What on earth had she agreed to? And how had Jasper possibly grown up into such a kind man? He had his moments of haughtiness and austerity, but he was as different from his mother as chalk from cheese.

Thinking back to Lady Mainwaring's parting words, she wondered if she ought to let her fiancé know that his mother had paid a call upon her.

Surely the lady would not jeopardize her son's reputation just for the sake of hurting their match. She was the matriarch of the family after all, so what harmed him harmed her as well.

But mothers had done less to ensure that their sons married where they wished. Lady Mainwaring, it would seem, was less concerned with her son's reputation than with her own.

Hermione might not be sure just how to respond to the lady's warning, but she did know one thing.

It was time that someone began to look out for Jasper.

And she was more than happy to be the one to do it.

When Jasper returned home from his visit to Sir Richard, it was to find his sister Evelina waiting for him by the front entrance.

"To what do I owe this pleasure?" he asked mildly once he'd handed his hat and gloves over to Greaves. "It isn't like you to lie in wait, Eve."

But Evelina shook her head, and wordlessly took him by the arm and led him into the small sitting room Greaves reserved for those guests who did not live up to his high standards.

"What is it?" Jasper asked, curious at his sister's actions. She'd seemed to have got over her pique at his betrothal to Hermione since he'd seen her last, but her peculiar behavior had him rethinking that assessment.

"Mama has just returned from paying a call on Lady Hermione," Evelina said, her brows drawn. "I do not know what was said, but when she returned she was in a towering rage. Muttering about headstrong young ladies without the sense to listen to their elders. And she wrote a note to Aunt Hortense."

His mother's sister, Hortense, was the second wife of the Marquess of Thayne, and one of the most powerful social leaders in the *ton*. A word in Hortense's ear would be enough to ruin a lady's reputation permanently. And he had little doubt that is what his mother hoped her sister would do once she received her note.

He swore, unsure whether he should go to Hermione, or attempt to intercept his mother's letter before the damage was done.

"Tell Greaves to send the footman to retrieve it," Evelina said, reading his mind. "I will stay here to watch for it."

"Why are you helping me with this?" he asked suddenly. It had seemed as if, when he broke the news of his betrothal to his family, that neither his sisters nor his mother would ever forgive him.

"Truth?" she asked with a rueful smile. "It occurred to me that ever since Papa died, you've always taken care of us. Perhaps it's time that someone decided to take care of you for a change."

Touched, Jasper gave his sister a quick hug. "Thank you," he said with a grin.

Then, retracing his steps into the entrance hall, he took back his hat and gloves and set out for Half-Moon Street.

Hermione was in the stable behind Half-Moon Street, when she heard the sound of a throat clearing behind her.

Turning from where she watched as a groom checked the hoof of one of the horses Lord Payne had sent to replace Rosencrantz and Guildenstern, Hermione saw that Jasper stood diffidently in the open area between the opposing rows of stalls.

"I don't mean to interrupt," he said with a smile. But she could see that his brows were furrowed, and that something was obviously bothering him.

His mother must have told him about her visit, she thought with an inward sigh.

Nodding her thanks to the grooms, she turned and indicated to Jasper that they should go back to the house.

Neither of them spoke until they reached the garden of the Upperton house, and Hermione had taken a seat on the bench beneath the rose arbor.

"My sister, Evelina, informed me that my mother paid a visit to you today," he said tightly. "And that the interview did not go well."

She took a moment to really look at him. To see the little furrow between his brows that appeared whenever he was worried or upset. And the way his fists were clenched at his sides. He was clearly unhappy about what had happened. But she was unhappy to realize that she did not yet know him well enough—or rather did not know his relationship with his mother well enough—to know whether his anger was at her, the situation, or Lady Mainwaring.

Deciding to give him the benefit of the doubt, she nodded. "Yes, she did. And unfortunately, I do not believe she was very happy with me."

"May I ask what it was she said exactly?" he asked, fidgeting with the quizzing glass that hung from his waistcoat. "I suspect it wasn't very polite."

"May I ask you something first?"

At his nod, she continued, "Why is your mother so distrustful of your decisions?"

He had been bracing for her question, and when he heard it, he sighed.

"May I?" he asked, nodding to the spot on the bench beside her.

At her assent, he lowered his tall frame to sit next to her. She felt the warmth of his body along her side.

They didn't touch, but his nearness was comforting somehow.

"When my father died," he began, staring out into the overgrowth of the garden, "I was just a boy. I was the earl, but unable to take up the reins of power until I reached my majority. My uncle was my guardian, but he left much of the day-to-day running of the estate to my mother."

She tried to imagine what Jasper must have been like as a child. What it must have been like for his mother—newly widowed—to be left not only with the well-being of three small children to see to, but also the day-to-day running of the estate. Surely there were stewards and secretaries, but even so it would be a great deal of work.

"And your mother became accustomed to being the one in charge?" she asked aloud.

"Indeed," he responded with a nod. "And when I came into my majority and began to make decisions on my own, she had a difficult time giving that power up."

"It's understandable, I suppose," Hermione said diffidently. As a woman who had fought against the seemingly arbitrary rules that governed patriarchal society, she could guess what it must have felt like to control the vast Mainwaring estates. What it had been like to command not only the household staff but also the running of the estate. And what it would have been like to give all that power away to her son when the time came.

"Of course," he responded with a wry smile. "And I admit that I was grateful for her counsel at first. She is not a simpleton, my mother. And having her input when I was struggling to figure out the best way to go about handling things was a relief."

He would have been a handsome youth, Hermione guessed. Perhaps a little gangly, not having grown into his height yet. And perhaps a little full of himself, as all young men are at that age. Even so, he would not have been cruel or indifferent to his mother. She couldn't imagine him behaving in such a way.

"But there came a time when I had to cut the apron strings," he said sadly. "And it was not pretty."

"Did she fight you over it?" Hermione wondered, looking to where his hand lay clenched on his thigh. Would he object if she were to take it in her own? Smooth out those clenched fingers?

"Worse," he said turning to look at her. "She challenged me in front of both the steward and my personal secretary."

"Oh no," she said, her heart aching for both mother and son.

"I had to speak to her in strong terms," he went on. "Otherwise I'd have lost the respect of every man on the estate."

"I take it she was not best pleased with your response?"

"She was devastated," he said with a sigh. "It was as if I'd denounced her before the whole of the world. Never mind that I was a grown man who had to take up the running of a massive estate. It wasn't that I didn't appreciate all she'd done for me. Of course I did. But there comes a time in every man's life when he must forge his own path. And so I asked her to reserve her future input for the housekeeper and maids. And that I thanked her but would appreciate her refraining from giving her opinions on matters that were none of her concern."

"Oh dear," Hermione said, wincing.

"It was not my most diplomatic maneuver of all time," Jasper said wryly. "And since then we've been at war in one way or another. We are constantly at cross-purposes, and she has grown more fractious as the years have passed."

"And so when you told her of our betrothal?" Hermione asked, almost not daring to hear the answer.

"She and both my sisters were quite vocal in their opposition to the match," he said, reaching out to take her hand in apology. "I'm afraid my sisters were upset on their own behalf, afraid that your notoriety would reflect on their matrimonial prospects. And my mother was angry out of sheer spite, I think."

"She told me that she did not wish for my family's infamy to further tarnish the Mainwaring name," Hermione told him. "Your own frequency at the tables having already rubbed some of the perfection off."

He pinched the bridge of his nose. "Do you ever wish that you could simply run away and leave your entire family behind to fend for themselves?" he asked.

"I believe you've met my father," Hermione said with a half smile. "I wish it every day. The only thing that keeps me from going is the fact that I would miss my friends. Leonora and Ophelia are closer to me than any real sisters I might have had."

Jasper nodded. "That's what Freddy and Trent and I used to say. Only substituting sisters for brothers, obviously. We would look quite silly in gowns."

"I don't know," Hermione said playfully, "you'd make a very pretty girl, I think. What with those long lashes and rosebud lips."

"Yes," he agreed, bringing their joined hands up to kiss hers. "Until my whiskers began to show, which happens around five o'clock in the evening. Then there would be some serious explanations in order."

Hermione tried to stifle it, but there was no help

for it. She laughed. And soon they were both wiping their streaming eyes.

"I'm sorry Mama was so awful to you, Hermione," he said into the companionable silence. "I cannot promise you that she will make your life as a Mainwaring easy. But I do think my sisters have come around. Well, one of them has come around. We'll have to see about the other."

"I know it had nothing to do with you," she said, kissing him impulsively on the lips. And when he brought his hand up to cup her cheek, and hold her close so that he could deepen the kiss, she let him.

When they were both breathless, he pulled back. "I think I am very glad we are planning to marry tomorrow," he said with a pointed look. "Otherwise I think we might find ourselves in a fair bit of trouble."

She had little doubt her cheeks were as rosy as her newly kissed lips. "Speak for yourself," she said with mock asperity. "I am quite able to control my impulses."

"Hm," he said with a wry grin. "Are you the same lady who let me put my hand—"

Her eyes wide, she put her hand over his mouth before he could finish. "Do not say that out loud," she hissed. "Anyone could hear you."

"Let them hear," he said. "It's not as if we aren't planning to wed tomorrow. But for your delicate sensibilities, I will refrain."

And the notion that Lady Hermione Upperton, newest member of the Lords of Anarchy, had any delicate sensibilities at all set her laughing again.

Fourteen

I t's lovely, Hermione," Ophelia said with an awe in her tone that made Hermione tremble a little.

"Truly, Hermione," said Leonora, who stood with her hands clasped before her, tears threatening.

Her friends had come hours early that morning, saying they were there to help her dress for the wedding, though Hermione was perfectly able to do so on her own.

Well, with her maid, but still . . .

"I was so hoping you would choose the deep blue. I'm quite pleased you did," Ophelia said now, stepping back to survey Hermione from the tip of her gleaming dark hair to her fine kid slippers.

"I may not be the fashion plate that you are, Fee," Hermione said with a half smile, "but I know what looks good on me, at the very least."

"You do indeed," said Leonora with a grin. "Who would have thought?"

"I hope you will agree," Ophelia said, turning to rummage in the bag she'd brought with her, then turning to raise a fine cashmere shawl in triumph, "that this looks good on you, indeed."

Without waiting for Hermione to respond, Ophelia opened the fine fabric and showed her the intricately patterned wrap. Unfurling it, she wrapped it carefully around her friend's shoulders. "There, that should do it."

"Something old," Hermione said, pointing to her gown.

"Something new," Ophelia said, gesturing to the filigree hairpin she'd given as a bridal gift.

"Something borrowed," said Leonora, arranging the ends of the shawl over her bosom.

"And something blue," said Hermione with a sweep of her hand to indicate the skirt of her blue gown.

"Can you use the same item twice?" Hermione wondered with a frown. She wasn't of a particularly superstitious nature, but considering the way in which this match had come about, she was not going to tempt fate if she could help it.

"Of course!" Ophelia said, though a small indentation between her brows belied her confidence.

"Your eyes count, do they not?" Leonora asked.

A wave of relief washed over Hermione. "Of course."

Then, stepping back a little to survey herself in the pier glass, she stared for a moment at her reflection. She'd never have considered herself to be a particularly timid person. It felt some days as if she had come out of the womb fighting and hadn't stopped since. But the beauty in the glass had a hint of doubt in her eyes. And for a moment Hermione wondered if this pretty girl would find it a bit easier to go through the world than the old Hermione had. She could not help but admit that a part of her was looking forward to marriage because it might give her the chance to re-create herself a bit.

Not that there was something wrong with the old Hermione. She had done what she had to do given her circumstances. But perhaps marriage would let her share the fight sometimes. Jasper's shoulders seemed strong enough for that.

A flicker of doubt made her wonder if it was a kind of betrayal to admit that she was tired of carrying the burden on her own all the time. But it was true, and she was deciding here and now that denial—which had been her constant companion since she'd got old enough to understand her father's vices—would have no more place in her life.

She only hoped that Jasper would make it a moot point anyway.

"Are you ready to go?" Ophelia asked, with a suspicious tremor in her voice.

Taking a deep breath, Hermione exhaled, took up her reticule and surveyed her bedchamber. Most of her things had been moved to the Mainwaring town house yesterday. It was not a room to which she'd had any great attachment, since she and her father had only moved there a few months ago. All her sentimental tears had been shed when they left the Upperton town house. Which made today's departure easier, to be sure.

"I am," she said, turning to give her friends both hugs. "Thank you for your help. Both of you. I could have done it on my own, or with my maid, but it meant more to have my dearest friends at my side."

"I wouldn't have missed it," Ophelia said with a grin.

"Now," Leonora said with finality, "let's go downstairs before some freakish mishap occurs and ruins your gown."

They were laughing as they descended the staircase, but the giggles died when they reached the entryway of the house and saw that Greentree was in deep conversation with a lady dressed in all black.

"Who is it, Greentree?" Hermione asked, a sense

of foreboding making her voice sound weak to her own ears.

"It is Miss Fleetwood from next door, my lady," said the butler with an air of disapproval. "I have assured her that you are not receiving but she will not take no for an answer."

Curiosity made Hermione step into the doorway so that she might get a better look at the woman whose scream she'd heard earlier in the week. "Nonsense, I have time for a short chat, though I do not think much longer than that."

She did not elaborate on what her reason was for cutting short the meeting, but figured an unexpected guest didn't deserve to know. "Come with me, Miss Fleetwood, and we can speak in the small sitting room. Do you mind if my friends accompany us?"

Perhaps startled at being welcomed so soon after being denied entrance, Miss Fleetwood nodded, bemused, and followed Hermione and the other two ladies into the sitting room.

"Pray be seated, Miss Fleetwood," Hermione said, gesturing to an armchair near the fire. "We haven't been properly introduced but I am Lady Hermione Upperton and these are my friends Mrs. Frederick Lisle and Miss Ophelia Dauntry."

She took a moment to examine her guest, now that they were in a well-lighted room.

The other lady was rail thin, and her complexion indicated that she'd had perhaps been ill, for there was a sallow look to it. Her light brown hair was shiny, however, and had been dressed by someone who knew what they were doing. And her gown was fine enough. Not for the first stare of fashion, but neither was it the work of some village seamstress.

"I thank you, my lady," said Miss Fleetwood, her voice hesitant, as if she hadn't spoken in some time.

"I can see that you and your friends were on your way to some social engagement. I do not wish to keep you. But I did so wish to thank you for coming to my rescue the other day."

"So it was you who screamed," Hermione said, a little bubble of triumph rising in her. She knew she hadn't imagined it. No matter what Mr. Fleetwood had said.

"It was," she said with a sheepish smile. "I know my brother lied to you, but he is very protective of me. And he has done his best to see to it that I'm not disturbed."

"And why is that, if you don't mind my asking, Miss Fleetwood?"

At her bold question, Hermione could feel Ophelia stare at her with shock. But the lady clearly wished to be asked about the matter and Hermione was not one to mince words.

"I have been ill, Lady Hermione," she said with a frown. "Very ill indeed. And unfortunately, I had news after your encounter with my brother that has not helped matters. My fiancé, you see. He was . . ."

The lady's voice trembled and, to Hermione's surprise, tears shone in her eyes.

"It's all right, Miss Fleetwood," said Ophelia, handing the other woman a handkerchief. "Take your time."

"Thank you, Miss Dauntry," said Miss Fleetwood, visibly reining in her emotions. "It's just that Tony's death was such a shock. I cannot imagine that anyone would ever wish to murder him. It's unthinkable."

"Murder?" Hermione asked. First Saintcrow and now Miss Fleetwood's fiancé? It was a wonder the streets of London weren't running with blood!

"Yes," Miss Fleetwood said with a sniff. "Tony, Lord Saintcrow, that is, was murdered in his own house. And the worst thing about it is that they do not know who did it."

At Miss Fleetwood's words, Hermione felt faint. "Did you say Lord Saintcrow?" she asked, trying not to show just how uncomfortable Miss Fleetwood's confession had made her.

"Yes," Miss Fleetwood said with a nod. "I understand that he had some business dealings with your father? That is why I am here, Lady Hermione. I wished to know if perhaps your father knew something that might help the Bow Street runner my brother has hired to find out the truth of what happened to him."

Good God, Hermione thought with an inward gasp. Mr. Rosewood had been hired by Fleetwood? What a coil!

"I'm afraid my father and I aren't that close, Miss Fleetwood," she responded truthfully. "Indeed, though I did know that my father had lost some horses to Lord Saintcrow in a card game, I have no notion of the particulars of the affair. I did meet your fiancé once, but it was brief. He was quite handsome, though."

She added that last in an attempt to say something good about the man. After all, she'd not been his biggest supporter after he stripped her of her grays in the presence of the entire membership of the Lords of Anarchy.

"Oh, he was handsome, indeed," Miss Fleetwood said with a flash of animation that made Hermione realize just how beautiful she must have been before her illness. "And he was a good man. If a bit wild. I blame his driving club for some of that, of course. Tony was never so ungoverned as he was after he joined the Lords of Anarchy."

Was there no other way in which the late Lord

Saintcrow might have been entangled in Hermione's life? she wondered. Perhaps he was secretly the editor of her friend Leonora's poetry. Or was Ophelia's long-lost brother? Must he also have been a member of the Lords of Anarchy?

Though, if that were true, why hadn't he been driving out with the club that day in the park? She was new enough with the club that she didn't know the name of every member, but if Lord Saintcrow was so involved with the club that his fiancée complained about his exploits with them then one would think he'd have been with them in the park.

Aloud she said, "I am well acquainted with the club." And since it would be easy enough for the other lady to find out, she added, "Indeed, I have only recently been admitted to the membership."

At Hermione's admission, Miss Fleetwood's eyes widened. "You? But you are a lady. Surely ladies do not belong to such clubs."

"It is only recently that they began admitting ladies," Leonora spoke up, loyalty for Hermione in her voice. "Indeed, Hermione was the first lady to be admitted to the club. It was a true honor, bestowed upon her because of her excellent driving."

A silence hung between them for a moment. Then, perhaps sensing that further condemnation of "such clubs" would do her no good in her present audience, she said, "I mean no disrespect. I am sure that you are not one of the members who pushed my Tony to take more and more risks. But there are some men among the membership who . . . well, I will say only that I hope you know what you are about."

"No insult was taken, Miss Fleetwood," Hermione said with a speaking glance at Leonora. Really, how was she to learn what the woman had against the club if her friends made her stop talking? "Perhaps you can tell me what happened and then I might be prepared for such behavior myself? For I admit I've only been a member for a few weeks. And I have not yet participated in any club activities."

But the moment had passed. "It was nothing, Lady Hermione. Truly. I was probably only imagining things. If I'd known someone like you was a member I would have been less foolishly afraid of the club. Indeed, I think ladies must always be a softening influence on men, do you not think?"

A memory flashed in her mind of just how very . . . hard Jasper had felt the other day in her arms. Was she blushing? she wondered. Then, she remembered. The wedding! Jasper!

"Oh dear, Miss Fleetwood," she said with an apologetic smile. "I am afraid that my friends and I must be off. I just recalled that we have a very important appointment."

She rose, and took the flustered Miss Fleetwood's hand. "I am so pleased that you stopped by. And I do wish to hear more about Lord Saintcrow and what happened to him. If there is anything I can do to make the situation more bearable, I hope you will let me know."

"You are too kind, Lady Hermione," said the other lady with a smile. "I vow, I do not have very many friends. My brother is often so protective that he frightens off anyone who dares to get close. That is why I was so happy to have Tony."

"Then you will have to come to tea once I am settled in my new home," Hermione said impulsively, even as she was thinking of how soon she could recount Miss Fleetwood's tale to Jasper. "I will be at Mainwaring House in Grosvenor Square."

The brunette's brow furrowed. "I do not understand."

"We are on the way to Lady Hermione's wedding to the Earl of Mainwaring, Miss Fleetwood," said Ophelia, clearly eager to be off.

Miss Fleetwood's gasp was evidence enough of her surprise.

"I'm sorry, Miss Fleetwood," Hermione said, even as she and Hermione were handed into the waiting carriage by the lingering footman. "Do come for tea, though!"

And leaving a stunned Miss Fleetwood in their wake, Hermione her friends set out for St. George's Hanover Square.

"Where are they?" Jasper demanded for the fifth time in four minutes as he and the duke of Trent stood, along with Lord Upperton in the vestibule of St. George's Hanover Square.

"I am sure my daughter will arrive soon, Mainwaring," said Lord Upperton with the grin of a man who was about to be relieved of a great responsibility. He was also, perhaps, pleased by the marriage settlements he and Jasper had worked out the day before which added to his personal coffers considerably. "I left orders for Greentree to have the carriage brought round at precisely nine-thirty."

"Perhaps there is traffic, Mainwaring," said Jasper's mother. Given the way she and his sisters had reacted to the news of his impending nuptials, he'd been surprised when all three requested to attend the ceremony, but he'd agreed easily enough. It would be better for everyone concerned if he and Hermione were able to begin married life on good terms with one of their families.

"She will be here," said Trent. "Just be patient. You know how Lady Hermione is. It's entirely possible she chose to drive herself."

At the notion of Hermione driving a coach and four to her own wedding, Jasper couldn't help but laugh. Leave it to him to marry the one lady in London who just might do so.

Even so, he doubted somehow that Miss Dauntry and Leonora would allow such a thing to transpire.

Just then, the doors were opened by a liveried arm, and a breathless Miss Dauntry stepped in, followed by Leonora.

And finally, Hermione.

Jasper took a moment to drink her in.

Her dark hair, which always appeared to be shiny and tidy, was today dressed in a looser, more feminine style which left a single curl to caress her neck. The blue morning gown was one he'd seen her in before, but paired with a brightly colored cashmere shawl it was more festive somehow. She was at once familiar and someone entirely new. And she would soon be his.

"Will I do?" she asked with a smile that told him she knew exactly what he'd been thinking.

"I believe you will," he said with a grin, offering her his arm.

"I am sorry we were late," she said in a low voice as they walked in an untidy procession to the front of the church. "I had a very interesting visitor. Which I will tell you about later."

"Tease," he said, not giving a fig who her visitor had been. All he cared about now was making this beautiful, stubborn, maddening woman his.

"I see everyone has arrived," said the bishop with a brisk nod, as Jasper and Hermione and their guests took their places.

And then the ceremony began.

If he were entirely honest, Jasper would admit that he did not recall a word of what any of them had said. At least not beyond Hermione's firmly uttered, "I will." When the clergyman was finished, he pronounced them man and wife, and before he knew what he was about, Jasper had lowered his head and kissed her—restraining the flare of passion he felt anytime she was in close proximity.

"Shall we repair to Mainwaring House for a celebratory repast?" he asked the others, tucking Hermione's arm in his.

After murmured assent, they all left the church and Jasper handed Hermione into his carriage for the short ride from Hanover Square to Grosvenor.

Almost as soon as the door shut behind them, he pulled her into his arms for a proper kiss. One that left them both breathless and Hermione's hand clutching his now horrifically rumpled cravat.

"There," he said with a grin. "I wanted to do that the moment you walked into the church, but I decided that might be a bit too much for the bishop."

Her cheeks pink, Hermione laughed, a low giggle that did nothing to cool his ardor. "I suspect that the bishop might have had some objections to a kiss like that in a house of worship."

"It would be worship," he said with a raised brow. "Just not worship of the Lord."

"I believe that breaks a commandment, does it not?" she asked saucily. "It is a good thing you chose to restrain yourself. I'd hate to begin our marriage with you excommunicated."

"We almost didn't begin it at all," he said playfully. "I do not mind telling you I had a moment of fear when I suspected you weren't coming."

"Do not be absurd. I wouldn't leave you at the altar," she said with a shake of her finger. Then, her eyes grew serious. "I was late because of a visitor. As I told you."

Seeing that the giddy mood had passed, he settled back against the carriage squabs, though he kept her hand in his. "Who was it? Not Rosewood again, I hope?"

"No," she said with a frown. "It was Miss Fleetwood, of all people."

That name put Jasper on alert, though he schooled himself not to show it. "As long as it was she and not her brother," he said with more sharpness than he intended. Calmer, he went on, "I still have reasons for wishing you to avoid Mr. Fleetwood."

"Even if it had been him," Hermione said with a show of her teeth, "I could not have turned him away. But in this case there was no need because it was Miss Fleetwood. And though Ophelia and Leonora and I were on our way out of the house, we decided to speak to her privately for a few moments at least."

"And?" he asked.

Quickly she revealed the conversation that had transpired between the four ladies.

"I am now not only pleased that you spoke to her," he said with a shake of his head, "but I wonder that you were able to tear yourself away in order for us to be married!"

At his jest, she rapped him on the knuckles with her fan. "I should have done so considering how lightly you speak of it," she said with a scowl. "But in all seriousness, did you know she was betrothed to Lord Saintcrow? What are the odds of such a coincidence?"

"I could calculate it, but there are too many variables for it to have a great deal of meaning," he said seriously.

At her raised brow, he shrugged. "Sorry, I am nothing if not a mathematician."

"It's the first I've heard of it," she said with a frown.

"It's hardly a secret," he said with a shrug. "It's how I win so often at cards. I'm able to calculate the odds of getting a particular card in my hand after seeing which ones have already been played. It isn't particularly difficult if you know what you're doing."

"If it weren't difficult," she shot back, "then everyone would do it."

He said nothing.

"I had no idea," she said with a shake of her head. "Me, married to a mathematician. It boggles the mind."

"Because you have a particular antipathy for maths?"

"Because I have a particular antipathy for maths," she confirmed.

"Then let us get back to the subject at hand," he said, drawing her against him, liking the feel of her warm body tucked up against him. "What did Miss Fleetwood have to say about Saintcrow? Or Fleetwood for that matter?"

It occurred to him that he'd perhaps been hasty in ordering Hermione not to have any dealings with the Fleetwoods while they were her neighbors. It had been a missed opportunity, he realized now.

Hermione told him about Saintcrow and the Lords of Anarchy.

"Do you think it's true that they encouraged him to take risks?" she asked, her body stiff, clearly not wanting to hear him confirm the report.

"It's possible," he said, not wanting to lie to her. "But I should have thought that after that business earlier this year, Lord Payne would wish the club to turn over a new leaf. Isn't that what you said was his intention in accepting ladies into their ranks?"

"Yes," she said, snuggling up against him. "And as far as I know they have been behaving themselves. Of course I've not had the chance to interact with most of them."

"Do you think Miss Fleetwood had any suspicions about her brother being involved with Saintcrow's murder?" he asked, wishing he'd been there to question the lady himself. Of course, it was likely she was far more forthcoming with Hermione than she'd ever be with him.

"I don't know. I had the feeling she was going to tell me something more," Hermione said. "But I recalled that we were late and fobbed her off with an invitation to come for tea once I was settled at Mainwaring House."

For a moment, he was struck dumb at the pleasure he felt at hearing her speak of her settling into Mainwaring House. But then the substance of what she'd actually said sank in. "My darling wife," he said with a bark of laughter. "You are utterly brilliant!"

"I am?" she asked puzzled at his sudden giddiness.

"One of the reasons I was so damned worried about you getting friendly with the Fleetwoods was that I did not wish for you to get caught in that house alone. Or rather, alone with him. He's a dangerous fellow and I worried for your safety. And I didn't feel much better about your safety in your own house."

"And inviting Miss Fleetwood to Mainwaring House removes that threat?" she asked, leaning back to look into his eyes.

"It does," he said with a grin. "And this way, I can speak to Miss Fleetwood as well. There was no way I could get into the Fleetwoods' house without raising his suspicions."

"I must admit to being baffled at having pleased you so much without even realizing what I was doing." She shook her head. "If this is a sign of how marriage to you will be on a daily basis, I suppose I will like it well enough."

"Well enough?" he asked with mock affront. "Damned with faint praise!"

"I can hardly be overjoyed at being unable to replicate my triumphs thanks to never knowing what it is about them that made it possible for me to enact them in the first place," she said, her brows drawn together.

"I shall be sure to give you some instruction on the matter just as soon as I am able," he said, kissing her on the nose. Then the mouth.

And they spent a very enjoyable few moments kissing before the carriage drew to a stop and Jasper reluctantly let her go.

"I suppose our guests await," she said with a sigh.

"They do, Countess," he said with a grin. "But, the good thing about that is that as the lady of the house, you can ply them with food and drink and then leave whenever you like."

"Won't that be a little scandalous?" she asked, shocked.

"Maybe a little," he said with a grin. "But you're only a newlywed once in your life. Why not take advantage of it when you can?"

And with that, he handed her down from the carriage and into their married life.

Fifteen

When the carriage arrived in Grosvenor Square, Hermione was surprised to see that the servants of the Mainwaring town house had been assembled in a line from the front door and down the wide black-and-white tiled marble hallway.

"Welcome to Mainwaring House, my lady," said the butler, Greaves, a short dapper man with more gravitas than many noblemen she'd met. "I hope that you will be happy here."

It was a good thing Jasper was there by her side, else Hermione would have been in real danger of turning and fleeing in the other direction. It wasn't that she was frightened. But more that she was unaccustomed to such ceremony. And certainly not in celebration of her.

Up until that moment, the swiftness of their betrothal and marriage had felt strange, even unreal—so if it were happening to some other Hermione who would be the one to deal with the details of the whole affair. But as she stood there in the ornate entrance of Mainwaring House, the weight of it landed squarely on her shoulders. With such force that Jasper turned to look at her, his expression worried.

"Are you well?" he asked in an undertone that only she could hear.

Was she well? Hermione hardly knew. But as she had often when in the face of situations that threatened to overwhelm her, she squared her shoulders and gave her best impression of what an Amazon warrior must look like on going into battle.

"Of course," she said, not letting one fraction of her fear show in her word or countenance. Turning to Mr. Greaves, she said warmly, "I thank you, all of you for your warm welcome. I only hope that I will endeavor to make the house a happy one."

And, though Jasper said it was unnecessary, she went down the line shaking every servant's hand and committing their names to memory. Or, as near as was possible. It was exhausting, but once she'd reached the boot boy, she felt reasonably able to recall their faces if not all their names.

"That was remarkable," Jasper said as they made their way to the great dining room where the wedding breakfast was to be held. "I think you charmed them all. Even the cook, who is always cross when he's expected to leave the kitchen for any reason."

Happy to have pleased him, Hermione beamed. "My mama always said you should be as kind as possible to the servants because their lives were difficult enough without having our petty slights heaped on top of it."

"An insightful lady," Jasper said, patting her hand where it rested on his arm. "How old were you when you lost her?"

"I was eight," Hermione said, thinking how pleased but worried about her her mother would be on this, her wedding day. It certainly wasn't how Hermione had envisioned her marriage coming about. Aloud she said, "I missed her today. But I also am grateful she wasn't alive to see my father behave in such a shocking manner. Of course, had she been alive, he likely wouldn't have done something as scandalous as wager my hand in marriage. I know it's difficult to imagine, but when she was alive he was a different person. More content with what he had. Less reckless."

"I think we both understand well how the death of one parent affects the other," Jasper said softly. He stopped just outside the door to what she presumed was the dining room. He looked down at her, his blue eyes serious. "I am sorry it came about this way, Hermione. But I'm not sorry for the fact of it. It wasn't the way I'd have arranged things, certainly, but I couldn't have asked for a braver, lovelier wife."

She was shocked. How could she not be, when it felt as if this whole affair had been outside their control from the start? Not to mention the way they'd started off things between them. It wasn't difficult to remember just how appalled he'd been on first learning that she aspired to belong to a driving club.

As if he could read her mind, he grinned. "I realize we have not always been the best of friends. Indeed, far from it at times. But I have always admired your tenacity and determination. And I should rather have a wife with a backbone than all of the prim and proper misses of the *ton* put together."

"I think there is a law against a marriage such as that, my lord," she said with an amused quirk of her lips. "But I hope that I will endeavor to make you a proper wife."

"It is not for you to endeavor in this, Countess," he said with a fierce expression that she didn't quite understand. "It is I who should endeavor to please you."

"But I should like to try anyway," she said seriously. "For if this marriage is to work, we both have a role to play. I think we have both seen what happens when one partner is absent, for any reason."

He looked as if he would argue, but after a moment of thought, he nodded. "All right. We will try it your way."

With a nod to the footman who stood at the door to the dining room, they entered while the servant announced them. "The Earl and Countess of Mainwaring."

It was odd for Hermione. But, she decided as they made their way to the table, not unpleasant.

Do you find your new home pleasing, Countess?" asked the dowager after the toasts had been drunk and the table had broken up into small side conversations. Hermione had been seated opposite Jasper and had her mother-in-law on her left and the Duke of Trent on her right. Trent was presently engaged in conversation with the younger of Jasper's sisters, Celeste.

"Indeed I do, Lady Mainwaring," Hermione said with diffidence. She was having a difficult time reading the other woman. One minute she seemed welcoming and pleasant, and the next dismissive and threatened. "I hope that you will help me as I become accustomed to the way the household works."

"Certainly, my dear," the older woman said with just a trace of condescension. "As long as I am here to do so. There is some question right now as to whether my daughters and I will stay on here at Mainwaring House or remove to another house so that we might leave the newlyweds to their privacy."

Since "privacy" was said in such a tone as to imply "orgy," Hermione was quite sure that the decision to leave had not been her mama-in-law's idea.

"I am sorry to hear it," she responded with what she hoped was deference without implying that Jasper was in any way at fault for making the suggestion. "I hope you will let me help you in your search for an appropriate house. I did the same thing when my father made the decision to let the Upperton town house."

But the dowager was not impressed. "I thank you, my dear, but I feel sure I will be able to find something suited to our needs. We are hardly in the same situation as you and your father were when you chose to find a new home, after all."

It was a good thing the dowager was going to be moving soon, Hermione thought, careful not to let her annoyance show in her expression. Else she might find herself in the position of being suspected in the murder of two people in the space of a few weeks. Only one of which she would be guilty of.

"Of course," she said with what she hoped was a bland smile. "And really, I cannot thank you enough for being so considerate. I feel sure that it will work out for the best once you and my sisters-in-law are settled into a home of your own. Why, you might even find you like it better."

But that was apparently the wrong thing to say. "I have been mistress of this house for some thirty-odd years, Countess," the dowager said with a chilly dignity. "It will not be easy for me to leave it. But far be it from me to refuse to step aside when my son asks me to. Indeed, I am a little surprised that he chose to do such a thing for a lady with whom he has only a passing acquaintance, but then we know how gentlemen are, do we not?" The knowing gleam in the dowager's eye implied that her son's reasons for marrying an earl's daughter with an unimpressive dowry and a reputation that was less than pristine were self-evident.

Better to be hanged for a sheep as for a lamb, Hermione thought with a hint of annoyance. "Lord Mainwaring and I have been friends for some time, Countess. I wonder that he didn't mention it to you. But I suppose that is just like him not to share every little detail of his life with his mother. After all, it would hardly do him credit to be a grown man still tied to his mama's apron strings. So to speak, of course—countesses do not wear aprons in my experience."

"As it is with most men," the dowager said, "my son does not tell me every small detail of his acquaintance. We are closer than some, of course, but he did not think it important to mention you, apparently. Perhaps you did not make as much of an impression as you'd hoped."

"But that matters not a bit now," Hermione said with a shrug. "We are married, after all."

"That you are." The dowager's glare could have cut glass.

"I was sorry Freddy and Leonora had to leave," said the Duke of Trent from Hermione's other side. "Leonora was unwell, I take it?"

"Indeed, your grace," Hermione said with relief at the change of subject. "Though I suspect it was more a matter of Lord Frederick being overprotective than actual illness."

"You are speaking of Lord Frederick Lisle and his wife?" the dowager asked with a frown. "I had heard that he'd married but it was some sort of scandalous circumstance, wasn't it?"

"Not the marriage itself, my lady," Hermione said, biting back her instinct to tell the other lady to pull in her claws. "I believe Lord Frederick and Miss Craven, now Mrs. Lisle, were betrothed once before.

They simply reconnected and decided to marry a few years later, from what I understand."

"Now I remember," the dowager said with a gleam in her eye. "Her brother was killed for being part of that driving club. The Lords of Anarchy, I believe. What a shame. I was quite fond of Mr. Jonathan Craven when he and my son were at school together. I had such high hopes for him. And to see him brought down in the prime of life by that monstrous club is truly a tragedy."

Since Hermione had herself been closely acquainted with Jonathan, she could do nothing but agree with her mother-in-law.

"I believe all such clubs should be abolished," the dowager said firmly. "Not only for the safety of their members but also for the safety of the general public. They are a nuisance and should not be allowed to roam free."

"I do not believe, my lady," Trent said with a wink at Hermione, "that abolishing driving clubs altogether should be the punishment for one rogue group. And from what I understand the Lords of Anarchy have even reformed their ways. Going so far as to welcome ladies into their ranks."

"Ladies?" the countess asked with a shudder. "What sort of low creature would accept such an invitation? I know in my day there were some scandalous goings-on, but we certainly knew what behavior was good for ladies and what was good for gentlemen."

Hermione was about to open her mouth and admit that she was one of those low creatures, when her husband stood.

I want to thank you all for coming today," Jasper said with a smile. "But the time has come for my bride and me to retreat. You are more than welcome to remain here and partake of my hospitality in our absence, however."

With that, he walked down to offer his arm to Hermione and they left the room together. "I hope you weren't frightened off by Mama," he said as they walked downstairs. "It was perhaps not the best idea to leave you to her tender mercies on your first day of marriage. She is not best pleased at being supplanted as countess I don't think."

"You are quite correct, there," Hermione said with a laugh. "I thought she would challenge me to a duel. Either that or poison my wine."

"She would never do anything so uncouth," Jasper said, leading her into the kitchens and out the door into the garden beyond.

"Where are we going?" she asked as they navigated the winding path through the surprisingly lush shrubbery and flowering plants.

"It's a surprise," Jasper said with a secret smile.

"I don't like surprises," Hermione said, though she couldn't help smiling back. "One never knows if it will be a good surprise or a bad surprise."

"This is a good one," he said, squeezing her hand. "I promise."

When they reached the back gate, and stepped out into the lane that ran behind the house, her heart began to beat faster. Because, as they crossed to the mews beyond, she saw that he didn't lie.

"I had to do a bit of negotiating to make this happen," he said as they stepped into the well-kept stables, which smelled of fresh hay, straw, and horse. "But I think it was worth it. At least I hope it will be."

She couldn't speak as he led her to stand before a pair of stalls. Almost afraid to peer inside, Hermione was unable to stop herself, however, and when she saw that they held her grays she was overcome with a wave of emotion so strong she thought she might collapse under the weight of it.

But the horses, their eyes bright and their ears turning this way and that to catch every murmur of sound, nickered and pressed inquisitive snouts over the stable door and demanded her attention. And she was helpless in the face of such recognition.

"Hello, my dears," she said through tears as she scratched first one, then the other between the ears and stroked down the muscular sides of their long necks. "I do not have an apple or any sugar lumps, my darlings, but . . ."

And Jasper was there, handing her first one half apple, then another, and she watched in awe as they chomped down the treat.

"They are yours again," Jasper said in a low voice. "I was able to buy them off Saintcrow's heir. A distant cousin with no use for curricle racing. He was happy enough to sell them and make room in his stables for his carriage horses."

"I will repay you, my lord," she said, unable to turn away from the wonder of seeing her horses again. "I promise."

"You will do no such thing," he said. "They are your bridal gift. And I will not hear anything more about payment. The very idea."

She turned then, to see if he was angry, but instead she saw that he was looking at her with a softness she'd never seen in him before. It did things to her insides. Made her think that perhaps he wasn't as indifferent as she'd thought he was.

"I don't know how to thank you," she said, and impulsively she threw her arms around his neck and hugged him close. She could smell the sandalwood and man scent of him, and felt the strength of his arms as they closed round her. "It's the nicest, best gift I've ever received."

"I didn't do it so you'd be grateful," he said into her hair. "I did it because I knew how much it hurt you to have them taken away. And I wanted to make it right, somehow."

How on earth would she be able to protect her heart from this man when he said such things? she thought. And she had to, because no matter how he might seem so very different from her father, the truth of it was that he was a gamester, too.

They stood there together for a moment. Just the two of them in the dark of the stables with only the horses looking on.

After the afternoon spent under the watchful eye of Lady Mainwaring and the rest of the wedding guests, it was a relief for Hermione to be there in some degree of privacy. She'd never been one to enjoy a crowd, but today had been less about numbers than being the center of attention. When she was driving, she had something to take her mind off the fact that she was the focus of the crowd. And at parties and balls she was only one of any number of other young ladies.

Today, however, she, along with Jasper had been the sole focus of the wedding guests. And though she was grateful to have him at her side, she still felt the scrutiny of them on her.

"Would you like to have some time to rest?" Jasper asked finally, pulling back from her. "It's been a whirlwind of a day."

And almost as if she'd been denying it for hours, Hermione felt herself aching with fatigue. "That sounds like heaven. I should like to settle into my rooms a bit."

"You could have a bath, as well," he said, and the

very fact that a gentleman was mentioning such a thing sent a flush of heat through her. "My father renovated the house not too long before he died. And the countess's bathing room is a sight to behold."

At the mention of the countess's rooms, Hermione flinched. "Was your mother very unhappy to be forced to give up her rooms?"

As they retraced their steps through the back garden and into the kitchen Jasper kept her arm about her waist.

"I won't lie and tell you she was ecstatic about it," he admitted. "But she knows her duty. And it's time for her to move on to the next part of her life. She'd become a bit too . . ." He seemed to search for the right word. "She's grown complacent. Not doing anything that would help her grow or change. And I must admit that I am somewhat relieved that she and my sisters have chosen to search for another house. It's not that I do not love them. I do. But they are . . . difficult at times."

Hermione could well imagine. Especially for the lone male in an all-female household.

"I won't lie and say I am not relieved to hear you say it," she said with a twist of her lips. "She was a little argumentative at the wedding breakfast. I had hoped that we would get along well since I have had no mother of my own for many years now. But I'm afraid that won't be the case with us."

She saw him frown at the mention of his mother's behavior at the breakfast. "I am sorry to hear it," he said. "I can only tell you that she will get better with some time. I'm afraid my announcement took her by surprise. I think she had come to think that she could carry on as mistress of the Mainwaring holdings for a good many more years."

"And she resents me for that?" Hermione asked,

curious. She had no wish to carry on a feud with his mother, but it would do her more good to be aware of which way the wind blew than to keep her head in the sand.

"Perhaps a little," Jasper said as they made their way up the stairs to the floor where the family bedrooms lay. "But she'll get used to it."

When they reached a doorway near the end of the hall, he stopped and opened it.

Preceding him in, Hermione was stunned into speechlessness for a moment.

"I had the drapers in to change the curtains and the bedclothes and hangings yesterday," Jasper said in a rush. Almost as if he were nervous. "It was a near thing to get the changes finished in time for your arrival today but it's amazing what can be done when there's a financial incentive. And I fear the fellow might have robbed Peter to pay Paul and gave us some things he'd been working on for another customer."

"Who obviously had exquisite taste," Hermione said, reaching out to touch the rich blue and cream floral fabric of the hangings. "It's the most beautiful room I've ever seen."

"There was no time to paint," Jasper admitted, "so I had to go with a similar color scheme. I'm not particularly skilled at decorating but my sister Celeste helped a bit."

"I love it," she said, turning to offer him a genuine smile before she ran her hand along the surface of the dressing table on the far wall. "I'm amazed you were able to have so much replaced in such a short period of time. I don't think I could manage half so much in half the time."

"So you're pleased?" he asked, as if he weren't

quite sure whether to trust her words up until this point.

"Absolutely," Hermione said, opening the door to what she supposed was the dressing room.

"This room shares a bathing chamber between our two dressing rooms," he said a bit diffidently. "I will do my best to ensure that you are not occupying the bath before I come barging in."

But she was too curious to see what this remodeled bath would look like to respond. Making her way through the dressing room, where her maid was there arranging Hermione's things in a large armoire, she opened yet another door to see a spaciously appointed room with a large plunge bath holding center stage.

Behind her, Jasper said, "It can be filled from the spigot there, without having to wait for water to be heated in the kitchens and carried up."

"Ingenious," she said with a shake of her head. "I must admit I am having a bit of trouble not pinching myself. Not only have you returned my grays, but you've also given me the most gorgeous bedchamber imaginable and now you tell me about this magical bathing apparatus. There can be no other course of action for me but to simply expire from shock and delight."

"Don't do that," he said, though there was a smile in his voice. Coming up behind her, he slipped his arms around her waist. "So I can take all that to mean that you are pleased."

"An understatement if ever there was one," she said with a laugh. "I cannot possibly let it go with such faint praise. Thrilled might be a better word. Or perhaps ecstatic. Pleased sounds almost grudging by comparison."

"Then ecstatic it is," he said, kissing her cheek and letting her go. "I'll be off to let you rest before supper. I thought instead of a formal dinner we could have a private meal up here in your rooms. Will that suffice?"

Unable to stifle a yawn, with a nod to her departing husband, she kicked off her slippers and climbed up onto the enormous bed and stretched out upon it.

What an extraordinary day it had been, she thought with a nervous laugh. And before he firmly shut the door behind him, she was fast asleep.

Sixteen

*J*asper would have liked nothing better than to remove his boots and climb up into the bed beside
Hermione for a cozy sleep.

Unfortunately, her conversation with Miss Fleetwood had given him enough concern over the possibility that the lady's brother might be involved in
the murder of Saintcrow that he found it imperative
to relate the information to the authorities at once.

This meant having his horse brought round and
leaving his home on the evening of his wedding night.

It couldn't be helped, but he felt a pang of regret
at leaving Hermione so soon after the ceremony. No
matter that he would return before supper. It simply
didn't feel right.

He was donning his hat and coat in preparation
to leave when he was delayed by his mother.

"Already going out?" she asked with a raised
brow. "I should have thought the chit would be able
to entertain you for a whole day at the least."

"Don't be nasty, Mama," he said without malice.
"I have an errand. And Hermione is resting at the
moment."

He hadn't been the only one to notice the shadows beneath her eyes, he was certain. His mother for

one was sensitive to such physical signs of weakness, since exploiting them was her stock in trade.

"I mean no disrespect," she said, affronted. "Can not a mother express concern when her only son marries in haste?"

"Of course you may," he said firmly, "but that does not mean you should cast aspersions on her ability to keep me 'entertained' as you put it. If I were interested in hearing your opinion on the matter I would ask for it. As you well know."

But the dowager only sniffed. "As if you would ask my opinion on anything," she said haughtily. "But, as it happens, I did not come down to question you about your new bride, but instead to inform you that your sisters and I will be attending the Hartford ball this evening."

Which was a fib, he knew, but he let her save face by not calling attention to the fact.

"I am happy to hear it," he said aloud. "I hope you will enjoy yourselves."

"The reason I mention it," she continued with a frown, "is that I feel sure we will be questioned about the match. Is there something you wish us to convey to those who question it? I know how you like to control what is said about you."

It was a fair question since there was little doubt that his swift marriage to Hermione would be the topic of conversation among the *ton* for some weeks. Especially given the way it had come about.

"Thank you for asking, Mama," he said sincerely. "If you are asked, simply say that it was unusual the way it came about but that Lady Hermione and I had formed an attachment long ago and this was simply an acceleration of what would have been a conventional engagement."

"I suppose that will have to do," the dowager said

with a moue of distaste. "I do wish you had consulted me before you went about it this way. I could have saved you both some degree of difficulty with the public's reception of the news. It is one thing to marry in haste, but to win your bride's hand in a card game is simply not the thing."

"But it is the way things happened," he said, pulling on his gloves. "And now, if you will excuse me, I must see to a few things before my bride awakens."

Hurrying from the house, he mounted Hector and rode the short distance to Lord Payne's residence in Berkeley Square. As the current president of the Lords of Anarchy, Payne would be one who would best be able to tell Jasper about Saintcrow's involvement with the club, and whether there was any truth to what Miss Fleetwood had said about the club being the cause of his recent wildness.

When he arrived, however, it was to find the house was lit up like a fireworks spectacle at Vauxhall.

A line of curricles being handled by tigers, or in some cases coachmen, stretched down the street and round the corner.

Directing Hector through the throng of traffic, Jasper handed the reins to a footman and mounted the steps to the door. When he handed the butler his card, the fellow said, "I regret to say, my lord, that Lord Payne is occupied at the moment."

Well able to see the raucous clusters of men in various stages of inebriation down the front hallway and huddled in the doorways on either side, Jasper was willing to bet that Payne was occupied. Even so, it was imperative that he speak to the man regarding Saintcrow, so he said, "I will only take a few moments of your master's time. He will be quite cross if you turn me away, I fear."

He watched as the butler, who was built more like

a prizefighter than the faithful retainer of a noble-man, seemed to think over what Jasper had said. Fi-nally, he gave a dour nod and instructed a footman to show Jasper into the playroom.

Because he was well-known amongst the *ton* for his skill at cards, Jasper found himself the recipient of a number of slaps on the back and a mixture of congratulations and commiserations regarding his marriage. None of them went so far as to mention the fact that Hermione was, because of her recent membership in the club, one of theirs. But he thought that might be because he was also known to be, if not an enemy of driving, at the very least a skeptic. He might not be considered a man one didn't cross, but he was most certainly not one that they would engage in open war without serious consideration.

The playroom, it turned out, was likely termed "the ballroom" on the blueprints for the large town house. But, sportsman that he was, Viscount Payne had transformed the large chamber into a sort of gen-tleman's amusement hall. In one corner, a pair of men whom Jasper knew slightly were stripped to the waist and dancing around one another in the stance championed by Gentleman Jackson in his saloon on St. James Street.

Still another pair, in the opposite corner, were re-ceiving instruction from the famous Angelo in the art of the sword. A third corner was set up with card tables, though how the men there could possibly hear the declaration of trumps or even the contents of their own minds, he had no notion.

Payne himself was involved in a heated discussion in the fourth corner with a man Jasper recognized from the morning Saintcrow took Hermione's grays. "I don't care how you make it happen," the viscount said in a harsh voice, "but you make it happen. If this business remains hanging round my neck like a bloody albatross I'll hold you personally responsible, Newsome."

As if sensing an outsider in their midst, both men looked up at Jasper's approach. Payne's expression turned from one of intensity to one of jovial welcome. "Well, damn my eyes, if it isn't Mathematical Mainwaring! Have you come to join us now that you've married into the club, so to speak?"

"Hardly," Jasper said with a shudder he made no attempt to hide. "I would sooner jump headfirst into the Thames."

At that the other man just grinned. He knew well enough that Jasper was not interested in coaching in the least. And since they'd been at Eton together when Jasper's father died, he knew the reason for it. Even so, he enjoyed inviting the other man to join the group from time to time. As if in the asking he was fulfilling some sort of obligation to welcome even those who despised the club's very purpose.

"Then I hope you are here to tell me your lady will be joining us on our next outing to Dartford," Payne said, indicating with a gesture that Jasper should follow him from the loud chamber and to the hallway beyond. "I do not mind telling you how disappointed I was that our newest member was unable to join us thanks to Saintcrow's untimely collection of her father's debt."

Once they were in what Jasper presumed was Payne's study, the other man poured them both a glass of whisky and indicated that his guest should have a seat.

"I confess that after seeing tonight's activities," Jasper said with a raised brow, "I am tempted to ask my new wife to renounce her membership in the club. If there were other ladies to lend some propriety to the group, it would be one thing, but all this tonight looks like a Roman bacchanal without the orgy."

"Oh, I suspect there will be an orgy later," Payne said, sipping his drink. "But it's a bit early yet."

"I rest my case," Jasper said to Lord Payne. It was one thing for Hermione to test her driving skills against the other members of the club, but quite another for her to be present at what was going on tonight in Payne's residence. He was hardly a prude, but this was insanity. And a group of men engaged in sport in large numbers like he'd seen tonight were prone to behave in reckless ways.

"Oh, tonight is not really a club function," Payne said, waving away Jasper's disapproval. "I decided to have a bit of a large-scale sporting evening tonight. I daresay there are any number of fellows here who do not even belong to the club."

"Which is why there are enough curricles to populate a small nation stretched round the square," Jasper said dryly.

"Well, not every fellow in London with a curricle belongs to the club, Mainwaring," said Payne primly. "But I daresay you are not here to discuss tonight's entertainment. Did you not celebrate your marriage today?"

It never failed to amaze Jasper how quickly gossip made its way through town. Even someone like Payne, who spent most of his time in company with men, was able to learn all there was to know almost as quickly as it happened.

"Indeed, I did," Jasper said, inclining his head. "But as it happens, my bride was visited this morning by her neighbor at her father's house. A Miss Fleetwood."

"And I am supposed to know the significance of this?" Payne asked, brows raised.

"She was the fiancée of the late Lord Saintcrow," Jasper said baldly. "The fellow who cut short Lady Mainwaring's first foray as a member of the Lords of Anarchy. The one who was murdered the following day."

"Aha." Lord Payne set his glass down on the desk before him. "A terrible loss for us, the death of Saintcrow. I was shocked to hear he'd been killed in his own home. What is to become of us if ruffians are willing to venture into a man's home and kill him without a by-your-leave?"

"Miss Fleetwood informed Hermione that Saintcrow had become increasingly reckless once he began associating with the Lords of Anarchy," Jasper informed the other man, watching carefully to see what his response to the accusation would be. "Do you have anything to say to that?"

"If I had a guinea for every time an overprotective lady blamed the club for her son, brother, husband, betrothed's descent into dissolution, Mainwaring, I'd be a wealthy man."

"So you disagree with her characterization of her fiancé's dealings with the club?" Jasper asked. He was not surprised that Payne had not seemed surprised at the accusation. Clubs like his were considered the bane of polite society's existence in some quarters. Certainly those of ladies whose menfolk were drawn into so-called wicked behavior by them.

"I don't deny that Saintcrow enjoyed driving fast and drinking loud toasts afterward," Payne said with a shrug. "But that hardly means he was headed for Hades. Indeed, if he was engaging in risky behavior it wasn't at club functions. He was not even a club member."

"So you are aware of his risk-taking in other

venues?" Jasper asked, hearing what the other man wasn't saying.

"Between the two of us," Lord Payne said, picking up his glass again and staring at the amber liquid within, "there is a small faction of club members who have been giving me a bit of trouble."

Jasper's senses went on alert. "How so?"

"You know what happened earlier this year when Sir Gerard was head of the club," said Payne, referring to the man whose tenure as the president of the driving club had led not only to murder but also to its dissolution in the face of accusations of illegal fighting and threats from one of the most dangerous men in the London underworld, Smiling Jack O'Hara.

When Jasper nodded, Lord Payne continued, "Well, most of us were glad to see Sir Gerard gone. He took what had been a pleasant diversion and turned it into a place where most of us had to worry from one minute to the next about getting on the wrong side of the law. And I don't mind telling you, I don't have the bottle for that sort of thing. I am quite happy with my life as it is. And I got damned tired of explaining why I kept coming home with black eyes and bruised ribs."

Payne might give the impression of being the sort of man who could hold his own—he was tall and beefy with the body of a laborer rather than that of a manicured aristocrat. Even so, looks didn't always hint at a man's true nature, and Jasper was well able to imagine that the viscount would not want the bother of involvement in illegal activities.

"So, there were others who were not so willing to leave the risk that Sir Gerard offered in the past?" he concluded.

"Precisely," Payne said with a shake of his head. "I warned them that they would not use the club to run their backroom dealings and secret boxing matches."

That explained what Jasper had seen earlier in the Payne ballroom. He was trying to keep the membership happy by conducting the sort of sporting activities the splinter group preferred out in the open where he could keep an eye on them.

When he said as much to the other man, Payne nodded. "And so far it's worked. With a few exceptions."

"I take it Saintcrow was one of the exceptions?" Jasper asked.

Payne nodded. "He was close with the leader of one of the smaller factions And he and Fleetwood were running an underground gaming hell."

That was a surprise. So Fleetwood had reasons besides loyalty to his sister for wanting to find Saintcrow's killer. It was entirely possible that Saintcrow was killed not for his involvement in the Lords of Anarchy, but for money collected in the course of illegal gambling.

"So Fleetwood was a member of the Lords of Anarchy?" he asked aloud.

"Not for long," said Payne. "He didn't last above a week before he quit, saying he'd found more excitement at Almack's."

"Ouch."

"None of my problem," the club leader said with a shrug. "I don't care if they take themselves off to do God knows what. But I will not allow it to take place in the club itself. They might like the cover that a group of this size gives them when the authorities come asking questions, but I'm damned if I'll let them use us for that. I try to stay within the bounds of the law and those that don't like it can take themselves off."

Thanking the other man for his time, Jasper stood and made his way back through the house and out to the street beyond. He gave a coin to the fellow who'd been holding Hector for him and made his way back through the tangle of curricles toward Grosvenor Square.

Once he reached Park Lane the traffic thinned out and though it was rather early the streets were relatively quiet. He wondered what role, if any, the subgroup of the Lords of Anarchy had played in Saintcrow's death. He knew that Smiling Jack had been very unhappy to find that Sir Gerard Fincher had been poaching on his turf. It would not come as a surprise to Jasper that the scourge of the Rookery would be equally unhappy to learn there was a competing gaming hell.

He had just rounded the corner of Grosvenor Square when a man leaped from the shadows and swung a large cudgel at him, connecting painfully with his ribs.

Spooked, Hector went up on his back legs, and it was all Jasper could do to stay on his back. His attacker, perhaps not having considered the response of a large horse to being surprised, hurried off. By the time Jasper had the horse under control once more, the man was long gone.

He was getting his breath back when he saw a slip of paper on the ground near where the fellow had been hiding.

Mindful that his mount was spooked, he swung down, painfully aware that the club had connected solidly with his ribs. And though it was not pleasant to do so, he bent forward and snatched up the paper.

The lamplight was too dim for him to see what it said, and considering that it would hurt far more to remount than it would to simply walk Hector the several yards to Mainwaring House, he tucked it into his pocket and made the trek home.

Hermione awoke with a start some hours later to see that it was dark outside. Scrambling off the bed, she rang for her maid and requested that the girl draw a bath for her and set out her clothes for the evening. She didn't specify that her attire should be night-clothes, but as it was her wedding night and she and Jasper were to have supper in her bedchamber, she supposed the girl would figure it out for herself.

She was seated at her dressing table, which had been laid out with all her familiar brushes and combs and the like from home, brushing out her hair, when she heard the connecting door between her own room and Jasper's open.

Turning, she saw that he had removed his coat, and was in shirtsleeves and waistcoat. It was a little thing, but as a man was considered to be shockingly undressed in such attire, it reminded her of the change in their status that had occurred earlier in the day.

Not to mention the fact that she was wearing a terrifyingly sheer nightrail with only a thin robe for cover in his presence.

Things had most certainly changed.

"I hope you rested well," he said, strolling farther into the chamber. "You look as if you did."

She winced. "I hope that doesn't mean I was looking haggard before," she said with a frown.

He grinned. "Not at all. You were lovely before and are lovely still."

"Diplomatically put, my lord," she said with a quirk of her lips. Why did her heart insist on beating so quickly? she wondered. It was only a conversation. And her nightclothes were more modest than some evening gowns she'd worn.

And yet, there was no denying that being here in her bedchamber with her husband of a few hours, with only lamplight to illuminate them, was thrilling in a way she'd not ever considered.

"No need for diplomacy when one is speaking the truth," Jasper said, offering her his hand. She saw that his hair was damp, perhaps from his own bath? And he'd changed into a different waistcoat from the bottle-green and gold embroidered one of that morning. This one was dark blue with silver and caught the light from the lamps that shone from the sconces on Hermione's bedchamber walls.

She took his hand and allowed him to pull her against him, her softness against his hard chest. When she slid her hands around his waist, though, instead of dipping his head to kiss her as she'd hoped he hissed inward.

Startled, she pulled back despite the fact that his arms had tightened. "What is the matter? Did I hurt you?"

"It's nothing," he said, though his hand unconsciously covered his left side. "I merely had a bit of an accident while you were sleeping. Don't worry over it."

She frowned. "An accident? How? Did you trip in the house somewhere? I should hope your servants know better than to allow carpets to bunch up."

"No, nothing like that," he said, shaking his head. Then, perhaps realizing that she would not be fobbed off with a half answer, he admitted, "I went to see Lord Payne. And on my way back I was set upon."

There was so much to unpack from those few words that Hermione didn't know where to start.

But that wasn't precisely true. "Let me see your ribs. Did they strike you anywhere else? Your head?"

He shook her off, however. "I had my valet see to

it," he said with a soothing hand on her shoulder. "He is quite used to seeing to my various aches and pains from riding and bouts and Jackson's and the like. I promise you. It was only that you surprised me."

"If you're sure," she said carefully. She did not yet know him well enough to know when he was trying to pull the wool over her eyes, so she would have to make do with that explanation. "But I am well able to wrap bruised ribs if it comes to that. Papa leads quite an exciting life at times."

That was an understatement, she knew, but she was not interested in going back through her father's many sins.

They were saved further conversation by the arrival of two footmen carrying a small table, and soon after the men had laid laying a tablecloth and set two places along with multiple tureens of delicious-smelling food, Hermione and Jasper were seated opposite each other.

She was far hungrier than she'd thought and after a pleasant meal of turtle soup, roast pheasant, ham, oysters, haricots verts, and a dessert of lemon ice, Hermione was ready to write a love letter to Jasper's chef.

When she admitted as much, he laughed. "Married only a few hours and already you are talking of love for another man?"

The mention of love brought her up short, however, for there had been no mention of affection between them up till now. Indeed, as with most marriages of convenience, it had been undertaken without consideration for their feelings.

He must have realized she was uncomfortable, for Jasper said, "Forgive me. I did not mean to suggest that you—"

"That I love you?" she asked, made bold by the

wine. "Think nothing of it. I am well aware that we entered into this marriage more as a matter of honor than from any affection on either of our parts."

"I wouldn't say that there is no affection between us, though," he responded with a frown. "Perhaps you do not feel any for me, but I certainly would not say that I am entirely without any sort of finer feelings for you. Not love perhaps, but still."

It was cutting rather close to her heart to admit that she, too, found herself thinking of him in more affectionate terms than one would normally consider in an average marriage of convenience. But that was the truth. Was she willing to admit as much this early, though? Perhaps not.

Instead, rising with her wine glass to leave the table for the servants to remove, and heading over to the small sitting area in the corner of her bedchamber, she said, "I did not mean that we are at daggers drawn, of course. But the truth of it is that we hardly know each other, my lord."

She was put in mind of a prowling predator as he followed behind her. Once she was tucked into a corner of a sofa, she expected him to take a seat on the chair opposite. But to her shock, he sat right beside her, stretched his long legs out before him, and leaned back against the cushioned back.

"We are certainly not at daggers drawn," he said, taking her wine glass from her suddenly limp hand, and placing it carefully on a low table behind her. "Are we, Hermione?"

Suddenly he seemed far larger and more intimidating than he had while seated politely across from her at the dinner table. She swallowed. "No, my lord," she said to his cravat, which was right at eye level now.

He slipped a finger under her chin and tipped up

her head. "I like to think that we are friends." She looked up into his smiling eyes and was breathless with anticipation. For what she knew not.

She licked her lower lip and watched as his eyes tracked there and darkened. "We are friends at the very least," she admitted, leaning closer without even being aware of doing so. It was almost as if an invisible thread were pulling her toward him. Toward their inevitable coming together.

His mouth when it touched hers was far gentler than she expected. Once, twice, his mouth caressed hers, and when she gasped at the connection, he took that as an invitation to slide his tongue, hot and silky, inside.

It was far more intoxicating than anything she'd ever imbibed, this gentle seduction of his that both claimed and calmed her. Perhaps she would have known better how to resist if he'd demanded, but the stroke of his tongue against hers asked a question that she found impossible to ignore. It was as if he enlisted her in her own surrender.

When her arms slipped around his neck, it was to pull him closer, so that she could have more of him. So that she could slide her fingers though his silky dark locks, so that she could press herself more firmly against the solid expanse of his chest.

He pulled back, surprising a mewl of frustration from her that Hermione hardly recognized as coming from her. "I think we should move to a more comfortable locale," he said, his voice harsh, unlike his usual amiable tones. Without waiting for her to answer, he pulled her up by the hand and led her to the bed, where seemingly unable to keep his hands from her, he lifted her up onto the cool sheets while kissing her at the same time.

As if by mutual agreement, they began to undress

him, she unbuttoning his waistcoat, he unwinding his cravat. And all the while they caressed one another. Finally, he stepped back and pulled his shirt over his head.

When he made to press her into the bed, Hermione held him back with one hand. "Wait, I want to see you," she said, taking in just how marvelously sculpted the muscles of his chest were. And as he stood impatiently, she took in the light dusting of hair that tapered from the middle of his chest and disappeared just below his navel into his breeches.

"Enough," he said, once she'd looked her fill, and now he stretched out alongside her, his hand stroking up the flare of her hip and gathering her breast in his palm.

Hermione had never been particularly fond of her bosom, finding it too large for the gowns that were currently fashionable. She supposed breasts were necessary for feeding babies, but since she had none, they were more often than not a source of annoyance.

But the moment Jasper's rough hand stroked over her nipple she knew precisely what other use they might be put to. Almost like they were joined with a thread made of nerves alone, the feel of his mouth when it suckled her through the sheer fabric of her night rail set the heart of her throbbing. For what she knew not.

She only knew that if she didn't hold onto him, she was in danger of flying away on the wings of the euphoria his hands, his mouth, his body were drawing from her.

Seventeen

He was quickly losing the ability to hold himself back, Jasper realized as his mouth covered her breast through the fabric of her night rail.

One of the things he'd always prided himself on as a lover was his ability to see to his partner's pleasure before his own, but he was damned if he didn't find Hermione's little gasps of pleasure each time he touched her more decadent than the most experienced courtesan's touch.

Almost from the moment they'd met he'd wanted her. Wanted to be the man who introduced her to the pleasure that was possible between a man and a woman when both their bodies and their minds were engaged.

And he'd not been disappointed in the way she responded to his kiss that day in her father's sitting room. It was one of the reasons he'd been so determined to go through with the marriage that had been arranged over a game of cards.

But even knowing all that, having mentally prepared himself for the intensity of the connection between them, he still found himself responding to her lightest murmur like a green boy with his first lover.

So, when her hand drifted down his chest to rest

against the eagerness of his erection, he was a bit more forceful than necessary with his grip on her wrist.

At her inhalation of dismay, he cursed himself and kissed her. "You can touch me," he said, his voice hoarse with passion. "Indeed," he went on as he moved his lips to the sensitive skin below her ear, "I want you to touch me. But I fear if you do so right now I will lose control. And I want to be gentle with you. I need to be."

"But I don't . . ." she began, only to stop when he touched his tongue to the skin of her neck. "I don't know what that means," she finally managed to get out.

"I want it to be good for you," he whispered against her ear, feeling her tremble at the sensation. "Surely your moth—"

And then despite his lust-addled brain's inability to do complex thinking, it occurred to him that she had no mother to speak to her of such things.

He uttered a very bad word.

And though it was perhaps the hardest thing he'd ever had to do, he pulled away from her and sat on the side of the bed. Facing away from her and thinking of every possible terrible erection-killing thing he could think of. For if he had to be the one to explain this to her, he'd better be at his most nonthreatening. And even he was aware that a man with a rampant erection was about as nonthreatening as a rhinoceros.

"Jasper?" Hermione asked, her voice sounding more timid than he'd ever heard it. "Did I do something wrong? I promise I won't touch you there again. Not if you don't want me to."

Of course she thought she'd done something wrong. He was a beast. Not least because he'd no ensured that she'd had some older lady—hell, even Leonora would do—to explain to her what happened between a man and a woman.

"It's not that," he ground out, every last bit of him demanding to know why he wasn't hiking up her skirts and pounding into her. "Just give me a minute."

"Did, did I hurt you?"

His erection now at least a bit more tolerable half-mast, he turned and took her hand. "You did not," he said gently. "I promise you. It's just that men have a difficult time . . . that is to say, I . . ."

"It's all right," she said with a nod. "I'll lie as still as I can if you wish to continue. I want to please you."

He was a beast.

"I do not want that at all," he said with a sigh. "I hadn't thought to ask if you had some female relative to speak to you about what happens between a husband and wife. I should have considered it, but there was so much else going on."

"I admit," she said with a smile, "my knowledge about the process is a bit limited. I have seen horses of course, but as they have hooves there was no question of the lady horse touching the stallion's . . ." She made a hand gesture meant to indicate the missing word,

"Quite," he said with a wince at the absurdity of this conversation. He ran a palm over the back of his neck. "It's not unlike horses, actually." He felt his ears redden in embarrassment.

"Only with people it's possible to . . . ah . . . be face-to-face."

Her eyes widened and he could almost hear the gears grinding in her head as she considered the possibilities.

"So," she said, tilting her head to the side. "You wanted to be gentle because it will hurt?"

"The first time, yes," he said, grateful that her question was something relatively easy to answer. He wasn't sure he was up to the rigors of explaining the variations of sexual positions at the moment. "But I will try to make it as painless as possible. Perhaps it would be better to show you rather than tell."

She nodded and moved back a little to make more room for him on the bed.

He was almost undone by the trust in her eyes as she watched him crawl toward her. Unable to stop himself, he kissed her. It wasn't as gentle as before, and to his relief she gave as good as she got. Perhaps their little conversation had removed some of her misgivings.

As their embrace intensified, he kissed his way over her chin and down to her breast again. And when she writhed beneath him, he slid his hands down over her legs, lifted her night rail and slid it upward. She lifted her bottom to help him whisk it over her head, and when she was naked before him, Jasper leaned back, unable to keep from finally looking his fill.

As he'd expected, her native athleticism, her handling of the reins and years of riding, had left her with shapely legs and arms. But it was her breasts that nearly took his breath away. They were large enough to cup in his hand, with dark rosy nipples that seemed to beg for his mouth.

"Gorgeous," he said, mindful of her sudden shyness. "You're beautiful, Hermione. I couldn't have asked for a lovelier bride."

She smiled shyly and reached out to stroke his chest. "You're rather a fine specimen yourself," she said pertly. "And in the interest of fairness you are wearing far more clothes than I am."

Leave it to his little trailblazer to demand parity

between them, he thought with a laugh. Quickly, he shucked his breeches and smalls, and before she could look for too long at what he knew was a raging erection, he climbed back up and covered her, reveling in the sensation of skin to skin.

"Ah God," he said, sliding a hand over her hip even as he kissed his way from her ear to her chin and down toward her breasts again. Listening to her response as he went, he slid his hand over the soft hair at the apex of her thighs, and despite her gasp, he cupped her mound and stroked his middle finger over the wetness there.

In response, she gasped again and lifted her hips, as if begging for more.

"Easy," he whispered against her bosom, using his teeth to scrape over her eager nipple. "Do you like it?"

Her moan when he pressed a finger inside her told him that the answer was yes, and for a moment he concentrated on alternating between his finger's movements and suckling her breast.

When she whispered "More," he added another finger, and when she moved her hips against his hand he knew she was ready. At least he hoped so.

Lifting himself up over her, he pressed his knees between her, and bracing himself above her with his left hand, he lifted her leg up over his hip with the other. "This might hurt," he whispered against her lips, "but it can't be helped. I'll be as gentle as I can."

Then, guiding himself into her wetness, he pressed forward.

Despite Jasper's warning of pain, Hermione was still shocked that something that began so pleasurably could possibly be so uncomfortable. Even so, she bit her lip and tried to relax as he pressed his body into hers. Bit by bit he forged ahead until, at last, she sensed that he was fully seated.

What an odd sensation, she thought as she gave a tentative flex of her muscles down there. His surprised intake of breath told her that perhaps he wasn't the only one with the ability to create feeling as part of this act. With her legs spread wide and the feeling of his strong body beneath her fingers, she felt closer to Jasper than she had to any other person.

"Is that all?" she asked when he seemed in no hurry to remove himself from her body.

His soft laugh made her feel a little foolish. It was bad enough he'd had to explain to her what any other young lady would have learned from her mother, but now she was asking foolish questions. Still, it was the only way she would learn things, wasn't it?

Rather than answer her, he pulled back and, to her shock, the sensation was not altogether unpleasant.

"No," he said with a quick kiss on her mouth. "Not by a long shot."

And he began to move within her, stroking in and out, the hot skin of his chest sliding over her sensitive breasts, and all the while, that part of her where he filled her starting to ache. When he pressed in, she wanted to hold him there. She even brought her legs up to hold him to her, trying to lock her feet over his buttocks. Her arms grasped his shoulders with the intensity of a falling woman clinging on for dear life.

And all through her she felt the beat of her heart, in tempo with the throbbing between her legs, beating a tattoo, keeping time with his every stroke. Again and again, he pressed into her, his body beginning to press harder, move faster, until there was no more pain, only urgency. Until her body almost quivered with the desire to hold him within her. And at the same time, she knew that if he stopped moving she would weep with the disappointment of it.

She was moving—they both were moving—toward something, though she had no notion of what it could be. Only that she had to keep moving against him or she would die. And then, almost as if some threshold had been crossed, she felt herself jolt out of rhythm and she was flung up into the heavens where her very essence splintered into a shower of small pieces where she could feel only a kind of otherworldly unreality.

And as if from far away she felt Jasper's thrusts speed up and then he cried out, holding still within her, gorgeous as his face shone with his own euphoria. Then, as if he no longer had the strength to hold himself up, he collapsed onto her.

Rather than discomfort at his heavy weight, instead she felt a wave of tenderness wash over her. And closing her eyes with her own overwhelming fatigue, she drifted into a dreamless sleep.

When she awoke for the second time in her new bedchamber it was to find herself stark naked, and tucked firmly against a very large, very warm male body.

She thought he must have been asleep, but he must only have dozed, for as if sensing her fluttering eyelashes, he kissed the back of her neck.

"Sleep well?" he asked in a possessive tone. Thinking back to what they'd done to make her so very sleepy, she felt herself blush.

"Yes," she said diffidently. "Quite well."

She heard rather than saw the grin in his voice. "Then I suppose I did my job well enough."

If that had been a job only done well enough, she feared a job done splendidly would have killed her outright, she thought to herself.

Aloud, however, she said only, "I suppose so."

It was then she became aware of a certain hard part of him pressing rather insistently against her backside. "Are you sore?" he asked against her ear, and she felt a shiver run down her spine at the sensation.

She should be embarrassed at the question, she knew, but after their discussion earlier, followed by that ultimate intimacy, she found herself unruffled by it. "A little," she confessed, but she added a slight thrust backward of her bottom to the words. "Not too much so."

She began to turn, but he held his arm firm against her belly. "Stay facing that way," he ordered. And she must be under his spell, she thought, because if he'd ordered her to do something any other day she'd have given him a dressing-down he wouldn't long forget.

Allowing his warm hand to slide under her top knee and bend it upward, she gasped when she felt him slide into her already desperate body. And unlike before, there was no pain, only delicious sensation as he stroked into her from behind. Again and again filling her, then pulling back out again.

In this position, she could only thrust back a little when he left her, and though it meant her role was limited, it also left her free to experience every last drop of sensation as he thrust up into her again and again.

Her climax, when it happened, was not so explosive as earlier, but with his arms wrapped around her it felt even more intimate in some way. And she was almost too overcome to realize when he stilled within her and exhaled his pleasure.

Jasper was deep in a dream involving unicorns and a curricle procession when a voice penetrated his consciousness.

"My Lord," his valet said in a stage whisper. "My lord, you have a visitor."

He opened his eyes, and suddenly the events of yesterday and last night flooded his brain. Which would explain why his legs were tangled in Hermione's while she lay with her back tucked tantalizingly up against his quickly awakening cock.

"This had better be good, Clarkson," he said in a low voice, not wanting to wake her.

"It's the Duke of Trent, sir," the manservant said, his tone of voice revealing that he knew just how utterly wrong it was of him to awaken his master in his current state.

As furious as he was to be pulled from bed on his wedding night, Jasper knew Trent wouldn't descend upon him unless it was absolutely necessary.

"I'll be down in a moment," he told the other man.

Carefully, he extricated himself from his delectable wife and climbed from the bed. Wordlessly he gathered up his breeches from the floor and stepped into them. Taking the banyan Clarkson offered, he thrust his arms into it and didn't bother looking in the glass to see if he was presentable. Guests who arrived in the middle of the night deserved no such niceties.

When he reached his study, where the underbutler had placed Trent, he looked inside and saw that the matter must indeed be grave.

Trent was a man who had spent nearly a decade

fighting the French in the army, and as such he'd seen his share of death and destruction and any number of generally grim situations. But his expression now was as bleak as he'd ever seen it.

"What is it?" Jasper asked, shutting the door behind him. "Is it Lisle?"

They'd lost the fourth member of their little group, Mr. Jonathan Craven, earlier in the year and to lose Lord Frederick Lisle would rock both men to their very cores.

The duke shook his head. "No, thank God. As far as I know, he and Leonora are fine."

"Then what?" Jasper asked, racking his admittedly fatigued brain to guess who else's loss would give Trent such a bleak expression.

"I'm afraid Lord Upperton has been attacked with a knife," Trent said baldly. "It's clear someone attempted to cut his throat, but was interrupted. I'm having him brought here. I thought you would want that. For Lady Mainwaring. I came ahead to warn you."

"Good God." Jasper shook his head in disbelief. "Where was he?"

"Wallingford's," Trent said grimly. "I followed him from here after the wedding breakfast. I didn't like his mood. He seemed a little too pleased at the way the marriage settlements had gone."

"That's because I gave the bloody fool ten thousand pounds," Jasper said, cursing himself. "I should have known better than to give him such a windfall. A man like that has no self-control at the best of times, but with a new fortune in his pocket he's a damned gun with a sensitive trigger."

"Which is why I tagged along," Trent explained as Jasper moved to the decanter of whisky he kept behind his desk. "I can't help but admit that he's good company in small doses."

"He isn't a monster," Jasper said, handing one of the glasses to Trent. "Just unable to control himself when it comes to games of chance. And I think he cares about Hermione in his way. Just not enough to stop him from hurting her."

He rang the bellpull and told Greaves to have one of the footmen fetch the doctor at once.

"I suppose the old saying about a fool and his money is true," he said, downing the rest of his drink. "I should have known better."

"I don't think it was for his money, though," Trent argued.

"But you said he was found outside the hell. I assumed he'd won and someone followed him out."

It was something that all men who engaged in deep play feared. It was one thing to leave with your pockets empty from losing. There was no stealing what didn't exist, after all. But anyone with a night's winnings in his pocket was careful to stay with the crowd or to take a hack rather than walking home. And someone who had been as frequent a gambler as Upperton would have known that.

"He lost," Trent said flatly. "I tried to convince him to use the money you gave him to pay off the rest of his debts. Or at the very least, to put it away for later. But there was no persuading him. He played until he lost the whole of it. I don't know that I've ever seen a man ride such a spectacularly dismal losing streak until the very bottom."

"Of course he did," Jasper said with a curse. "And I made that possible."

"You were trying to give the man a second chance," Trent argued, drinking the rest of his alcohol in one gulp. "It was kindly meant. And if he'd been any other man he would likely have done the right thing with it. Unfortunately, Upperton is nothing if not foolish with his money."

Lowering himself heavily into his desk chair, Jasper scrubbed his hands down over his face. "What the devil am I going to tell her?" he asked grimly.

"She knows what he is," Trent said firmly. "The man lost her hand at the tables. If anyone knows about his proclivities, she does."

"But you said it wasn't because of his money?" Jasper asked, recalling his friend's exact words. "If he wasn't holding any money then why was he attacked?"

"That's the question," the duke said with a sigh. "I don't know what the motive could have been. He had no money on him, and though he lost, he was in good enough spirits when he left with Fleetwood. They were going to walk home together since their houses adjoin. It's why I didn't think to follow him home. I remained behind to finish my own game. I was still there when one of the other men came in to tell us that he'd found Upperton and that he was badly injured."

At the name Fleetwood, Jasper's ears began to ring. "And what of Fleetwood?"

Trent shrugged. "He was gone. I assumed he'd fled when the attack happened. Or left while Upperton smoked a cigar. There was one burning there when we found him."

Jasper swore fluently. "He's the one who did it. He must have been interrupted before he could finish the job."

Quickly he filled Trent in on the investigation into Fleetwood, Saintcrow, and the horses. "And now Hermione's father was nearly killed because we couldn't find enough evidence to take Fleetwood into custody."

"Don't blame yourself," Trent said. "From what you say, Fleetwood has been wily. And by hiring the runner to investigate Saintcrow's death himself, he predisposed the magistrate to assume he's innocent."

"Yes, but that's no excuse for my lack of progress." Jasper pinched the bridge of his nose. "I have been distracted. And that might have cost a man his life tonight."

At that moment, the sound of a commotion at the front door alerted them to the fact that the carriage carrying Upperton had arrived.

"Let me know if there is anything more I can do to help," Trent said, squeezing Jasper's shoulder. "I can be here in a moment's notice if need be."

Grateful for his friend's support, Jasper nodded. Then hurried off to tell Hermione what had happened.

Eighteen

"But I don't understand," Hermione said, shocked by the news that her father had almost been killed. "Papa spends a great deal of time in gaming hells, but he is hardly violent. I cannot imagine why someone would wish to harm him."

She'd awakened alone in her bed, disappointed in spite of her determination not to be the sort of wife who clung to her husband's every word. She'd tried to go back to sleep, but the unfamiliar room, coupled with anxiety over her new situation, kept her awake.

When Jasper returned some moments later, she knew at once that he had bad news to share.

"Hermione," he said, sitting down on the side of the bed and taking her hands in his. "I'm afraid your father has been attacked."

"What?" she gasped. "What do you mean? Is he alive? What's happened?"

"He is alive," he assured her, chafing her hands between his. "The physician is with him now. Trent had him brought here where we could look after him. We agreed that would be best for him instead of sending him to Half-Moon Street where he would have only the servants to look after him."

She knew she should get up and go to see him, but

she was numb with shock. Hermione had become accustomed to the ups and downs of life with her father and his gambling habits. But it had somehow never occurred to her that his behavior could lead him into danger. He was often desperate for funds, of course. But she'd never connected that desperation with the other people who frequented the same spots as Lord Upperton.

Of course he'd come into contact with dangerous people, though. What a naïve fool she'd been.

"Thank you," she said numbly, grateful that he was alive and not dead in an alley somewhere. "That is best. Greentree would see to him, of course, but it's best that he's here. With me. Do you know how badly he's hurt?"

"I haven't been to see him yet," Jasper told her, his voice gentle. As if he were afraid she'd go into hysterics. Though Hermione knew she was far too shocked for that. "But I believe it was a near thing. His attacker was interrupted, Trent said. So he hadn't the time to finish his task."

The task of killing Lord Upperton, he meant. Unbidden, the memory of Lord Saintcrow's lifeless body rose in her mind. And she began to tremble.

"Come here," he said, gathering her against his body, holding her close. How long had it been since she'd had someone she could go to when she needed comfort? She had Leonora and Ophelia, of course, but she couldn't tell them about her darkest fears. The ones relating to her father's worst excesses. "He is alive. That is the important thing. He was attacked but he survived."

"I need to see him," she said against his shoulder. "I need to see for myself that he is still breathing." And to replace the image of Saintcrow's body with her father's face that had set up shop in her mind. "Please."

"Of course, my dear," he said, moving aside and offering her his hand.

When she was on her feet, she rang for Minnie, and as soon as she was dressed she let Jasper lead her to the guest room where her father had been taken.

"I am Dr. Braeburn, my lady," said the russet-haired man who stood at Lord Upperton's bedside. He stepped back to the foot of the bed so that Hermione could stand near her father's head. "Your father is a lucky man."

How Lord Upperton would regret the missed opportunity to try that luck at the tables, she thought wryly.

He was quite pale in the lamplight. With a wide white bandage wrapped around his neck.

"So someone tried to cut his throat?" she asked gravely.

"Aye," the physician said matter-of-factly. "The cut was shallow, however. He lost a great deal of blood, but so long as he is kept quiet and receives a daily diet of red meat to enrich the blood, I think he can make a full recovery."

When had her father begun to look so old? she wondered, stroking her thumb over the thin skin of his hand. It was as if the attempt on his life had turned him into an invalid over the course of a few hours.

"He should get as much rest as possible," Dr. Braeburn said to Jasper, who had come to stand beside her. "And I cannot stress enough how much he should be kept calm. His body needs time to rejuvenate itself. And too much excitement could inhibit that process. I understand he was found outside a gaming hell. It goes without saying that he should refrain from cards or games or any activity that might raise his heart rate."

"We will see to it that my father-in-law receives the best care possible," Jasper assured him, while Hermione continued to observe her father. "And I can assure you there will be no gambling while he is in this house."

When the doctor had gone, Hermione sank greatfully into the chair Jasper brought for her at Lord Upperton's bedside.

"I've never known him to look so frail," she said softly, tracing the outline of her father's bushy eyebrows. "For all that I was so frequently frustrated with his behavior, it never occurred to me that he might be harmed in some way. That he was as vulnerable to danger as the next man. He was always my invincible Papa."

"It is difficult to see them for the fragile beings they are," Jasper agreed, placing a strong hand on her shoulder. "Especially when they spend a great deal of their time trying to convince us that they are anything but. A man like your father spends his days bluffing— that is, pretending to be richer, more clever, more prosperous, wiser than the other men at his table. It is part of what makes a successful gamester. You musn't chide yourself for believing the lie. Men far more attuned to such practices have been fooled."

Something occurred to her. Looking up at Jasper, she saw that he was, for the moment, utterly without guile. And the look of naked pain in his face nearly broke her heart. "You're speaking of yourself, too," she said softly. "You believe that you are just as guileful as he is. But you know that's not true."

"I know nothing of the sort," he said sadly. "We spend a comparable amount of our lives at the tables. And there is not all that much difference in the way we play cards."

"There is a vast difference," she said, turning to really look at him. "You once told me that you use mental calculations to choose which card to lay down, which to discard. I don't think Papa could do that to save his life. He hasn't got the mathematical skills to do what you do. The only weapon in his quiver is guile. Don't you see?"

"That doesn't mean that I am somehow nobler than he is," Jasper returned. "I am a cardplayer just as he is. It's true that it has not become as necessary to me as breathing, certainly not as necessary as it has become to him. But do not make the mistake of judging me less harshly, Hermione. I am culpable for my own behavior. Perhaps more so because I have the ability to leave it without looking back, but I choose not to."

He stepped away, far enough out of reach that she could not touch him. "I will leave you to spend some time with him," he said sadly. "Perhaps I can find out something more about the man who tried to kill him."

Before she could object, he was gone. And though she turned her gaze back to her father, her mind was on Jasper.

I believe there is some merit in what you say, my lord," said Mr. Rosewood as Jasper stood before him in the tiny office in Bow Street.

After he left Hermione at her father's bedside, he'd put on his hat and coat and gone in search of the runner. It was obvious to Jasper that Hermione's erstwhile neighbor was the likeliest suspect in the murders of both Lord Saintcrow and now the attack on Lord Upperton. And since Rosewood had been hired by Fleetwood, he already had the man's trust.

"So, you will agree to work for me instead of Fleetwood?" Jasper asked the investigator. He had come to the conclusion that the only way to lure Rosewood to his own side would be to offer the man twice what Fleetwood was paying him. "Not only is it in your best interest with regard to your pay, but it also will save you from knowing you've aided and abetted a murderer."

"All right, my lord," the other man said with a brisk nod. "You've convinced me. I will do what I can to help you."

"And I do not wish you to inform Fleetwood of your decision," Jasper told him. "Indeed, you must behave as if you are still doing your best for him. I wish for Fleetwood to be unaware that you and I have had any dealings with each other."

"If that's what you want, my lord," the other man said with a shrug. Clearly he didn't understand what Jasper was intending. Which was just as well.

"Now," Jasper said firmly, "I want you to go to Fleetwood today and inform him that Lord Upperton has been murdered. He is still alive, of course, but Fleetwood doesn't know that."

Perhaps if Fleetwood believed everything had gone according to plan, he would relax a bit, and make a mistake.

"I want you to watch his reaction to the news," he continued. "And send me word of what his response is. And if he leaves at all, I want you to follow him. I suspect he will go to his partner and inform him that this latest mission has been accomplished. So take note of who he is going to see."

"Aye, my lord," the investigator agreed. "I'll do exactly as you say. And if I can't get away, I'll send word to ye."

"Good." Jasper picked up his hat, gloves, and walking stick. "Now, I must be off."

When he was back out on Bow Street, Jasper handed the urchin holding Hector's reins a coin and threw himself up into the saddle.

There was something about those horses. Something that was worth killing one man for and nearly killing another. And now that they were in his own stables, he would take every precaution to ensure that he and his family remained safe. To that end, he'd arranged with Mr. Rosewood to post runners at his London residence, and before he left that morning, he'd instructed Greaves not to let any of the ladies leave the house today.

They would not be best pleased, but when the choice was for them to remain indoors but safe or venture outdoors at the risk of their lives, he would choose indoors every time.

He made his way to Tattersall's in record time, and since there were no auctions taking place today, he was able to speak to the head auctioneer, Mr. Sam Vernon, without fear of taking the other man away from his business.

"I'd like to know whatever you can tell me about the sales history of a pair of matched grays that were purchased from here a few months ago," he said, showing the man the bill of sale for Hermione's grays, by name Rosencrantz and Guildenstern. It listed Tatt's as the seller, and Jasper had a sneaking suspicion that they had not originated at the auction house.

Putting on his spectacles, the dapper little man examined the paper and nodded. "That was the pair bought by Mr. Wingate, for Lady Hermione Upperton, correct?" At Jasper's nod of assent, he stepped over to a large filing cabinet and began to search through documents.

Finally, he found the page he was looking for. "I recall that sale quite clearly," Mr. Vernon said with a brisk nod. "I believe Lady Hermione is a driver and was in need of a coaching pair."

"Those are the ones," Jasper said, trying to curb his impatience with the man's laconic manner. "What can you tell me about the horses? How did Tattersall's come to broker the sale?"

Shuffling through the documents before him, Vernon nodded. "I recall now. We purchased this particular pair from a gentleman here in London, who said he had bought them from a breeder in Yorkshire. Poor lad could no longer afford to keep them. And young gentlemen being young gentlemen, he had no kind of pedigree papers for them. But they were such fine horses, and so easy to drive that we took them without. Which is unusual for us, but a bird in the hand and all that."

"In fact," Vernon continued, scratching his chin, "there was another man who'd heard about them from a friend, and he came the day after the sale went through in hopes they'd still be for sale. When I told him they'd already been sold, he was that angry."

"Can you recall the man's name?" Jasper asked, his senses on alert.

"I'm sorry, my lord," Mr. Vernon said mournfully, "but I cannot. I know he was a titled gentleman, but I speak to so many in the course of my work."

Jasper almost groaned in frustration. "Then can you tell me the name of the young man who sold them to you?"

"Of course," Vernon said. "His name is right here in the record. Robert Fleetwood. I thought perhaps he'd have tried to come buy them back again, but he never did. I suppose he was on to other things and had his eye on some other pretty bits of horseflesh by then."

Or he'd wanted those horses in particular back so he killed Saintcrow in order to get them. It was the fellow's reason for selling them and wanting them back again that made no sense. What was it about those horses in particular that made them special enough to commit murder for? And who was the man who had come the day after the sale to inquire about them?

Why did it feel as if this case were becoming more complex and not less?

"My dear, you must not stay here in the sickroom all day," the dowager Countess Mainwaring said to Hermione late that afternoon. "You will be of no use to him if you wear yourself down while he is unable to even know you are here."

Hermione had been surprised but touched when her mother- and sisters-in-law had come to inquire if there was anything they might do to help her while her father was ill.

The dowager had even suggested that Hermione go for a walk in the garden for a short while just to get her out of the sickroom. "I don't know how much my son told you about his father's death," she said in a low voice, once her daughters had gone. "He did not die immediately following the accident, but lingered on for several days before he passed. It was an awful thing to see the vibrant man I'd married waste away like that."

"No," Hermione said, aghast. How hard it must have been for Lady Mainwaring to stay by her husband's side during those days. "I am so sorry."

"I have made my peace with it," Lady Mainwaring

said with a sad smile. "It was a trying time for all of us. And I'm afraid I took a great deal of comfort in the running of the estate once my husband was gone."

Hermione thought back to her conversation with Mainwaring about his conflict with his mother.

"I began to see it as the only thing keeping me from falling back into the pit of despair that had nearly consumed me when Philip died," the dowager said sadly. "And when Jasper reached his majority and—as was reasonable—tried to take control of the estate, I fought him. It was not well done of me. And I fear that I may have said some things that I've come to regret."

"But why have you not told Jasper this?" Hermione asked, knowing that he would be grateful to mend fences with his mother.

"Because I haven't wished to remind him of it," the dowager said with a shrug. "I have tried to stay out of his way, and let him do whatever it is he feels is best. Though I fear I did not help matters by ripping up at him when he informed us of his forthcoming marriage to you."

Not something that came as a great surprise to Hermione, considering the uncomfortable visit the dowager had paid in Half-Moon Street.

"I was wrong then, too, Hermione," her mother-in-law said with tears in her eyes. "My only excuse is that ever since I lost my husband, my nerves have seemed to be strangely out of joint. And I have felt things more deeply than other people seem to. It's as if my skin has suddenly disappeared and I am moving through life with all that raw viscera exposed to the air."

Hermione had never heard emotions described in such a way, but there had been times in her life when

she had felt just as the dowager said. She couldn't
imagine just how painful it would be to spend days,
weeks, months feeling that way, rather than just
hours like Hermione had done.

"I know it is probably too little, too late," the
dowager Countess of Mainwaring continued. "But I
do hope that one day soon you will be able to find it
in your heart to forgive me. I think this attack on
your father has served to jolt me from my self-
indulgent bubble. And I mean to show both you and
my son that I need not be a burden on you. I hope
you'll let me start by allowing me to relieve you for
a short time in your sickroom duties."

Unable to hold herself back, Hermione threw her
arms around the older lady and hugged her. "You cannot know how relieved I am to hear that you don't
despise me, as I thought you must on that day you
called in Half-Moon Street. I have no wish to come
between you and Jasper. Or Jasper and his sisters."

"Of course not, my dear," said the dowager. "And
I feel sure my daughters, now that the marriage is a
fait accompli, will come around."

"I hope so," Hermione said with a shy smile. "I've
never had sisters, you know. And I lost my mother
when I was but a girl. I would be grateful to know
I'd gained both with my marriage to Jasper."

With one more grateful hug for her mother-in-law,
Hermione hurried out of her father's sickroom, and
fetched her pelisse and hat to prepare for a turn in
the garden.

Since there had been no time last night, Jasper
hadn't given her a tour of the back garden of the
Mainwaring town house. Like the house in Half-
Moon Street, this one also backed up to a mews. But
this house was far larger, and the carriage house and
stables were twice as big as Hermione's had been.

The garden itself was also larger, with landscaping in the romantic style, which meant that it looked on the surface as if it had been allowed to grow wild, but in actuality had been carefully cultivated to look that way.

But though she appreciated the loveliness of the greenery, she gravitated, as she always did, to the stables for her comfort.

She found, to her surprise, that for a man who did not enjoy the sport of carriage driving, Jasper owned multiple vehicles and many more horses—both coaching and riding.

"My lady," said one of the grooms, who was busy repairing a bridle just inside the entrance. "How can I help you?"

"I've just come to say hello to Queen Mab and Rosencrantz and Guildenstern," she said to the young man with a smile. "I know where they are, you needn't let me interrupt your work."

And with a nod, he let her wander along the row of stalls, crooning and scratching the noses of curious horses until she came to where Rosencrantz and Guildenstern were housed side by side.

"Hello, my beauties," Hermione said with a grin as the two grays nickered in greeting to her. Standing before the wall that divided the two stalls, where she could pat and scratch each horse at the same time, she laughed when they shook their heads and snuffled against her hand in search of treats.

"I'm afraid I wasn't able to bring apples this time," she told them mournfully. "But I assure you that shall bring them next time. I promise."

As was his habit, when she tried to scratch Rosencrantz on the top of his snout just below his eyes, he shook his head in annoyance. "All right, all right," she told him with a frown. "I won't do that. I'm sorry."

For a few minutes, she talked to them in nonsense words and crooned and had a lovely time of it. What was it about animals that could so help one regain a sense of balance, a sense that there was hope in the world? Perhaps it was because animals were so helpless when it came to taking care of themselves.

Oh, she had little doubt that if Rosencrantz and Guildenstern were set loose on Dartmoor they'd soon enough learn to get along well enough. But even out there, where they were free to feed themselves, there were still those tasks that were beyond them. Like removing a stone from an injured hoof, or brushing out their coats with a curry comb.

How much darker her life would have been if she'd never discovered just how much she could rely on these marvelous creatures.

Even Rosencrantz and Guildenstern in particular, who had been the cause of one man's murder and another's near murder.

What on earth about these horses inspired such violence?

"All right, pretty boy," she told Guildenstern with one last pat on the nose. "I must be off before Lord Mainwaring comes home and finds I've left the house."

But before she could turn around, she felt a hard object connect with the back of her head, and she desperately struggled to remain upright while the reality was that her body was sliding slowly to the ground.

And her last thought was that she wished she could have seen his face.

Nineteen

"What do you mean you don't know where she is?" Jasper demanded once he'd returned home.

Knowing now just how determined someone was to kill or injure anyone with anything to do with Rosencrantz and Guildenstern, he had walked into the house wanting nothing more than to set eyes on Hermione. Just to reassure himself that she was alive and well.

But when he went to his father-in-law's room, she was not there. Nor was she in her bedchamber. Or any of the other places where she might seek a few moments of solitude. And a quick check with his mother and sisters revealed that they'd not seen her for at least a couple of hours.

"When last we spoke," his mother told him with a frown, "I urged her to take a turn in the garden. She'd spent nearly all day in that stuffy room with her father. And so to ease her mind, I sat with him for a little while, then left when the nurse you hired came to take over. I thought she'd been back for a long while now."

"And you didn't think to check to see if she'd come back?" Jasper asked, clutching his hair in frustration.

"She was only going into the garden, Mainwaring,"

his mother said tartly, "not to Paris. I thought she'd take a turn through the flowers, then come inside and maybe rest for a little while."

"Think," Jasper told himself. "Think."

The garden. She'd enjoyed the garden at Half-Moon Street. But when he'd gone in search of her there she was often to be found instead . . .

"The stables," he said aloud. And calling for the Bow Street runner who had been watching the front of the house, he hurried through the French doors to the terrace leading into the back garden, and toward the lane that ran behind the house separating the garden from the mews.

"My lord," said Jenkins, his head groom, when Jasper stepped inside the stables calling out for Hermione. "I was just about to come for you. Someone's stolen her ladyship's coaching pair."

"Show me," Jasper demanded, following the big man into the heart of the stables to the stalls where Rosencrantz and Guildenstern had been housed.

Holding up a lantern, the groom showed him the empty stalls, but there was no sign of Hermione.

"Ask your men if Lady Mainwaring has been here this afternoon."

When Jenkins made as if to respond, Jasper cut him off. "Just go ask them."

He scanned the area himself, and began to open the stalls of the horses who still remained. When he got to Hermione's mount, Queen Mab, he opened the gate of the stall to see a dark form on the ground at the edge of the stall.

Moving closer, he saw that it was Hermione.

"Jenkins!" He called for the groom, who came hurrying and quickly led Queen Mab from the stall while Jasper stepped inside and lifted Hermione into his arms.

"Jasper?" Hermione asked once he had her up close to his chest. "What happened?" "

"Shhh," he soothed. "Don't talk right now. Let me get you inside and have the doctor look at you."

"Where am I?" she asked, frowning. Then opening her eyes, she saw that he was carrying her through the stables. "Wait! Jasper, someone hit me in the head. Has something happened to Rosencrantz and Guildenstern?"

"Settle down, my dear," he said, trying to sound calmer than he felt. "I will tell you everything I know when we get inside."

And, as if it were too much for her to deal with, she closed her eyes again. "All right, I can wait," she said softly. "But I do have the most awful headache."

Jasper had never felt so ready to do murder in his life. Whoever had attacked her, he was going to find out who it had been, and make them pay.

That was a promise.

"Other than a bump on the head," said Dr. Braeburn a short time later, "I believe Lady Mainwaring is in fine health. Though I must insist that she retire early and take it easy for the next couple of days."

Hermione wondered if the physician thought it odd to be called to the same house twice in the same day. If he did, he didn't show it.

Once Jasper had carried her into her bedchamber and her maid had helped her into her nightclothes, Hermione had listened in horror as Jasper explained that her horses had once more been removed from her possession.

"But what is it about them that is so special that these people will go to such great lengths to take them?" she wondered aloud once Dr. Braeburn had gone. "I cannot understand it. Surely no horse is worth killing over."

Quickly, Jasper told her about his conversation with Mr. Vernon at Tattersall's.

"So you think it was the man who came the next day?" she asked with a frown. "Can he really have been so angry at missing the original sale that he would kill because of it?"

"Either that," Jasper said, "or there might be some other reason that we haven't considered."

"But what could that be? I just don't understand."

Seated on the side of her bed, Jasper looked a little sheepish. "There is something I haven't been truthful with you about," he said finally. "I have been investigating your neighbor Fleetwood, Saintcrow, and the Lords of Anarchy in connection with a ring of horse thieves."

Hermione's eyes widened. "What? Are you telling the truth?" she demanded.

So many things made sense now. Mainwaring's irrational request for her to stay away from the Fleetwoods. His sudden appearance at Lord Saintcrow's house that day. Even his quick thinking when his father's attack was discovered.

"But why are you telling me about this now?" she asked, puzzled. "I assume it was something you were not supposed to reveal to me. What has happened now that makes it all right for you to inform me about the investigation?"

"Someone hurt you," Jasper said, his jaw clenched in fury. "I have been telling you as little as possible because that is what I am supposed to do for the sake of my position. But if keeping the truth of the matter from you means that you don't know what is necessary for you to stay safe, then it's a foolish rule.

don't want to see one more person hurt by these thieves who are more concerned with their own hides than the safety of innocent strangers."

"Oh my dear," she said, cupping his face in her hand. "I am fine. But I am grateful you've told me, because we can work together now."

"Now, Hermione," he warned. "There will be no working together. I told you so that you would stay safe. Which will not happen if you go off trying to solve the thing yourself."

"I simply cannot believe Fleetwood lived next door the whole time," she said, her eyes round with shock. "That cannot be a coincidence."

"I doubt it," Jasper agreed. "And for some reason he wanted the horses back after he sold them."

"Hmm," Hermione said with a frown. "What reason could a man have for wanting to renege on a sale of a coaching pair?"

"If they were stolen," Jasper posited, "then maybe there was another buyer who would have paid more."

"But unless the money was a goodly sum that wouldn't be enough to murder over," Hermione argued.

"If the horses were stolen, perhaps they were afraid someone would be able to tell," she continued. "As if there were some distinctive marking or some other identifying characteristic that would make it easy to tell it was the missing horse."

"Like what?" Jasper asked, bending down to take off his boots, then climbing up beside her on the bed. "Do either Rosencrantz or Guildenstern have any distinguishing marks? I know there are no blazes or socks . . ."

Hermione moved into the circle of his arm and

leaned her head back against him. "Other than Rosencrantz's dislike of having his snout rubbed, I can't think of any. They are wonderful horses and easy to drive, but I cannot think of anything that particularly distinguishes them from any others. And one can hardly call being adaptable to various harnesses a distinguishing characteristic."

She yawned. "Maybe we should sleep on it."

"Maybe you should sleep on it," Jasper corrected, kissing the top of her head.

Too tired to argue, she closed her eyes. And just before she drifted off, she heard him say, "Don't scare me like that again. I don't know what I'd do without you."

Hermione came awake some time later with a start, as her mind and body jolted with the memory of being struck upon the head. For a moment, her pulse raced and she felt herself falling to the floor of the stables again, and she cried out in protest.

"What is it?" Jasper asked.

And she realized that she'd been asleep in his arms, her head pillowed against his naked chest. "A bad dream," she said, pulling away to get her breath, and let her nerves settle.

"You were remembering," he said softly, stroking a hand over her back.

"How did you know?" At times it was unsettling how he seemed to know just what she was thinking. For someone who had been forced to fend for herself for so long, it was at once comforting and disturbing.

"For days after the accident that killed my father," Jasper said, his hand warm through the fine lawn of her night rail, "every time I tried to sleep I would start awake with the memory of impact, of hurtling through the air. It was as if my mind were trying to rid itself of the recollection, but the only way to do it was to experience it again."

"That's it exactly," Hermione said, turning to look at him. "I feel it all again, the blinding pain, the sensation of my legs giving out from beneath me, of falling to the floor."

Wanting the comfort of his arms around her again, she went to him, tucked her head into the crook of his neck. Had it really been only a few days since they'd shared this bond? This closeness?

"I am sorry you had to go through that," he said, his voice rumbling beneath where her ear lay against his chest. She felt him kiss the top of her head.

Lying there in his arms, feeling his strong body against hers, inhaling his scent that was unique to him, she suddenly wanted to feel more of him.

She lifted her head and though her heartbeat now quickened for a different reason, she embraced boldness and met his gaze. There was heat there, and affection, and suddenly she knew that if she did not kiss him she would go mad with wanting.

He watched her through heavy-lidded eyes as she touched her lips to his. Once, twice, before gently opening her mouth over his and darting her tongue out to stroke along the seam of his lips. And suddenly all diffidence was lost as she gave herself up to their shared passion.

She felt his hands slide up to pull her closer, and she gave a little whimper as his tongue slid over hers and their kiss grew hotter and more intense.

Her breasts peaked against the hard warmth of his chest, and suddenly she had to be skin to skin. Pulling back, she moved to straddle him, the texture of his breeches slightly rough against the sensitive skin of her thighs.

"Let me help with that," Jasper said with a growl that made her center clench. And taking each side of her night rail's neck in his hands he ripped it down the middle.

At her astonished gasp, he pushed the gown off her shoulders and moved his mouth close to her ear, whispering, "Gowns can be replaced."

And then they were fused together, their mouths eager, their hands exploring, their hearts beating to the same frenzied rhythm.

"So beautiful," Jasper whispered as he kissed and licked his way down to the spot where her neck met her shoulder, scraping his teeth over the prominence of her collarbone.

Hermione's hands threaded through his hair as she felt his mouth close around her nipple, and at the suction there, she bit back a cry. Every pull of his lips sent a throb of awareness through the very center of her, and before long, she found herself shifting against him, restless and needing to be touched.

"Don't worry, sweet," Jasper said against her breast, "I'll take care of you."

And she felt his hand slide down to stroke over her where she needed him most. His fingers slid along her wet core, the teasing touch sending every ounce of Hermione's concentration there where her body strained to meet his hand.

Her hips bucked when he lightly scraped his teeth over her sensitive nipple, while at the same time his finger stroked into her, where her body craved him.

When he lifted his head, she almost wept, though her movements below didn't slow. But he was only moving to offer the same attention to her other breast, and when he connected there, he stroked a second finger inside her.

"I need more," she gasped as she continued to move against him. "I need you inside me, Jasper."

"Then you shall have me," he said in a low growl.

Panting, Hermione moved off him so that he could strip off his breeches and smallclothes, and she stared in the lamplight at his freed erection.

Unable to stop herself, she reached out to stroke her thumb over the bead of moisture glistening there. And she could tell from the way his breath changed that he liked it.

But when she enclosed her fist around him, Jasper took her hand by the wrist and gently pulled it away. "I like it very much," he told her in a strained voice, "but I want to lose myself inside you."

And then he was kissing her again, and Hermione felt her world shift as he reversed their positions until her back was against the softness of the sheets.

Pulling him to her, she gasped with pleasure at the feeling of his skin against hers from head to toe. And when he slid his body down, the friction of it was almost too much to bear.

But when she felt him kiss his way down over the slight roundness at her belly, headed lower and lower, she protested. "What are you doing?"

He looked up at her, and Hermione almost forgot her pique at the sight of him braced over her spread legs. "Do you trust me?" he countered, his blue eyes dark with intent.

"Yes," she said, though her heart beat furiously at what he might intend to do. It was one thing for him to touch her there, but . . .

"Then let me do this," he said, lightly kissing her hipbone. "I promise that if you don't like it, I'll stop."

Then her traitorous body clenched at the possibilities of his intent, so Hermione nodded. And when she felt his hot breath against her most sensitive skin, and then the stroke of his tongue, she knew she'd give anything to keep him from stopping.

Over and over again, he licked and bit and sucked until her hips began to buck, only moving more when he added his fingers into the mix. But when he closed his mouth over her sensitive bud, it was simply too much to bear, and as her body pulsed around his fingers, she floated away in a tide of mindless pleasure until nothing existed but feeling.

When she came back to herself, Jasper had moved up to brace himself over her, his mouth covering hers. Tasting her own pleasure on his lips was more intoxicating than whisky.

"I take it you liked it," he asked with a self-satisfied grin. "I didn't hear any objections."

"You know I did," she said primly. "Now," she continued, lifting her knees to come up on either side of his hips, "I want you."

"Then," he said, his eyes dark with desire, "have me." And in one thrust, he pressed into her, the pleasant stretch of fullness heightened when the pulses of her earlier orgasm reignited.

Jasper kissed her, and began to move, the friction of every thrust setting off waves of pleasure where they joined. And every time he pulled out, she lifted her hips, and her inner muscles clenched as if trying to hold him inside a moment longer, until they were moving together in a perfectly calibrated dance of desire.

Every thrust edged her closer to the brink of some unseen precipice, as she strove for something she could not name. All she knew was that if she stopped she'd die. And when he began to press harder, gripped her hips with his strong hands, to hold her in place, Hermione felt herself begin to splinter. Her body began to pulse around him again, and when he moved his hand between them to stroke his thumb over her there, she cried out. Her hands gripped tightly to his shoulders as she felt herself throb around him and she tumbled over the brink into the abyss.

Twenty

I think," Jasper said into Hermione's hair once they had regained their composure, "we are very good at that."

"I don't know what to say to that," Hermione responded with a laugh. "Having had no other experiences of it, who am I to say that you are a better partner for me than some other man?"

He tightened his arms around her, possessiveness overtaking him at the thought of any other man taking his wife to bed.

His wife. The very word brought forth a maelstrom of protective feelings, urged him to cling tight to her lest some other man try to take her away.

"You'll never know," he said when he found his voice, "because you'll always belong to me. Till death do us part."

At the mention of death, he felt her sigh. "Speaking of death," she said softly, her fingers toying gently with his chest hair, "there is something I'd like to ask."

He didn't like to hear that serious tone in her voice, but Jasper could hardly fault her for it given the events of the past two days. Not only had her father been almost killed, but she, too, had suffered a serious attack.

"Hermione," he said, "you need never be afraid to ask me something. Or speak to me on any subject. I realize that your life with your father has been somewhat . . . difficult at times. But you should never worry about angering me or upsetting me. I will always listen to you with an open mind."

Jasper wasn't sure what sort of household Upperton had run, but he hadn't been long acquainted with the man before he realized that he would not be an easy man to live with. The irregular hours he must necessarily keep thanks to his gambling, coupled with his personality, would have made life troublesome for a daughter like Hermione. Who longed for nothing more than to be taken seriously.

"I am so grateful for that, Jasper," she responded. "Especially since, as you say, life with my father has been unpredictable. And though I know you have assured me that you are not the same sort of gamester as he is, I cannot help but admit that I do feel some degree of trepidation at the fact that I've married a man whose favorite pastime is gaming."

It was hardly a surprise she felt this way considering her father had just been attacked outside a gaming club—not to mention that the only reason they were here together now was because of her father's habit. But he wasn't ready to admit that the card game he'd played Upperton for her hand had been a mistake. Anything but, when he considered just how right it felt to hold her against him now.

"What can I do to alleviate some of that worry?" he asked her, knowing that by asking the question he was opening himself up to the possibility that she would ask him to give it up. The one thing he'd always been good at.

Her hand on his chest slowed, as if she were con-
centrating. "I do believe you when you say that you
are not as desperate for games of chance as my father
is," she said softly. "And that you are not so much doing it out of a sense of need as for entertainment . . ."

"But?"

"But," she said carefully, "I wonder if maybe you
're not as aware of your reasons for doing it as you
might think. What I mean is, what if you are so keen
to play games of chance because you need them just
as much as Papa, but you do not realize it?"

"Are you asking me if I can stop, Hermione?" Jasper asked, just as carefully.

It had been a long time since he'd allowed anyone
to dictate his behavior for him. His mother had tried
all those years ago when he reached his majority, but
once he'd finally told her that he was taking over the
running of the estates without her input, it had become easier and easier to tell her no.

But a wife was a different matter.

Yes, the law said that he could do whatever he
liked without considering her feelings, but he wasn't
such a boor that he'd ride roughshod over Hermione's wishes just so that he could pursue his own
pleasure. But the idea of leaving behind his time at
the tables was jarring.

"I suppose I am," she said at last, a note of apology in her voice. "Or perhaps I want to know why
you do it, so that I might understand better. Because
as you've said, I've spent my life so far with my
father's predilections and look what has happened
because of that. I lose my horses, and Papa is lying
injured."

"And you are now married to a man you would
never have considered otherwise," he said tightly.
"Let's not forget that."

Perhaps he was more uneasy about their reasons for marrying than he'd thought.

But Hermione looked up at him, smiling sweetly. "That is the only thing that's happened as a result of Papa's gaming that can be accounted a success, as far as I'm concerned."

And to his surprise he saw that she did sincerely mean it. Unable to stop himself, he kissed her. "That's quite the nicest thing you've ever told me," he said with an answering smile.

"But," he continued, "I'm not sure that knowing my reasons for gambling will give you any more reason to trust me and my gambling habit than you do your father's."

She wasn't going to let the matter drop, however. He saw that in the set of her mouth.

"At least give me a chance," she said. "Let me know this part of you."

"Only if you will tell me what it is about driving that you are so desperately attached to," he returned. "For I find it just as frightening to think of you speeding along the road at breakneck speeds as you find the notion of me in gaming hells at all hours of the night."

She nodded. "I can agree to that."

Hermione sat up so that her back was against the pillows, beside Jasper.

He seemed unfazed by her demand to know his reasons for gambling. But she also knew that he was quite good at hiding his emotions when he wished to. He was a very good card player, after all.

"There's not all that much to tell," he said after moment of thought. "What is it you wish to know exactly?"

"Why do you feel the need to do it?" she asked.

"Why cards instead of some other hobby? Like fencing or riding or hunting? What is it about cards that draws you—besides your superhuman ability to calculate odds. For I can only imagine that would become boring after a bit."

Jasper sighed, and rubbed a hand over his face. "Well, I suppose I prefer cards because it's what I'm best at. And I discovered that at school, when I was desperately in need of something to make me stand out from the other chaps."

"At Eton, you mean?" Hermione asked, curious about what he'd have been like at that age. "That's where you met Freddy and Trent and Jonathan Craven, wasn't it?"

"Yes," Jasper agreed. "But before I met them at Eton, I was on my own. And I do not like to admit it, but twelve-year-old Jasper was not quite the strong, handsome fellow you see before you today."

"I'm sure you were sweet," she responded with a grin. She could just imagine his dark curls all mussed from roughhousing and his cheeks flushed from running.

"Too sweet," Jasper said with a frown. "And I'd just lost my father so that meant I'd just come into the earldom. Which did not make the other boys bow to me in condescension. If anything, they saw it as a reason to treat me even more badly than they'd done before."

He did not go into detail about just how the older, stronger boys had asserted their dominance over him. There were some things that a man didn't talk about. And those first few months at Eton were among them.

"Oh dear," she said, taking his hand in hers and gripping it. "I am so sorry. I didn't know."

"How could you?" he asked with a shrug. He'd

got over that trauma years ago. And there was no reason to let Hermione take that on as her own burden, too. "I survived it. And one of the reasons why is cards.

"You see," he went on, "at school, you need a way of making a name for yourself. A way of making you stand out, so that the other boys will admire you. And if they admire you then they want to be your friend. My skill was cards."

He thought back to the days when he'd first realized he possessed that particular affinity for numbers that allowed him to guess almost without fail which card another boy held, or which card was still hiding in the deck. It had been almost as great a thrill as the first time he'd kissed Hermione.

"I was soon the talk of school," he continued. "We weren't allowed to gamble in the open, of course. So we held secret games after hours. Or when we could get away for the weekend. And I found that I was no longer the one who was the butt of every joke. Instead, I began to make friends, like Freddy and Trent and Craven, and eventually became a leader. After that, it became as familiar to me as driving is to you, I would imagine."

"I had no idea," she said, her expression serious. "I knew you were good at it, but it never occurred to me that it would have been the way you managed to make friends, and become a man."

"But that was a long time ago," Jasper said, needing to let her know how important she'd become to him. "If you wish me to stop gambling in order to feel safe, then I will consider doing it. I'm not sure what I'll do with myself instead, but I do not want you to think that your wishes are unimportant to me. Or that I care more about cards than I do you."

Hermione stared at him for a moment, and Jasper wondered if he'd said the wrong thing. They'd only been married for a couple of days, after all, and here he was talking about feelings and such. Clearly he was an idiot.

"Neverm—" he started to say, before she threw her arms around his neck and kissed him.

"Not that I mind," he said when she pulled away, "but what was that for?"

"I believe my question has been answered," she said, her eyes glistening with tears. "I don't think in all the years I begged Papa to stop that he ever once told me that he loved me more than cards. In fact, I am quite sure he does not. Oh, he cares for me after a fashion, but not more than he does those squares of paper."

"Well," he said, relieved that his words hadn't sent her over the edge. "I am pleased to know you are pleased."

"I am," she told him with a shining smile. "So pleased. And I do not need you to give up cards. Though I do reserve the right to revisit this conversation if I feel you are skirting toward becoming the sort of player my father is."

"My dear," Jasper said in all seriousness, "if I begin to become the sort of player your father is, I will quit the game myself. Because I have absolutely no wish to lose everything I hold dear for the sake of a game."

"I suppose I owe you an explanation of why I enjoy driving so much, then," Hermione said, once she'd settled back against the pillows.

"Tit for tat," Jasper said with a shrug.

"It's not all that different from your story," she said, plucking at the bedclothes nervously. "I was a rather lonely child. And unlike you, I didn't go away to school. I had governesses of course, but my favorite thing was when I could go to the stables to see the horses. And when the head groom taught me to ride, and then to handle the ribbons of the gig, I became even more interested."

"How did you come to know how to drive a curricle, though?" Jasper asked. "I did wonder, since your father hardly seems like the sort who would teach you. And if he himself didn't drive overmuch then I didn't know why he'd have a curricle."

He felt Hermione still beside him. And he suddenly guessed what she would say next.

"I've been friends with Leonora for a long time," she said finally. "And her brother, Jonathan, too. Since we were in our early teens at least. We met in the park one day when we were all three on horseback. And soon I was spending a great deal of time at the Cravens' house."

"So Jonny taught you to drive a curricle," Jasper guessed. He'd known his friend had played a part in Hermione's life. Though it hadn't been until after Jonathan's death that he finally met the girl his friend had spoken of so often over the years.

"He did," she said softly. "He was a good teacher. Patient and easygoing, though he could get worked up if he thought I was taking too many risks. Or driving too fast. It was all well and good if he drove recklessly through town, but if I tried it, I'd get a horrible scold."

"He could be tough," Jasper said, recalling how intense Jonathan could be at times. Especially when it came to horses and driving.

It was driving that had eventually killed him.

"He could," Hermione agreed. Then, turning to look at him, she continued, "There was never any understanding between us, Jasper. You have to believe that. Though I did love him. And I believe he cared for me."

"Then why didn't . . ." He couldn't quite finish the question.

"I think deep down he must have known he wasn't long for this world," she said sadly. "I always got the sense that Jonny was driving so fast because he felt he had to in order to get all his driving in while he still could. Does that make sense?"

Thinking back to how his friend had lived, Jasper nodded. "I think that's a fair assumption."

"So, when he died," she continued, "I wasn't heartbroken. Though I was terribly, terribly sad."

Jasper took up her hand and kissed it. "So was I."

"And the reason I drive," she said, "is because, like you, it's the thing I am good at."

"You are good at a great deal of things, my dear," he said with a smile. "And I have little doubt you'll discover many more."

"I am glad to hear you say it," Hermione said, "but please don't ask me to give it up. For unlike you and gaming, I'm not sure I don't have Papa's inability to quit."

He stared at her, this woman who had bewitched him body and soul. And tried to imagine what she would be like if he attempted to rein her in, as she did with her horses. The very idea was inconceivable.

"Hermione, I could no more ask you to stop driving," he said to her, "than I could ask the sun to stop shining or the stars to fall from the sky."

She raised a brow. "This is England. The sun will stop shining whether you ask it to or not."

"Saucy minx," Jasper said, leaning forward to kiss her. "Just know that I don't want you to change. Or rather, I don't expect you to. It isn't a requirement for my happiness."

"You are a wonderful man," she said, kissing him back. "My father couldn't have chosen better."

Jasper could have informed her that it hadn't really been her father who made the choice, but figured they'd shared enough secrets for one night.

The next afternoon, after checking in on her father, whom she found sleeping peacefully, Hermione came downstairs to find the dowager Lady Mainwaring seated in the drawing room with a needlepoint frame before her.

"I hope you are feeling better after your unhappy encounter in the stables, my dear," her mother-in-law said with a frown. "To think that someone was so bold as to attack a countess like that. It's shocking."

"Aside from a small headache," Hermione said, hiding a smile at the other lady's indignance, "I am feeling much better, thank you."

"I am pleased to hear it," the dowager said, not looking up from her embroidery. "I don't know what this world is coming to when thieves and brigands feel free to attack ladies like that. It makes me quite frightened for the state of things."

"It is troubling, indeed," Hermione said. Then, hoping to change the subject, she asked, "I don't suppose you know what has become of Jasper? He was already gone when I came down to breakfast."

"I believe he said something about going to speak with the Bow Street runner," the dowager said, looking up with a questioning gaze. "You aren't already bickering, are you?"

Thinking back to their lovemaking and heartfelt conversations of the night before, Hermione blushed. "Certainly not. I must admit that I slept later than usual thanks to the bump on my head, though, an

I had hoped to ask Jasper if he had learned anything about the attack on Papa."

"Not that he told me," said the older lady with a scowl. "I hope that these ruffians are caught soon. How we are to sleep soundly knowing that such villans are roaming around the city, I do not know."

Hermione was saved from reply by the arrival of Greaves, who informed her that Ophelia had come to call.

"Oh, do send her in," Hermione said with relief.

Looking up, the dowager gave Hermione a short nod and rose from her place before her sewing. "I will leave you to your friend's tender care. Please do let me know if you hear anything from my son. I cannot like that he is out and about while those fiends are still at large."

Impulsively, rose and hugged her. "Thank you. Truly."

"I'm sure I don't know what for," the older lady said, but she looked pleased.

She greeted Ophelia as they crossed each other in the doorway, and was gone.

"I am so relieved you are getting along with her," Ophelia said with a sigh. "I was concerned that you were trapped here with no one for comfort but Jasper."

"And what is the matter with Jasper?" asked Hermione with a raised brow.

"Oh, I mean him no ill will," the other lady said with a shake of her head. "It's just that he's a man. And he has his estates to run and his masculine pursuits. I know you have not been used to having a mother and sisters, but having other ladies to confide in makes one's day-to-day life so much easier. If you get along. And I am pleased to hear that you do."

"I suppose you have a point," Hermione said with a frown. "But never having had them, I don't know that I'd have known the difference. At any rate, I am quite pleased that we will not be constantly at daggers drawn for I might be able to endure it, but I'm not sure Jasper would,"

"Where is Jasper?" Ophelia asked, unable to disguise the censure in her voice. "I thought after what happened to you yesterday he would be watching you like a hawk."

"Pray do not fly into the boughs," Hermione said dryly. "He did not abandon me in my hour of need. He left to go speak with the Bow Street runner, Mr. Rosewood."

"I won't apologize," her friend said, her lips pursed. "I cannot help but look out for you. I only have so many friends in this world, and you are one of them."

"And I do appreciate it," Hermione said with a fond smile. "But you may as well know that Jasper and I have progressed quite a bit from the first time we met. Indeed, one might even go so far as to say we care for each other."

"Oh, that is interesting," Ophelia said with a raised brow.

To Hermione's annoyance, she felt her cheeks heat.

"Yes, well," she said defensively. "We are married, you know."

"Oh, I am well aware of the fact," said Ophelia with a knowing smile. "And in the interests of friendship, I would like you to expound on that a little."

Hermione laughed. "Not for the wide world. I will leave that to your mama once you are betrothed."

"You're just as bad as Leonora," Ophelia groused. "I had hoped that you'd see the logic in letting me know what to expect."

Hermione thought about her own worries regarding wifely duties—at least, her worries before Jasper had kissed her for the first time.

"I will tell you that it is nothing to fear," she said, hoping that Ophelia would take what she said to heart. "And it is quite . . . ah—"

She was saved from continuing by a knock on the door followed by a footman with a note.

Thanking the young man, she ripped it open.

"It's from Miss Fleetwood," she said to Ophelia with a frown. "She asks if I might meet her at her house. Alone."

"That's odd," Ophelia said, her brows drawn together. "What do you think she wants?"

"I did inform her that she could find me here," Hermione said thoughtfully. "Perhaps she wishes to talk about Lord Saintcrow or the Lords of Anarchy."

She didn't say that she now knew the lady's brother was suspected of wrongdoing by the Home Office.

"I don't like it," Ophelia said, frowning. "You were attacked yesterday, and today you get a note from a lady you don't know very well asking you to leave your protected home to visit her alone? It is suspicious."

Hermione secretly agreed, but she was tired of sitting still while Jasper did all the work. And she'd genuinely liked Miss Fleetwood the day she came to call in Half-Moon Street. If the lady was ill, and left to the tender mercies of a brother who had shown himself to be a ruffian—as the dowager would call him—then Hermione wasn't sure she could let her request for company pass unheeded.

But she had an idea for how to stay within the bounds of Jasper's request that she stay away from Fleetwood, and yet still check in on Miss Fleetwood.

"I need to go get some of Papa's things for him,"

she told Ophelia after a moment of thought. "What if I go to Papa's rented house and ask Miss Fleetwood to come next door? That way, I won't be endangering myself needlessly, and if she is too unwell to come, then I will simply send my regrets and use the opportunity to get some work done."

"Hm. That does sound better than going to the Fleetwoods' by yourself, but I don't really know how remaining next door will be all that different," Ophelia said. "Though they are two separate houses. And I suppose you lived there for months before Jasper even warned you about them."

"I will be right as rain, I promise you," Hermione said.

Twenty-one

What do you mean she's gone?" Jasper demanded, his fear for Hermione's safety overcoming his good manners.

"She took a footman," Trent said patiently as he and Jasper discussed Hermione's disappearance from the house in her husband's absence. "Ophelia said that she tried to dissuade her from going, but that Hermione was insistent. You know how persuasive she can be."

He did know, and that's what made him so damned afraid. Not only was she persuasive, but she'd use that skill to convince the footman to let her go inside the Fleetwood house on her own just to issue the invitation for the lady to join her next door. After all, it was only a visit to a sick friend, he imagined her saying with that winsome smile she used when trying to wheedle. Damnation. He should never have let her out of his sight this morning.

"Don't think the worst, Mainwaring," said Trent, whose calm was quickly becoming an open invitation for Jasper to plant his fist in his face. "Fleetwood is a questionable character, I agree, but if the note really did come from his sister, then Hermione is very likely only visiting a sick friend as Ophelia said. Let's just go after her now and you can see that for yourself."

With a grim nod, Jasper climbed up into Trent's curricle with no hesitation whatsoever. He needed to find his wife and he was damned if he'd wait for his horse to be saddled, no matter how much he might dislike traveling by coach.

When they arrived in Half-Moon Street after a brisk drive that saw Jasper holding onto the sides of the vehicle to keep from being thrown out, the two men hurried up the stairs of the Upperton town house and their brisk knocks were rewarded with a confused Greentree.

"Where is my wife?" Jasper demanded before the man could even speak. "She should be here with Miss Fleetwood as her guest."

"I'm sorry, my lord," said the butler with a frown, "but we haven't seen her today. Perhaps she called next door and was detained?"

Not waiting for the older man to finish his query, Jasper turned and hurried over to the house next door, followed by a grim-faced Trent.

In answer to his knock, the Fleetwoods' butler opened the door.

"Where is my wife?" he asked.

"And who might that be, sir?"

"Lady Mainwaring," Jasper said through clenched teeth. "Is she here?"

"I'm sure I don't know—" the man began, but Jasper and Trent pushed past him into the foyer, which was the mirror image of the same room in the house next door.

As they hurried toward the stairs, Jasper saw Hermione coming down them, her arms akimbo. "What on earth do you mean causing such a ruckus in a house where there is a sick lady?" she demanded in a loud whisper. "Miss Fleetwood is quite ill. And you have upset the poor girl greatly."

But Jasper was only interested in clutching her against him. "Thank God." He sighed. "Thank God you are well. I thought . . . well, I cannot tell you what I thought."

She was stiff in his arms at first, but as his worry communicated itself to her, she began to relax. "I am perfectly fine," she said, patting his back. "Truly, fit as a fiddle. Nothing has happened."

When he finally accepted the fact that her visit to the Fleetwoods hadn't, in fact, done her any irreparable damage, Jasper allowed her to pull away. Trent, he saw, was leaning against the wall, his arms crossed over his chest as he watched them. He gave his friend a sheepish look, to which Trent simply offered a shrug. As if to say "it could happen to any of us."

"Do you mind telling me what that was all about?" Hermione asked, after she'd gone to assure Miss Fleetwood that the commotion had been a misunderstanding. "For I don't mind telling you that you frightened the life out of me."

"Perhaps we should go next door?" Trent asked. "Or rather, the two of you can go next door. I will take myself off if you have no further need of me, Mainwaring."

With a nod of thanks to his friend, Jasper slipped his arm through Hermione's and they all three left the house. Trent going back to his curricle and Jasper and Hermione going into the Upperton House.

They were greeted with welcome from the servants who asked after her father's health. After a few moments assuring them that he was resting comfortably, Hermione asked the housekeeper for a pot of tea and she and Jasper retired to the drawing room where they'd met with Rosewood only a few days before.

And almost as soon as the door closed behind them, Jasper pulled her into his arms and kissed her with every bit of the relief he felt on finding her safe.

When they came up for air, she pulled back a little to look into his eyes. "You were really frightened, weren't you?" she asked.

"Of course I was," he said, leading her to the sofa and pulling her into his lap. "I came home to find you'd gone, and though I'd asked Trent to keep watch on you, you'd managed to slip through the net."

"I didn't realize you were having me watched," she said with a frown.

"For your safety," he said firmly. "And I could trust no one but Trent to do it properly. Or couldn't as it turned out."

"Don't blame Trent," Hermione said. "I went out the back door so I could look at the scene of my attack. Just to see if I could remember anything else. And when I could not, I asked the coachman to bring me here."

"Why would you go there alone when you've already been attacked there once before?" Jasper asked in exasperation.

"The reason for my attack—the coaching pair—was gone," Hermione explained with a frown. "And you can hardly keep me prisoner. I am allowed to come and go as I please."

"I don't want you to feel like a prisoner," he said. "But I do want to keep you safe. It won't be forever. Just until we can catch these ruffians."

"I don't understand," she said with a frown. "Why in God's name is this person so willing to hurt—kill—other people over those horses?"

She shivered at the notion and Jasper took her hand in his, offering her comfort.

"I've learned," he said, "that the mysterious Fleetwood happens to be the younger brother of Lord Payne."

"Of the Lords of Anarchy?" Hermione asked, puzzled. "What an odd coincidence."

"Does it not puzzle you that it was Payne's brother who sold them, then tried and failed to buy them back?" Jasper asked. Then, careful about the way he worded his next question, he continued. "And only a short time later Payne, his brother, offered you membership in his club?"

She gasped. "Are you implying that the only reason he invited me into the club was so he could have access to my horses?"

Jasper winced. There was simply no delicate way to put it. "Not to say that you couldn't drive circles around every member of that club," he said, "but did it not strike you as odd that you are the only female member? If he really was interested in opening up the club to all sorts of people, would he not have welcomed more than just one lady into the membership?"

Hermione was silent for a moment, and Jasper worried that he'd gone too far.

"I cannot believe I was so gullible," she said finally, in a scandalized whisper. "How utterly self-important of me to think I was the only lady with the skills to be invited into the club."

"Do not be too hard on yourself," he said, soothing her with a stroke down her back. "He was very persuasive, I'm sure."

"But how could having me as a club member help him get my horses from me?" she asked, still confused.

"It's not as if I'd simply give them over to him because I was a club member."

"No," Jasper said, wrapping his arms around her. "He wanted you in the club so that he could claim friendship with you and then perhaps convince you to sell them to him."

"But he never even asked!"

"There was no time to do so," he explained. "Before you could even go on your first promenade with the club your father lost them to Lord Saintcrow."

"So, it was Lord Payne who killed Saintcrow?" she asked, shocked. "I must confess, I hadn't thought him capable of such a thing. He isn't an especially warm man, but I didn't think him a killer."

"And he may not be," Jasper assured her. "I think it was actually Fleetwood who killed Saintcrow. According to Payne, the two were thick as thieves. And the man at Tattersall's said it was Fleetwood who was there the day after Mr. Wingate purchased the grays on your behalf. I think it likely that Fleetwood sent Saintcrow to persuade your father to worst them and then Saintcrow double-crossed Fleetwood."

"But why?" she asked. "They are beautiful and spirited, but they are hardly the most brilliantly pedigreed horses in the world. I thought I was getting a bargain because of it, but clearly someone thinks they are valuable enough to kill for them."

"Do you recall how I told you I was looking into Fleetwood for the Home Office?" he asked. "I believe that Payne is somehow involved with the theft ring and that someone—perhaps Fleetwood—mistakenly put your grays up for sale at Tatt's."

"What's so damning about that?"

"Tattersall's is one of the most prestigious venues for horses to be bought and sold. And I think someone didn't wish your grays to be looked at too carefully. Which is not likely at someplace like that. Certainly not in a place where their horses are seen by hundreds of men in a day."

"You mean they were afraid their true owner would recognize them?" she asked, frowning.

"Precisely," he agreed. "Or that they would realize that they didn't start off life as pure grays."

She frowned. "What do you mean?"

"Do you recall how Rosencrantz always grows uneasy when you attempt to scratch him between his eyes?" Jasper asked.

"I thought he just didn't like it," she admitted. "Some horses don't. So I just stroke his neck."

"I think your Rosencrantz began life with a white marking between his eyes," Jasper said. "And I think someone dyed it before you bought him at Tatt's."

"So they're not matched?" she asked.

"Very likely not," Jasper said with a nod. "I believe their distinguishing marks were covered up so that their true owners wouldn't recognize them."

"Does Papa know?" she asked, a hand to her chest. "Was that why he was so keen to wager with them?"

He wanted more than anything to let her have the illusion that her father had been acting in her best interests. But he knew she would not like being lied to again. "I don't think he knew when he lost them to Saintcrow, no."

"But Saintcrow knew," she said with a frown. "Because he was working with Fleetwood from the start. And instead of giving them back to Fleetwood when he won them from Papa, he double-crossed him?"

"I think it's very likely." Jasper nodded. "Perhaps Saintcrow wanted more money than Fleetwood was willing to give him for managing to win the horses from your father. It's a risk a man involved in any sort of criminal dealings must take when he trusts someone else."

"Perhaps we'll never know why," Hermione said thougtfully. "If Saintcrow was planning to marry Miss Fleetwood, then perhaps he was going to attempt to turn over a new leaf. And he needed the extra money to do it."

"And before Fleetwood could manage to get the horses from Saintcrow's stables," Jasper said, "I bought them from Saintcrow's heir."

"And now Fleetwood has stolen them again," she said, shaking her head. "Do they not consider that by stealing them they are just alerting us to the fact that there is something amiss with them?"

"I think at this point, he feels he has nothing left to lose," Jasper said grimly. "One man is dead, another is lying abed with a cut across his throat, and they risked injuring you. That's the murder of one peer and the attempted murder of two others. Once they're caught they will be shown no mercy."

Hermione was quiet for a little while.

Finally, she asked, "Why attack my father? He was no longer in possession of the horses when he was waylaid. And he never even went to the stables to see them once while I had them."

"I believe that once he learned of Saintcrow's murder, your father figured out that there was something amiss with those horses." Jasper frowned. "Unfortunately, knowing your father and his constant desire to have more money with which to gamble, I am afraid he figured out who it was that killed Saintcrow and decided to blackmail them."

Hermione gasped. When her eyes filled with tears he pulled her against him. "I am so sorry, my dear. I would not tell you such a thing for the world, but I'm afraid it's the only thing that makes sense."

"Foolish, foolish man," she said through her tears. "He was so desperate for the next game. The next win. And it almost killed him."

"But he survived," Jasper said, kissing the top of her head. "That is the important thing. And I will make sure that the man responsible for hurting him is brought to justice."

"If not Fleetwood, then who?" she demanded.

But before Jasper could speak, a throat cleared, startling them both.

"I hate to interrupt this charming little tête-à-tête," said Lord Payne from behind them. "But I'm afraid I'll have to stop you now."

Twenty-two

$\mathcal{H}$ermione leaped up from Jasper's lap and Jasper stood, slipping his arm around her waist.

"What a sweet couple you make," said Payne with a shake of his head as he leveled his pistol at them. "I truly did not have anything against you, Lady Mainwaring. If I had to open the club to a lady, you were as fine a driver as any lady I'd ever seen behind the reins."

"But you only invited me to join because of Rosencrantz and Guildenstern," she said flatly.

If she thought he'd be shamed by her accusation, Hermione was to be grossly mistaken.

"I'm afraid so," he agreed. "But truly, you are a splendid driver. It's too bad you had the bad fortune to buy those bloody grays out from under me. I'm still not sure how they made it to Tatt's. My ridiculous brother, in all likelihood. But the minute I saw them I knew they were the ones we'd nicked from Lord Carston in Yorkshire. And I couldn't take the chance that he'd see them being driven about town. Imagine my shock when your man of business bought them before they were even put to auction."

"What must you have thought when you saw me

drive them to the promenade that day," Hermione said with a shake of her head.

"I'm afraid what I was thinking wasn't fit for a lady's ears," he said with a rueful grin. "I was so relieved when Saintcrow came and took them before the procession could begin. It's too bad my brother had to kill him, but the damned fool got greedy. He had agreed with Robert to hand them over when he won them from your father, and then once he had them in his possession he threatened to turn us all over to the authorities if we didn't pay his price. And we couldn't let that happen. They hang horse thieves, you know . . ."

Clearly he assumed that she'd not realized the horses were stolen because she was a silly lady, Hermione surmised. She never thought she'd be grateful for being thought foolish because of her sex, but she would be more than happy to accept his derision in this instance.

"Why didn't you take them from Lord Saintcrow's stables immediately?" Jasper asked, keeping Hermione close to him.

"Robert was interrupted at Saintcrow's house," said Payne with a grimace. "I ended up slipping out through the servant's entrance. Was a close thing, too. And then whoever it was contacted the authorities and neither of us dared to go back until it was too late. By the time I got there Saintcrow's damned heir had already sold them to you, Mainwaring. I have to admit you were the last man I'd expected to buy them considering your antipathy for driving."

"They were a wedding gift for my bride, Payne," Jasper drawled. "Unfortunately they were stolen from my stables not long after."

"Sorry about that, old fellow," Lord Payne said with a laugh. "Nothing personal, you understand."

"I'm afraid I find assaults on my wife very personal indeed, Payne," Jasper said with a growl.

Hermione was startled to see that instead of remorse, Lord Payne looked like a schoolboy who'd been caught in a prank.

"I couldn't very well let her see me," he said reasonably, as if it could all be explained away. "Besides, she seems well enough now. If you want her out of harm's way, then keep her on a shorter leash."

She felt Jasper stiffen beside her. She knew he was angrier with Payne than he was letting on. It was one of the reasons she loved him.

The thought startled her and she realized it was true. She loved her husband.

If only she hadn't been so foolish as to realize it when they were being held at gunpoint.

"I'll have to keep your advice in mind, Payne," Jasper said, drawing her from her thoughts. "But just now, I think I'd prefer it if you would simply put down your pistol and let Lady Mainwaring and myself go on about our business."

But Payne wasn't in any mood for giving concessions. "I'm afraid I can't do that, old fellow," he said with a smile that didn't reach his eyes. "You two know far too much about my business now. Do you really think I would have told you all of that if I intended to let you go on about *your* business?"

"I think you don't wish to compound your crimes with the murder of a lady," Jasper said firmly. "I think you are, despite your illegal behavior thus far, a man who abhors hurting women. Else you'd have killed Miss Fleetwood when she discovered her husband's involvement with your schemes."

At the mention of Miss Fleetwood or rather Mrs. Fleetwood, Hermione couldn't hold back a gasp of shock. But it must be true because Lord Payne's jaw tightened and if his eyes were able to fire bullets Jasper would be dead.

And suddenly she recalled that day she'd seen Mr. Fleetwood kissing his sister in the garden. Of course they were husband and wife.

"I might have known you'd guess my sister-in-law's true relationship with my brother," Lord Payne said with a scowl. "If you were hoping to save yourself and your lady wife, I fear revealing that was not the way to go about it, Mainwaring. Their brother and sister act came in handy. With Saintcrow and with you. Indeed her faux betrothal to Saintcrow allowed us to learn what your little wife knew about our movements on the day of your wedding."

"I should have known she was lying," Hermione said with a shake of her head. "She was trying to gain my trust and sympathy. And even today I came to see if she needed my help."

"I fear she was truly asking for your help, today," Payne ground out. "And she will pay for that as soon as I dispense with the two of you."

"Oh, but I disagree," Jasper said coolly. "For I fear that at the moment Miss Fleetwood is in the capable hands of my friend the Duke of Trent."

Hermione was shocked to see that Payne's expression could turn harder. "What do you mean?"

"Just that the Duke of Trent has removed Mrs. Fleetwood from her husband's house and has taken her to stay in a safe location. I have every reason to believe that she has been filling his ears with all sorts of tales. And no doubt Trent has alerted my friends at the Home Office to the fact that you are currently here in the late Lord Upperton's home."

Instead of looking unhappy at Jasper's revelation Lord Payne actually smiled. "But there is no reason for that to alarm them," he said, grinning. "I own this house."

Hermione's heart sank. She'd had no idea that Lord Payne owned the house she and her father had rented. Could Lord Payne really talk his way out of the grasp of the authorities by explaining his presence in the house? She could almost hear him revealing that he thought he'd come by to look over his property now that Lord Upperton was dead and that he'd thought he heard intruders. It would be so terribly easy. Especially since most of the servants had come with the house and were loyal to him.

But Jasper didn't seem to notice. "I know that," he said with an answering smile. "And the one next door. Do you think we would have investigated Fleetwood without finding out who owned his rental house? Sometimes it's the small connections between people that end up tying the noose, so to speak."

"Then what do I possibly have to lose?" Lord Payne asked with a snarl. And to Hermione's horror, he lifted his pistol and aimed it at Jasper.

"No!" she cried out, even as Jasper pushed her to the floor. And before she knew what was happening a loud gunshot rang out.

"Jasper!" she shouted, struggling to her feet, not caring if Lord Payne came at her. He'd used his shot, now he would have to kill her with his bare hands.

"Easy," Jasper said, helping her to her feet. "Hermione, it's all right. I haven't been shot."

And to her shock, when she opened her eyes, she saw that he told the truth. He was whole. And unarmed.

Turning, she saw that Lord Payne was on the floor, gaping wound in the back of his head.

"Don't look," Jasper said, turning her head into his shoulder.

"But how?" she asked, gripping him hard against her in gratitude for his being unharmed.

"That was me, I'm afraid, Lady Mainwaring," said the Duke of Trent from the doorway. "I'm sorry for the mess, but I couldn't let him make a widow of you so soon after the wedding. What sort of friend would I be if I allowed such a thing to happen?"

The absurdity of it made Hermione laugh. Which quickly turned into crying.

Jasper held her tight against him and soothed her, stroking his hand over her back. "I think it's time I took you home," he said in a low voice.

And to her surprise, he slipped his hands beneath her knees and lifted her into his arms.

"I'm taking your carriage, Trent," he told his friend.

And to Hermione's astonishment, her husband, who did not drive, lifted her into the curricle, and climbed up beside her and drove them home.

"I told you before, my dear, that just because I choose not to drive does not mean I cannot," Jasper said as he carried Hermione from the carriage and into his town house.

Not batting an eyelash, Greaves gave no indication that there was anything unusual in having the master of the house carry the lady of house inside. "Shall I have cook send supper to her ladyship's bedchamber, my lord?"

"Yes, thank you, Greaves," he said, not bothering to stop. "And please tell my mother and sisters that we are not to be disturbed."

It was likely that Sir Richard would require him to answer some questions but the Home Office could wait until tomorrow to debrief him about what Lord

Payne had confessed to. From what Trent had said, Fleetwood had been apprehended and he would likely keep them quite busy for the rest of the evening. He would certainly have a great deal more to tell them than Jasper would. He had little doubt that Payne had told his tale with an attempt to paint himself in the cleverest light possible. Unless Fleetwood told the unvarnished truth, they might never know the whole story.

"All this time," Hermione said, once he'd set her down on the counterpane of her bed, "I thought you were so traumatized by your father's death that you'd avoided driving altogether."

"It isn't something I enjoy," he admitted, removing his boots then climbing up onto the bed beside her. When she turned to wrap her arms around him, he felt a peace that he only knew in her presence. "But I can do it. If absolutely necessary."

"Evidently," she said with a shake of her head. "And this whole time I was feeling superior because I had this skill that you didn't."

"I'm hardly as skilled as you are behind the reins, my dear," he said, kissing the top of her head. "In fact, I doubt there are many men in the country who are better than you. And that is not just a husband's pride speaking."

He watched with pleasure as she preened. How on earth had he managed to exist without this woman in his bed, in his life? He knew he had done so, but it was difficult to imagine his life if she were to suddenly vanish from it.

"A penny for them," she said, looking up at him from beneath her dark lashes.

He kissed the end of her nose. "I was thinking that I'm very much afraid you've become indispensable for me."

He watched as his words sank in, caused a blush of pleasure to rise in her cheeks.

"Truly?" she asked in a soft voice.

And suddenly he knew that he couldn't go one more minute without telling her exactly how he felt.

"The thing is, Hermione," he said carefully, not wanting to ruin the most important words of his life, "it's been some time since I was able to think of my life without you in it. I very much am afraid I've fallen in love with you."

And to his horror, her eyes filled with tears.

Damn it, he cursed himself. It was too soon. He'd known it was, but he'd been buoyed by the moment and the excitement of the afternoon.

"It's all right," he said hurriedly. "You don't have to feel the same. Please pretend as if I never said anything."

But to his shock, she sobbed harder. "Please, Hermione. Don't."

"I'm not crying from sorrow, you silly man," she said, slapping him without much force on the shoulder. "I'm crying from happiness."

"Why?" he asked suspiciously, not ready to believe the evidence of his own eyes quite yet.

"Because I love you, too, Jasper," she said with a watery smile.

"You do?" he asked, shocked despite himself. He was so sure she'd be resistant to the idea.

She shook her head sadly. "It looks as if I'm going to have to spend the entire evening proving it to you," she said with a sigh.

"I think that would be for the best," he said with a grin. "In fact, I really think you'll need to do it every evening for the rest of our lives."

And that's just what she did.

Epilogue

"How pleasant it is to enjoy the open air without fear that one or the other of you will be assaulted by a crazed murderer," said the Duke of Trent from his lounging position on the edge of the picnic blanket.

In celebration of the fine weather, and the apprehension of the remaining members of the gang of horse thieves run by Lord Payne, Hermione and Jasper had organized an outing for their close friends in Richmond.

"If not for some quick thinking from you, Trent," Jasper said as he peeled an apple for his wife, "I don't think we'd be here right now." He exchanged a meaningful look with Hermione as he handed her the skinless fruit.

It had been two weeks since their dangerous encounter in Half-Moon Street, and in the interim, the newlyweds had only grown closer. Hermione had even begun to teach Jasper the finer points of curricle driving, though she acknowledged that he was competent without her suggestions. He simply claimed he wanted to be better. And Hermione did not argue.

"Have you learned any more about what might happen to Miss . . . that is, Mrs. Fleetwood?" Ophelia asked, her brow furrowed. "I could not help but like her that day we met her. And it cannot have been easy for her to refuse her husband's demands for her to assist them in their plots."

"But going so far as to seduce Lord Saintcrow?" Leonora asked with a shudder. "That must have taken a great deal of poise on her part. I'm not sure I would be able to do the same in her position."

"You might if your life was being threatened," Hermione said. "I did sense that there was some underlying sadness about her. But I assumed it was from the death of Saintcrow. Now of course we know that she was constrained to act on her husband's orders. It must have been awful. No wonder we heard her crying out that day in the Fleetwood garden."

"I believe the lady has been given a great deal of latitude by the authorities," Jasper said, slipping his hand into Hermione's. "I think it likely she will escape without any punishment."

"Let us talk about something more cheerful." Leonora said, leaning back against Freddy's strong chest. "Like how we all intend to spend the summer."

London society was notoriously empty during the warm summer months. And many families used the time to retreat to their country estates.

"We will be leaving for the Lake District in a month or so," Hermione said with a nervous smile. "It will be my first trip to the Mainwaring estates as countess. I hope the servants there will not find the transition to a new mistress terribly difficult."

"This self-doubt from the first lady to gain entrance in the Lords of Anarchy?" Jasper teased. "I am shocked!"

Hermione rolled her eyes. "I am quite confident about my ability to control a curricle, Jasper. A country estate will be an entirely new experience for me."

"But how will your mother take the transition

Mainwaring?" asked Freddy with a wink. "I believe that is the thing you heirs are forced to deal with. Much better, to my mind, to be a younger son with no fear of war between one's wife and one's mother."

"Mama has been surprisingly sanguine about allowing Hermione to take the reins, so to speak," Jasper said. "In fact, I believe she plans to remove to the dower house when we travel to Keswick. Which is something I never thought I'd see happen."

"Perhaps she had a meeting of the minds with her daughter-in law," Ophelia said with a grin. "We all know how persuasive Hermione can be when she truly wants something."

The murmured agreements made Hermione throw up her hands. "I am not that bad," she said, her cheeks pink.

"Not bad," Jasper said, bussing her on the cheek. "Just determined."

"Speaking of determined," Trent said once the laughter had died down. "How is Upperton getting along?"

Hermione's father had spent his convalescence at the Mainwaring town house, but almost as soon as he was able, he took rooms at the Albany Hotel. The house in Half-Moon Street, as part of Lord Payne's holdings, was tied up in probate, and besides that, Upperton was hardly eager to live in the house where Payne had lost his life. No matter how much of a villain the man might have been.

"He seems to be faring well enough," Hermione said with a shrug. "He has told me he plans to curb his time at the tables, but I will wait and see."

"I would think having one's throat cut would put a damper on his desire to visit Mrs. Wallingford's establishment," Freddy said with raised brows.

"We all know there are dozens more places for

him to find a game," Jasper said, with an apologetic look at his wife. "Though I do believe he limits himself to small stakes these days. Rome wasn't built in a day."

"And he has promised to come to the country with us," Hermione added with a smile. "He hasn't been out of London in I don't know how long. So I do have some hope."

"What of the rest of you?" Jasper asked. "Any great plans for the summer?"

"We will be traveling to Pemberton House," Leonora said, naming the country estate of Freddy's parents, the Duke and Duchess of Pemberton.

"Well, I shall be stuck here in London while all of you are gone away to the bucolic countryside," Ophelia said wryly.

"I think 'stuck' is not quite the right word," Hermione said with a speaking look at her friend. "Considering that you will be doing what you love best in the world."

"And what is that, pray?" the Duke of Trent asked with interest. "I do not believe I've ever heard Miss Dauntry express a great love for anything in particular."

"Don't be an ass, Trent," Freddy said without much heat.

But Jasper trained his quizzing glass on his friend with a speaking look, until Trent rolled his eyes and protested, "I will not retract the question, but perhaps my tone was less than respectful. My apologies to the lady."

"If you must know, duke," said Ophelia with dignity, "I write occasionally for a ladies' newspaper the *Genteel News*. And I will be spending the summer as guest columnist while my colleague is away in the country."

"A newspaper writer?" Trent said, his head tilted in query. "I had no idea, Miss Dauntry. But the mystery of how you became friends with Leonora is now solved. Your association with Hermione, however, is still inexplicable."

Hermione threw the core of her apple at him. "We met through Leonora, you great gudgeon. And just because I am a driving aficionado does not mean I am illiterate."

"I never said as much, Countess," said Trent with a staying hand. "Pray, why are the ladies all suddenly on the attack?"

"You brought it on yourself, old fellow," Freddy said with a shrug.

"Our ladies do not take insult without a fight," Jasper added.

"I would hardly cast aspersions on the countess's driving anyway," Trent said, looking put out. "It would quite hypocritical of me to do so."

The rest of the group exchanged puzzled looks. Trent was many things, but known for his driving skills was not one of them.

"Oh ye of little faith," said Trent with a shake of his head. "I beg leave to inform you that you are looking at the new president of the Lords of Anarchy."

"The devil!" Jasper said. "You're joking."

"I am absolutely not joking," said the duke with all sincerity.

"Why?" Freddy demanded, with real concern. "Do you have a wish to find yourself sent away or murdered? For I am sure you know that the men in that position do not survive for very long without suffering either fate."

"If you must know," Trent said with a lift of his shoulder, "I've been bored. You ladies might not be aware of it, but estate business can be dashed dull. And I miss the camaraderie of the military life."

"But surely you can find a better way to have it than to lead the most notorious driving club in town," Hermione said with a shake of her head. "I *like* you, duke. And I actually think you're a good enough driver to belong, but that club seems to be cursed."

"Then we'll simply have to see if I can pull it off," Trent said with a grin. "And perhaps you will consider rejoining the club once all the excitement of Fleetwood's trial has died down, Lady Mainwaring."

Hermione looked at Jasper. Who put up his hands. "Don't look at me. You can make that decision on your own. Though for what it's worth, I feel less queasy about you joining while Trent is at the helm than I did when Payne was the leader."

"Since Lord Payne was a murdering scoundrel," Trent put in, "I should hardly take that as a compliment. But thanks all the same, Mainwaring."

Hermione looked from one man to the other, and finally grinned. "Then I accept your offer, your grace."

She only hoped that Trent's tenure with the Lords of Anarchy would prove less volatile than the two previous presidents'.